WILLIAM W. JOHNSTONE

LAW OF THE MOUNTAIN MAN

Pinnacle Books
Kensington Publishing Corp.
http://www.pinnaclebooks.com

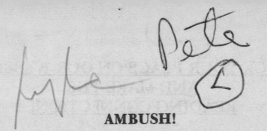

AMBUSH!

Smoke Jensen exploded out of the brush, his knife in his hand.

The bounty hunter wheeled around, his eyes wide with panic, the rifle in his hands coming up. But Smoke's forward charge knocked the man sprawling, loosening his grip on the Winchester. The man opened his mouth to yell a warning. With one hard swing of the long-bladed knife, Smoke ended the life of the hunter.

He took the man's rifle, pistol and ammo, and then dragged the body into the brush. Once more he headed out for the woods.

Smoke knew the time had come to show Jud Vale what he thought of a man who would declare war on women and young boys.

And he would write the message in blood!

I feel an army in my fist.
Friedrich von Schiller

Dedicated to Johnie and Molly Matthews

1

He hoped this would be the last winter storm of the season. Probably wouldn't be, but there is that line about hope springing eternal.

He just wished it was spring. Period.

Smoke Jensen sat in a cave over a fire and boiled the last of his coffee. He knew he was in Idaho. He guessed somewhere south of Montpelier. All he knew for certain was that he was cold, and he was being hunted by a large group of men. He knew why he was cold; he didn't really have a clear idea why he was being hunted.

He poured a cup of scalding strong coffee and fed a few more sticks to the fire, then leaned back against the stone wall of the cavern and once more went over events in his mind.

Sally's parents had come out from the East for a visit. Why they had chosen to come to northern Colorado in the middle of winter was still a mystery to Smoke. It was so cold during the winter, that when someone died the body was placed in a cave until spring when the ground thawed and a hole could be dug.

It was colder here in Idaho, Smoke mentally griped, his big hands soaking up the warmth from the tin cup.

Dagger, Smoke's big mountain-bred horse chomped on

some grass Smoke had dug up for him.

Then the baby had taken sick—some sort of lung ailment—and Sally's father had suggested they go to Arizona for the winter. Smoke had no desire to go to Arizona and there were a few things he needed to tend to around the spread.

With the house empty and matters tended to, Smoke became restless. The pull of the High Lonesome tugged at him. He saddled up and rode out one cold but sunshiny morning.

He didn't have any particular place in mind. He just wanted to be one with the mountains again. Damn near got himself killed doing it. And wasn't out of the fire yet.

He had headed northwest out of Colorado, staying on the west side of the Continental Divide, angling northwest. He did all right until he came to a little town on the Bear River, just about on the border, he reckoned. He had stopped at the general store to resupply and then to have a drink of whiskey. Not normally a drinking man, Smoke visited the saloons more for news than for booze, although in this sort of weather, a shot of whiskey did feel good going down.

Smoke was tall, broad-shouldered, lean-hipped, and ruggedly handsome, with cold brown eyes. Smoke Jensen, called the last mountain man by some, was the hero of countless penny dreadfuls sold all over the country. He was also known as the fastest gun in the West. He wore two guns: on the left a .44 worn high and butt-forward for a cross-draw, on the right a .44 worn low and tied down.

When Smoke had been just a young boy, he was taken under the wing of a cantankerous old mountain man named Preacher. Preacher had taught the boy well, watching him practice with those deadly guns as they traveled all over the Northwest.

Outlaws had raped and killed Smoke's first wife and cold-bloodedly murdered their newborn son. Smoke had tracked them all down and killed them, then rode into the outlaw town that had been their headquarters and shot it out with the killers' friends. His reputation was then carved in granite.

He poured another cup of cowboy coffee and let his mind drift back a few days.

"Whiskey," Smoke told the barkeep. "Out of the good bottle."

The saloon had quieted as Smoke walked in, something that did not escape his attention. He paid little mind, though. A stranger appearing out of the dead of winter always drew attention.

Especially one who wore his guns like Smoke wore his.

"We don't serve no Box T riders in here, mister," the barkeep warned.

Smoke's eyes turned colder than the weather outside. "I don't ride for the Box T. I don't even know where it is or what it is. Now pour the drink." He laid money on the bar.

A man walked up behind Smoke, spurs jingling. "I say you're a liar. I say you're one of that old man and woman's hands. And I say you ain't gonna buy no drink in here. I say—"

Whatever the loudmouth was going to say, he didn't get the chance to finish it. Smoke spun and hit the man smack in the teeth with one big, work-hardened fist. The cowboy's eyes were rolling back in his head and he was out cold before he hit the floor.

Smoke shifted positions, moving to the end of the bar closest to the door so he could keep an eye on the rest of the riders in the room.

"Pour the damn drink!" Smoke told the barkeep. "And make it out of a new bottle. Let me see you pry the cork and pour!"

"Yes, sir!" the barkeep barked. "Right now. Then will

11

you please get the hell out of here?"

"I'll think about it." Smoke held the glass in his left hand. His right hand was hidden by the bar. His right hand was close to the butt of his .44. Out of habit, he always slipped the hammer-thong from his .44 as soon as his boots left the stirrups and touched the ground.

Preacher's lessons stayed with him.

"Mister," the voice came from a table near the back of the room. "That there is Jud Vale on the floor. He's gonna kill you when he gets up."

"If he doesn't handle his guns any better than he flaps his mouth he's going to be in for another surprise."

"You won't say that to his face!"

Smoke laughed at the man.

"You can't take all of us," another voice added.

"Bastard looks like Perkins, don't he?" yet another said.

Perkins? Smoke thought. Who is Perkins? "Maybe not. But I can kill the first six or eight. Anybody want to start?"

Apparently, no one did. No more voices were heard.

Smoke sipped his drink as Jud Vale moaned and stirred on the floor. "Isn't anyone going to help this stumblebum up?"

Several men stood up and warily approached the groaning Jud Vale. All of them keeping an eye on Smoke, who was standing by the bar smiling at their antics. Whoever this Perkins person was, he was respected, for sure.

"You a dead man, Perkins, or whoever you are," one of the men said, helping Jud to his feet. "You got one boot in the grave now."

Jud Vale, his bloody mouth puffy, glared at Smoke. "I'm gonna let you ride, you punk!" he snarled. "Take this message back to Burden: I'm gonna kill him and then run that old broad off the land. You tell him I said that."

Smoke started to tell the man that his name wasn't Perkins and he didn't know anybody named Burden.

12

Then he thought better of it. He'd play along for a time. The idea of somebody like this loudmouth Jud Vale bothering some old couple rankled him.

Smoke nodded, finished his whiskey and then backed away from the bar, finding the doorknob with his left hand. He stepped out into the cold blowing winds and closed the door behind him.

He stopped at a farmhouse a few miles from town, spotting a man carrying a slop bucket out to his hogs.

"Mister, where can I find the Box T spread?"

"South of here. It's right around Bear Lake. You got any sense you'll stay away from there."

"Why?"

"'Cause Jud Vale wants it, that's why. And whatever Jud Vale wants, he gits. Now you git!"

Smoke got.

Jud Vale's men came after him hard. So far, not a killing shot had been fired from either side, but Jud's men kept Smoke in a box, warning him back with well-placed rifle shots and causing Smoke to wonder what in the hell was going on.

He was south of Montpelier, a town settled by the Mormons back in '63, first known as Clover Creek and later as Belmont; Brigham Young gave it its present name. He was not too far from the Oregon Trail. Smoke was close to Bear Lake and the Box T spread, but could not figure out a way to get to the place without killing some of Jud Vale's men, and that was something he did not want to do. Not just yet, anyway.

How do I get myself in these messes? he wondered, drinking the last of his coffee. All I wanted to do was see some country, not fight a war.

13

He walked to the front of the cave and looked out. It was getting light, and soon the hunt would continue. Smoke sighed and did his best to keep his patience. He didn't want to get riled up. When Smoke Jensen got angry, somebody was sure to get hurt.

Dagger snorted and scraped a steel-shod hoof on the floor of the cave. The big horse was getting restless, and was letting Smoke know it.

"All right, Dag," Smoke said, turning to walk back into the wider area of the cave. "I'm getting tired of it myself."

Smoke packed and saddled up, then checked his guns. He led the big horse outside and swung into the saddle, riding with his Winchester across the saddle horn.

"We're headin' for the Box T, Dag. And come Hell or high water or Jud Vale, we're going to make it."

The big horse shook his head as if in agreement.

He had not gone a mile before he saw smoke from a fire. Dagger's ears perked up as he caught the scent of other horses. Smoke smiled grimly. "You wanna go visit that camp, boy? All right. Let's just do that."

When he got close, Smoke dismounted and slipped nearer—on foot. A half-dozen of Vale's men were huddled around a fire, drinking coffee and eating bacon. Smoke recognized several of them from the saloon.

He lifted his rifle and plugged the coffeepot, then dented the frying pan with another round. He put several more rounds directly into the fire, scattering hot coals all around the clearing and sending gunhands scrambling for what cover they could find.

He emptied his rifle into a tree where the horses were picketed and several of them panicked, reared up, and broke loose, taking off into the timber.

Chuckling, Smoke ran back to Dagger, swung into the saddle, and skirted the camp, heading for the Box T range on the Bear.

He had sure ruined breakfast for those ol' boys.

14

As he rode, he saw smoke from several more fires, but decided not to press his luck.

Twice he heard the sounds of horses and men and both times he slipped back into the timber and waited it out as the men rode past him. And they came close enough for him to see that Jud Vale really meant business. He recognized Don Draper, the Utah gunslick, and Davy Street, the outlaw from down New Mexico way. As the second bunch rode by him, Smoke picked out Cisco Webster, the Texas gunny; Barstow, a no-good from Colorado; Glen Regan, a punk kid who fancied himself a gunfighter; and Highpockets, a long lean drink of water who was as dangerous as a grizzly and as quick as a striking rattler.

What the hell was going on in this part of southeastern Idaho?

Smoke rode on as the day started to warm some.

He began to see cattle wearing the Box T brand, really no sure sign that he was on Box T land, for cattle wandered miles to grass, but Smoke figured he was getting close.

Then he found out why the cattle were so scattered—miles of cut fences. Somebody, probably Jud Vale and his men, had really caused some damage.

He topped a ridge and could see, far in the distance, a house and barn, and off to the south, a winding road leading to the house. He cut toward the road, riding slowly and cautiously, for if those in the house were under siege, he would probably be considered hostile.

He stopped several times as he drew nearer, taking off his hat and waving it in the air.

Nothing from the house.

He came to a closed gate and stopped, dismounting. He wasn't about to open that gate unless invited to do so.

But no invite came.

The snow was just about gone from the ground, but the wind was still whistling around him.

"Hello, the house!" Smoke yelled.

He was just about to call again when the response came. "What do you want?"

A female voice. And not an old voice.

"Some food and coffee would be nice," Smoke called.

"Have this instead," the voice said, sending him a bullet that had Smoke diving for the ground.

2

Several more slugs cut the air above his head. Smoke noticed that none of the slugs came close to Dagger. The big horse trotted away a few yards and looked back at Smoke, his expression saying, "What have you got us into now?"

"I'm friendly!" Smoke called, crawling to his knees. "I mean you no harm!"

"You ride for the Bar V?" This time it was a man's voice.

"Hell, no! They've been chasing me all over the country for the last week."

"Why?"

"Because they think I'm somebody named Perkins!"

A full minute ticked by. "All right, mister." This time it was the female voice. "Get into the saddle and come on in. But you put a hand on a gun and you're dead. And close the gate behind you."

It suddenly came to Smoke. Perkins! Clint Perkins. The outlaw that some called the Robin Hood of the West. He was always helping farmers, nesters, and the down-and-outers. He would rustle cattle from big land barons, butcher the carcass and distribute the meat to the needy. He'd been known to give the money to the poor, after holding up rich folks.

But what connection did Clint Perkins have with the Box T?

Well, he might find out . . . providing he didn't get shot first.

He swung into the saddle, leaned down and opened the gate, and rode on in, carefully closing the gate behind him. He walked Dagger toward the house. Smoke stopped at the hitchrail and sat his saddle. Damned if he was going to get down until invited.

"What's your name?" the voice came from inside the house, speaking from behind the open but curtained window.

"Mamma," a child's voice said excitedly. "I seen him on the cover of a book. That's Smoke Jensen!"

After a lot of apologies and much embarrassment on the part of those in the house, Smoke was invited to sit down and eat. A small boy took Dagger to the barn. Children could handle the big mean-eyed stallion, but Dagger would kill a grown man who tried to mess with him.

Smoke tried to put some family resemblance between the young woman and the old couple. He could not see any. And he didn't ask; none of his business.

Smoke put away a respectable bit of food and started working on his third cup of coffee.

"I like to see a man eat well," Alice Burden said. "Our boy used to eat like that."

Walt gave his wife a warning look that closed her mouth.

Smoke picked up on the glance but said nothing.

"Just passin' through?" Walt asked, lighting his pipe.

"Something like that," Smoke sugared his coffee. "'Til I had a run-in with a loudmouth name of Jud Vale. I busted him in the mouth and put him on a barroom floor."

"I'd sure like to have seen that," Walt said with a sigh. "That man has sure caused us some problems."

"Why?"

The old man shrugged his shoulders. "He wants our land. Jud Vale wants everything he sees. Including her." He cut his eyes to Doreen, a slim but very shapely woman who looked to be in her mid-twenties.

Got to be more to it than that, Smoke thought. "What has Clint Perkins got to do with all this?"

Walt looked at his coffee cup. His wife busied herself at the sink, washing dishes. Doreen met Smoke's eyes. "He's my husband. Sort of."

Odd reply, Smoke thought. "Father of the boy?"

"Yes."

"Clint is from this area, right?"

"Not too far from here," she replied. "It's a long story, but I'll make it short. When Clint was just a boy he saw his father and mother killed by greedy cattlemen who wanted their land and didn't like farmers. The boy took to the high country and raised himself. He hates rich people to the point of being a fanatic about it. But he has a few good points. More than a few. I married him, but it just didn't work. He refuses to stop his outlawing. I just couldn't live like that."

"So you took the boy and left?"

"Yes."

Smoke didn't believe her. She was lying through her teeth, but damned if he knew why.

"This is a big spread, Mr. Burden. Where are your hands?"

"Don't have none no more. Jud's men run them off; killed a couple. They're buried on that crest to the east."

Smoke had seen the graveyard. More than two crosses there. "And Jud's men cut your fence?"

"Yep."

"Tell me about this Clint Perkins?"

"What is there to say?" Walt said. "Nobody 'ceptin' Doreen has seen his face in fifteen years."

"You two look alike," Doreen said. "I can see where someone might think you were him."

What to do? Smoke thought. All three of these people were lying to him. But why? What were they hiding? Walt and Alice Burden were too old for Clint Perkins to be their son. So that was out. So where was the connection? There had to be one.

"How'd you get here?" he asked Doreen.

"Runnin' from Jud Vale," she answered simply. "Walt and Alice took me and Micky in and let us stay."

Why? Had they known Doreen that well? Had they been neighbors? What? Too many unanswered questions. It made Smoke uneasy. Very uneasy.

"You have any idea how many head of cattle you have?" Smoke asked the old man.

"Not no more. Jud and his gunhands been runnin' 'em off for a year or more. The one herd they can't get to without a lot of fuss is west of here, next to the Bear River."

"How are you getting your food?"

The question seemed to make all three of them nervous. Walt finally said, "Friends slip food to us."

Smoke nodded, not satisfied with the reply but sensing he wasn't going to get much more out of the trio. Micky was outside, playing. Smoke figured the boy to be about eight years old.

"There is no point in my trying to restring the wire," Smoke said. "Without hands to ride fence, Jud's people would just cut it again come night."

"True."

"Do you have the money to pay hands, providing I could find some who'd work for you?"

"Oh, sure. I got money up in Montpelier. That's a Mormon town. Jud ain't gonna mess with them folks."

Smoke knew that for an iron-clad fact. Mormons tended

to stick together, and folks who thought they wouldn't fight because they were so religious soon learned how wrong they were—providing they lived through it.

Walt was saying, ". . . You ain't gonna find no one to work for me, anyways, Mr. Smoke. Jud's got the folks around here buffaloed."

"You let me think on that for a few hours. You just might be wrong." He smiled. "However, the hands I get might not be the type you're used to seeing."

Smoke stowed his gear in the bunkhouse and fired up the old potbelly stove in the center of the room. Dagger was warm and content and chomping away on corn in a hay-filled stall in the big barn.

Smoke had noticed that at one time—not too long ago—the Box T had been a money-making spread. So why the sudden downfall? Was it just because Jud Vale wanted the land? Smoke didn't believe that for a minute. There was more to it than that; a lot more.

Smoke hated bullies. If it were just a simple matter of Jud Vale's greed, the problem could be easily solved—with a gun. Smoke wanted the whole story, though, before it came to that, if it came to that. And he sincerely hoped it would not. He, however, had a hunch that it would. Usually all loud-mouthed, pushy, bullying types could be handled without being killed, for bullies are cowards at heart. Give them a good beating and you've got their attention. But Smoke felt that Jud wouldn't go down that easily. If Jensen stayed around, he would have to drag iron against Jud Vale.

He felt pretty sure he was going to stick around. Nothing like a good mystery to pique one's interest.

Over supper, Smoke asked, "Lots of small farmers in this area, huh?"

"Oh, yeah," the old rancher said. "Most of them just

21

barely hanging on. That's another thing that got me in trouble. I never minded farmers like a lot of ranchers seem to. Never had any trouble with them. I used to help a lot of them time to time. A little money, food, clothing, what have you. Used to hire some of the kids during the summer to work on the spread."

"Does Montpelier have a newspaper?"

"Sure."

Smoke nodded. "I'm going to be gone for several days." He noted the alarm that quickly sprang into the eyes of those around the table. "But I'll be back," he assured them. "And that's a promise."

"Jud Vale is a no-good," the farmer said bluntly. "And I'll say it to his face."

"Chester . . ." his wife warned.

"No, Mother," the man in the patched overalls shook his head. "Time for backing down is over. Mr. Burden is a good man who's hit on some hard times. We can't just turn our backsides to him and forget all the times he's helped us. 'Sides, we need hard cash desperate."

"Ralph is only twelve years old," she reminded him.

"And been doin' a man's work since he was nine. You seen how excited he is about Mr. Smoke's offer. And you heard Mr. Smoke say he ain't gonna put the plan into action unless the newspaper agrees to print the story and send it out to other papers."

"Well . . ." She shook her head. "I just don't know, Chester."

"Aw, Mom!" the boy finally spoke. "I can handle a gun good as the next feller!"

"No guns!" Smoke said it quickly and firmly. "If it comes to gunplay, I'll handle that. Any boy who shows up with a gun doesn't work."

"Yes, sir!" Ralph said. "You're the boss, Mr. Smoke,

for sure."

"You pass the word around to your friends and neighbors. And keep it inside the circle. We want this to be a total surprise to Jud Vale when we spring it."

The farmer grinned and stuck out his hand. Smoke shook it. "You got it, Mr. Smoke."

The editor of the newspaper chuckled and rocked back in his swivel chair. "I like it, Mr. Jensen. I really like it. Jud Vale doesn't throw that big a loop around this town, but he's made life pretty miserable for those in his area. I've been curious about just why he hates Walt Burden so. Of course I'll print the story, and I'll send it out to newspapers all over the state. We want to be sure those young boys are safe. And there is nothing like the power of the press to insure that. Hire your . . . cowboys, Mr. Jensen, and put them to work. I'll ride down and do a follow-up on the story in a few weeks, to keep interest alive."

"Damnedest bunch of cowboys I ever seen in all my born days," Walt said, looking at the new hands.

"Looks like we better get to cooking, Doreen," Alice said. "Some of those boys look like they haven't had a decent meal in weeks."

The youngest was ten and the oldest was fourteen. Of the boys, that is. In Montpelier, Smoke had rounded up three slightly older punchers. Dolittle, Harrison, and Cheyenne were in their sixties . . . they claimed. Smoke suspected they might be a tad older than that. He didn't know much about Dolittle and Harrison, except that they could sit a saddle and knew cows, but Cheyenne was quite another story. Smoke remembered Preacher spinning yarns about a mountain man he knew by the name of Cheyenne O'Malley from back in the '40s. Cheyenne was one of those born with the bark on, he didn't have to grow into it; mean from the git-go.

Cheyenne was about seventy, Smoke reckoned, and looked so skinny he might have to drink a glass of beer to keep his britches up. But he still wore his Colt low and tied down and Smoke knew the old mountain man could and would use it.

"All right, Cheyenne," Smoke told him. "You're the range boss on this job." Cheyenne nodded. "You boys know what that means. Cheyenne tells you to make like a frog, you just jump as high as you can. You don't have to ask if it was high enough. If it wasn't, he'll let you know. Dolittle and Harrison will be carrying orders from Cheyenne to you boys, and you boys will be spotted all around this spread.

"Now then, the first thing we're gonna do is round up some horses and top them off; settle them down for you." Smoke glanced at the animals the boys had used to get over to the Box T. Mules and plow horses. "Then you boys can turn your own animals out to pasture and let them rest." He looked at Walt. "All right, Boss, what's the first order of the day?"

The old rancher smiled. "The wife says the first thing we do is feed these boys."

All the boys cheered at that.

Jud Vale balled the newspaper up and hurled it into the fireplace. "That no good—" He proceeded to cut loose with a stream of cuss words that almost turned the air blue.

When he had calmed down enough to try to catch his breath, his foreman said, "Boss, this is bad. If one of them kids gets hurt by a bullet, the governor will send the law in on us, that is, if some vigilantes from around here don't hang us to the nearest tree first."

"I know, Jason. I know. That damn Smoke Jensen!

Jesus God, why didn't I recognize him right off and let him alone?"

"Didn't none of us recognize him, Boss. But we should have, I reckon." He wore a sheepish look. "Damn bunkhouse is full of them penny dreadfuls writ about him."

"I better not see any of them around!"

"I'll pass the word."

"Do that. Damn!" Jud yelled. "Pass the word, Jason: stay off of Box T range and don't bother the boys. Don't even go near them. Jensen can't stay up here forever and them damn kids got to go back to school come fall. We can wait."

"Them high-priced gunhands is about next to worthless when it comes to workin' cattle, Boss. Most of 'em is just salivating to get a chance to brace Smoke Jensen."

"I'll give a thousand dollars to the man who kills Jensen. You pass that word along, Jason."

"That ought to get something stirred up, for sure!"

While in Montpelier, Smoke had arranged for a wire to be sent to Sally, advising her where he was, and for a courier to bring any reply to the ranch.

One was forthcoming quickly.

Darling Smoke stop Doctors say baby must remain in a warm dry climate for at least two years stop Mother and Father arranged to stay with me stop Father bought a bank here in Prescott stop We are fine stop Miss you terribly stop Come when you are finished stop Love Sally stop.

"Bad news?" Doreen broke into his thoughts. He had not heard her come up.

The girl moved like a ghost.

"Yes and no. Our baby has to stay down in Arizona for quite a long time. Lung problems."

"Then you'll be leaving . . . ?" She let that trail off with a catch in her voice.

"No. Sally knows I don't go off and leave a job half-finished. I'll see this through. If it hasn't ended by midsummer, then I'll finish it."

She didn't have to ask how he would do that. She knew. "That is very kind of you, Smoke."

She moved closer. Doreen was a mighty comely lass. Smoke could smell the lilac water on her. Mayhaps, he thought, her middle name was Eve.

He moved back just a tad. "That is, I'll make up my mind about staying when and if you people ever get around to telling me the truth."

Her eyes turned frosty as an early morning chill. She spun around and stalked away, her rear end swaying like women's rear ends have a tendency to do.

Mighty shapely lassie. And Smoke didn't trust her any further than he could pick up his horse and toss him.

3

On the first full day of work, Smoke didn't know whether to laugh or cry.

The boys were sure willing enough, but the trouble was that none of them knew diddly-squat about ranch work. They were farm boys, used to gathering eggs and slopping hogs and plowing and such as that.

Little Chuckie fell off his mount, and landed in a fresh horse pile. The only other britches he had were hanging on the line to dry. He had to work the rest of that morning dressed, from the waist down, in his longhandles. With a safety pin holding up one side of the flap.

Of the boys, Jamie was the oldest and the strongest. He was built like the trunk of a large tree. And he could ride and was a fair hand with a rope.

Matthew was a frail young man who wore glasses and was in dire need of boots.

Smoke was making a list of what the boys needed; and he was going to see to it that they got it. One way or the other.

Ed meant well and tried hard, but it was plain that he would never be a cowboy. Smoke put him to running errands and taking messages back and forth.

Leroy would do. He never complained, even after being

tossed a half-dozen times. He just got back up, dusted himself off, and climbed right back in the saddle and stayed there until he showed the bronc who was running this show.

Eli was the son of a carpenter and, like Ed, was no horseman. Smoke put him to work fixing up the place, and there was a lot of fixing up to do. A ranch starts to run down mighty quick, and this spread had been neglected for a long time.

Jimmy and Clark and Buster would do fine, Smoke concluded.

Cecil was fourteen, like Jamie, and solid and mature for his age. A fair horseman.

Alan was a grown-up thirteen, from a hardscrabble farm family. A good solid kid.

Rolly, Pat and Oscar were all twelve and showed promise.

All in all, Smoke thought, a pretty good bunch of kids. But, he had to keep this in mind: they were kids. He could not chew on them like he would adults. He didn't want them screwing up their faces and bawling like lost calves.

"All right, Cheyenne!" Smoke called, with Dagger under him. "Take the men to work!"

Smoke rode over to a three-building town located on Mud Lake, leading a pack animal. He would buy the boys as much clothing as possible here. Maybe all of it if he were lucky. And he could pick up any talk about how Jud Vale was taking this new twist.

As soon as he walked in, he could tell by the barkeep's reaction that the name Smoke Jensen was known. Somebody had been talking about him, and fairly recently.

The barroom was separated from the general store by a partition, so the men could talk and cuss without bothering any ladies who might be shopping in the store. The only door connecting the store and saloon was closed.

Smoke ordered a beer and leaned against the bar, observing the very nervous barkeep draw the suds. Three men were sitting at a table in the back of the room. It was gloomy in the small saloon, and the men were shrouded in shadows, but Smoke could see well enough to recognize the men as part of one of the groups who had chased him all over half of the southeastern part of Idaho days back.

And one of them was Sam Teller, a gunfighter from over Oregon way. Sam wasn't known for his easy disposition and loving nature.

A local man, a farmer by the look of him, opened the door and stepped inside, closing the door behind him. He stopped cold when he saw the tall man at the bar. His eyes cut to the three gunslicks sitting at the table. He swallowed hard, then walked on to the bar and ordered a beer.

"All of a sudden it smells like a hog pen in here," one of the gunhawks commented.

The farmer's face hardened but he was smart enough to keep his mouth shut.

"What'll it be, neighbor?" the barkeep asked.

"Beer." The farmer took a position at the end of the bar, near the curve of the planks, so if matters deteriorated into gunplay, he could hit the floor and be out of the line of fire.

Smoke was a cattleman, so he could understand, at least to some degree, why ranchers disliked farmers. But Smoke Jensen was living proof that rancher and farmer could live side by side and be friends. And he knew that not all of the blame for the hard feelings could be laid at the doorstep of the ranchers. Some farmers flatly refused to work with the ranchers, fencing off the best water; homesteading in lineshacks that the ranchers had built and maintained; and sometimes rustling cattle, not always for food to feed hungry families. Sometimes just to aggravate the rancher.

The bartender had moved to the end of the bar, just as far away from Smoke Jensen as he could get.

Smoke sipped his beer and waited for the gunplay that he knew was just around the corner, lurking in those invisible shadows that drifted around and clung to those who lived by the gun.

"There ain't much to that pig slop, Burt," Sam Teller said. "Hell, he ain't even packin' no gun."

Burt. Smoke searched his memory. Could be Burt Rolly. Smoke had heard of him. A gunfighter of very limited ability, so he'd been told. Usually a back-shooter.

"You're a long ways from home, Jensen," Sam said. "I figured you was still in Colorado, hidin' under your wife's dresstail."

"You figured wrong on a lot of counts, Sam," Smoke told him. "But then, the way I hear it, you never were very bright."

"Huh?"

"I said you were stupid, Sam. Dumb. Ignorant. Slow. Mentally deficient. Am I making myself clear now?"

The farmer moved further away from Smoke and if the barkeep pressed any harder against the rear wall he was going to collapse the entire end of the store.

"I don't think I like you very much, Jensen," Sam said, finally realizing he was being insulted.

"I don't like you at all, Sam. And I'm not real thrilled with those half-wits with you."

Burt pushed back his chair and stood up, his hands at his sides. "You take that back, Jensen! I ain't no half-wit."

Smoke smiled at him. "You're right, Burt. You're not a half-wit."

Burt relaxed.

"You're all the way a fool," Smoke finished. "The best thing you boys could do is pay for your drinks and ride out of this area of Idaho. Forget about Jud Vale and Walt Burden. And for damn sure, forget about trying to brace me."

The third man at the table slowly stood up and walked to another table. He sat down and placed both hands on the table.

Smoke recognized him. "Smart move, Jackson."

"The timin' ain't right, Smoke," the gunhand said. "Man, you're walkin' around with your tail up in the air, huntin' trouble. That ain't like you. What's got you on the prod?"

"I don't like Jud Vale." Smoke spoke to the man without taking his eyes off of Sam and Burt.

"Hell, I don't like him either! But he's payin' top wages for fightin' men."

Smoke laughed. "To fight an old man and an old woman? To fight a young woman and her eight-year-old kid? For that, Jud Vale hires two dozen gunnies? He must be a mighty skittish man."

"They's a lot more to this than that, Smoke."

"I figure so myself. One of these days somebody's going to tell me the whole story."

"I'm tired of all this jibber-jabber!" Burt shouted, just about scaring the pee out of the barkeep. "I'm a-gonna kill you, Jensen!"

Smoke stood tall and straight, facing the two men standing by the table. "No, you're not, Burt. All you're going to do is get buried. Think about it, man. I've faced more than a hundred gunhands, most of them better than you. They're all dead, Burt. Every last one of them. Pike and Shorty. Haywood and Ackerman and Kid Austin. Canning and Poker and Grisson. Clark and Evans. Felter and Lefty and Nevada Sam. Big Jack and Phillips and Carson. Russell and Joiner and Jeff Siddons. Jerry and Skinny Davis and Cross. You want more names, Burt? All right. Simpson and Martin and Reese. Turkel and Brown and Williams and Rogers. Fenerty and Stratton and Potter and Richards. And a half hundred more whose names I

31

can't recall or never even knew. They're all dead and rotting in the ground. But I'm still here."

"Listen to him, boys," Jackson spoke the words softly. "I'm tellin' you, the timin' ain't right just yet. Back off."

"You could buy in!" Sam said hoarsely.

"Not just yet."

"Then you jist yellow!"

"No. But I'll be alive," Jackson told him.

The farmer was on the floor, belly down. The barkeep had slipped down to his knees and was peering around a keg of beer.

"Make your play, damn you, Jensen!" Sam yelled.

"Your deal," Smoke replied. "Bet or fold."

Sam and Burt grabbed for iron. Smoke's guns roared and belched fire and death. Sam stumbled back against the wall, his gun still in leather. Burt was plugged twice in the belly. He fell down on the floor and began squalling as the intense pain reached him. Sam cursed Smoke and managed to clear leather and level the pistol. Smoke shot him in the head. Burt tried to lift his pistol. He managed to cock it and fire, shooting himself in the foot, the slug tearing off his big toe. He dropped his gun to the floor and started yelling in pain.

Smoke glanced at Jackson. The man's hands were still on the tabletop, palms down.

"Holy Hell!" the barkeep hollered.

The farmer was praying to the Almighty.

"Can't say I didn't warn 'em," Jackson broke the silence.

"For a fact," Smoke replied, punching out empty brass and reloading. "Is there a bounty on my head, Jackson?"

"Thousand dollars."

"I don't have to ask who put it there."

"I 'spect you know."

"I imagine the bounty is gong to go up on me after this."

"It wouldn't surprise me none."

"What about them?" Smoke jerked his head at the dead and dying gunslicks.

"Don't ask me, Smoke. Hell, I didn't take 'em to raise!"

"I'll bury 'em iffen I can have what's in they pockets!" the barkeep said.

"Suits me," Smoke told him. He picked up his beer mug and drained it, wiping his mouth with the back of his hand. He set the mug back on the plank. "Fill it up, barkeep."

"Git it yourself! It's on the house. I ain't movin' 'til I know all the lead's through flyin'!"

Smoke walked around the bar just as the farmer was getting up off the floor. He looked at him. "You want another beer?"

"Hell, no!" The farmer hit the air and didn't look back.

"I'm gonna stand up now, Smoke," Jackson said.

"Go right ahead."

"Then I'm gonna walk out the door and get my horse and go."

"See you around, Jackson."

"Maybe. I ain't made up my mind about this job. You showin' up sorta tipped the balance some."

"Whatever pops your corn, Jackson."

The gunfighter nodded, turned, and left the smoky barroom. Within ten seconds, the sounds of his horse's hooves echoed down the short silent street.

Burt started hollering something awful.

"Ain't he gonna die?" the barkeep asked. "I'd lak to have them boots of his."

"Sooner or later. Is there any hard candy for sale in the store?"

"Hard candy!"

"Yeah. I got some kids working for me. They all probably have a sweet tooth."

"Hell, I don't know!"

33

Smoke shrugged and walked into the store area of the building. He was thinking that he'd better buy a couple boxes of .44's. Way things were going he'd probably need them.

The news of the gunfight had reached the ranch before Smoke returned. Walt and Cheyenne met him in the barn.

"Did you run into some trouble, boy?" the old rancher asked.

"Couple of two-bit gunhands who thought they were better than they really were." Smoke stripped the saddle off Dagger, hung up the reins, rubbed him down, and began forking hay into his stall.

Cheyenne and Walt were silent for a time. Walt broke it. "Swenson came by here, all flusterated. Said you cut them boys down faster than the blink of an eye."

"Like I said, they weren't as good as they thought they were."

Cheyenne grunted and spat a brown stream onto the barn floor. "I knowed Burt Rolly's dad. He wasn't no good neither. Utes kilt him years ago. Died bad. They never sung no songs about him. What was that other hombre's name?"

"Sam Teller."

The old mountain man and gunfighter shook his head. "Must not have been much to him. I never heared of him."

Cheyenne limped off. He still carried a Sioux arrowhead in his hip. Slowed him down when the weather changed.

"Doreen finally got around to telling me that you two had a little run-in, Smoke."

"Not much of one. I would just like to know why everyone is lying to me."

The rancher was silent for a time. "You want to explain that remark, Smoke? 'Cause if you don't, old man or not, I'm goin' in the house for my six-gun and call you out!"

34

Smoke chuckled. "Yeah . . . you probably would, too, Walt. But I'm going to let my statement stand. None of you have leveled with me. I've seen the quick looks passed between you whenever I touch on certain subjects. What's going on, Walt?"

"Doreen is a good girl, Smoke."

"I never said she wasn't."

"She isn't married to Clint Perkins."

"I didn't think she was. The boy is a wood's colt, huh?"

"How'd you guess?"

"Just that, a guess. Is the boy's father Clint Perkins?"

"Yes. They went together for a time—on the sly. Then he got her all puffed up and ran out on her. He kept tellin' Doreen how they was gonna move to California and he was gonna change and . . . lies and lies, that's all they was. He'd climb a telegraph pole for a lie and leave the truth layin' on the ground."

"So Doreen figured that a make-believe outlaw husband was better than no husband at all?"

"That's about it. Clint is a no-good, Smoke. He started out doin' good, I'll give him that much; he really did do good. Then he turned bad. The young man is not right in the head."

"All that about him seeing his parents killed and running off into the timber . . . ?"

"Lies. You got to understand something, Smoke. I was the first white man to settle in this part of Idaho. Back in '38. The first one. I built me a cabin and got settled in and then went back for Alice. When we got here, the Injuns had burned the cabin down. We built again and fought off Injuns until they got to where they'd leave us alone. I prospered. Found some color and panned it. Found some more color and mined that out. I got money, Smoke. Plenty of it. I got money in a half-dozen banks. Hell, I don't need this ranch or the cattle. I kept on to it for my boy."

The old man paused to light his pipe and Smoke waited.

"But he married into trash. Pure trash. That woman—damn her black heart wherever she is—wasn't nothin' but a whore. That's all she was. Anyways, they had a son. Clint. His name ain't Perkins, it's Burden. But she run off with him and changed it."

"Wait a minute, wait a minute! This is getting confusing. Back up. Where is your son?"

"Dead. Ten years back. He turned into a drunk after that woman run off and left him. Staggered around here drunk and crazy in the head and heart for years. He never hurt nobody. He was just a fool there at the end. Jud Vale killed him. Shot him for sport one night over at the tradin' post where you was this day. Made it last a long time. Shot his legs out from under him, then busted his hands and arms with .44's. It was a awful thing for one human to do to another. Jud and that no-good foreman of his, Jason, just left my boy there in the mud to bleed to death. He ain't never hired nothing but trash over there at the Bar V. Most of them runnin' from the law somewheres."

"Where does Clint fit into all this?"

The old man laughed bitterly. "That's funny, son. Really funny. You see, I hired some fancy detectives to hunt that witch-woman down and bring my grandson back to me. They found her and brung him back. Bad seed, Smoke. He's just bad. But the more I got to lookin' at him, the more I began to suspect he wasn't none of my blood. The day he run off for the last time, he told me. My boy Clint didn't father him. Jud Vale did."

4

Smoke walked outside the barn with Walt and paused to roll a cigarette. "Does Jud Vale know about Clint being his son?"

"Oh, yeah. That's why he wants Clint dead and Doreen his so bad. He suspects, and rightly so, that I changed my will leaving everything to Doreen. He don't want no wood's colt hanging around, messin' everything up. And with Doreen his woman, willing or not, he could produce a false weddin' license and claim it all. At worse, he could tie it up in court for years."

"Jud sounds like a real nice fellow."

"A regular Prince Charming," the old man said sourly.

"I'm glad you told me this, Walt."

"Me and the old woman talked about it last night. We agreed that it wasn't right for you to come in here and lay your life on the line for us, and us not to level with you. I'd have gotten around to tellin' you, son."

"You say you found gold around here?"

"A small pocket of it. I panned it plumb out. There was enough for me to invest in one thing or the other and become a well set up man. That's another thing, Smoke. Jud Vale knows about me panning the gold. But I never could convince the hard-headed no-good that there ain't

37

no more gold. The gold I panned washed in here from God knows where, and the small pocket I mined is gone. Nature is a funny critter, Smoke. She'll sometimes put precious minerals in a place where they just ain't supposed to be. And when it's gone, it's gone forever. There just ain't no more."

"But Jud Vale doesn't believe that." It was not a question.

Walt sighed. "No. The man's a fool when it comes to money. Greediest man I ever saw in all my life. Got hisself a regular palace on his spread. And Doreen believes the man is in love with her; obsessed, is the way she put it. He's finally found something that he can't have; he can't buy it or steal it, and he's furious about it."

"He might try to take her by force."

"That thought has come to me from time to time."

"You going to tell her that you leveled with me?"

"Yes. Oughta ease the tensions around here."

"For a fact. Let's go all the way with it and then we'll speak no more of it. How were you getting your food in here?"

"Shoshone friends of mine. But rations was gettin' kinda sparse since Jud found the trail they was usin' and posted guards on it."

"Toward the end of this week, once the boys have settled in, we'll take a ride to the trading post and stock up. I imagine Alice and Doreen would like a little outing."

"I reckon so. Ain't none of us been off this spread in months. And them boys you brung eat like starvin' animals!"

The boys settled right in and soon needed very little supervison. They began stringing wire and doing a good job of it. Smoke took Cheyenne and several of the older boys and went looking for Box T cattle. He felt he knew

38

where most of the cattle would be, and his hunch paid off.

"We been on Bar V range for a time," Cheyenne pointed out.

"And seeing more and more of Walt's cattle. Jamie, you boys start hazing them out and bunching them."

"Yes, sir, Mr. Smoke."

They hadn't gone another half-mile before Jud Vale and half a dozen of his hardcases came galloping up, punishing their horses needlessly. That was another way you could judge a man's character—by the way he treated his horse. Smoke's dislike for Jud Vale deepened as he looked at the lathered-up gelding he was riding.

"What the hell are you doing on my range, Jensen?" Jud demanded.

"Looking for Box T cattle, Vale. And finding them. You got any objections?"

Cheyenne had shifted positions so the muzzle of his Winchester was aimed right at a Bar V rider's belly, and the Bar V man didn't look a bit happy about it.

Smoke had pulled his Winchester out of the boot and had his thumb on the hammer. Jud didn't seem to be too terribly thrilled about that either, since the muzzle was pointed in his general direction.

"Yeah," Vale finally replied. "I got objections. I can't help it if that old coot's cattle wandered onto my range, eatin' up all my grass."

"Well, then, you should be glad to see us, Vale. We're going to take them back to home range and then you won't have to spend your nights worrying about them. Now we can either do that, or I can wire the territorial governor and ask for range detectives to be sent in here. How do you want it, Vale?"

The man puffed up like a 'possum and gave Smoke some dark looks. "Well . . . git your damn cattle and git the hell off my land then. I'm tired of lookin' at your damn ugly face, Jensen."

"Unless you want us over here every day for a couple of weeks, Vale, why don't you have your boys assist us? It would move a lot faster."

Cheyenne's leathery old face struggled to hide his grin. Smoke was pushing the big blow hard into a corner and the man couldn't find a way out.

Vale blustered and hissed like a spreadin' adder and shifted around in the saddle. "I ain't helpin' you do nothin', Jensen. I don't give a damn how often you come over here. You just make sure all the beeves you push across the crick are wearin' Box T brands, or by God, you'll answer to me."

"We can do that now, Vale," Smoke told him. He booted the Winchester and dropped his right hand to his thigh, close to the butt of that deadly .44.

Jud didn't like that idea at all. It was seven against two, for a fact. But it was also a fact that this was a no-win situation. Cheyenne was an old he-coon from 'way back. Jud's men might take him, but the old man was sure to empty two, maybe three saddles before he went down; and even down the old goat was as dangerous as a cornered grizzly. Even dying, if you got too close to the old bastard, he'd sure likely come up with a knife and cut you from brisket to backbone.

Smoke Jensen was quite another matter. Everybody knew he'd been raised by Preacher, and Preacher was a legend. Jensen had killed more than a hundred men—and that wasn't counting Injuns. Jud Vale knew the first thing to happen should he grab for iron, was that Smoke was going to blow him right out of the saddle.

And there just wasn't no percentage in dying.

"Round up your damn cattle and get off my range," Jud finally backed down. He savagely jerked his horse around and galloped off, his men following him.

"I hate a man treats a horse like that," Cheyenne said. "A horse or a dog. You show me a man who's unkind to animals and I'll show you a man that just ain't no damn good."

"I'm going to have to kill that man someday, Cheyenne. I can see it coming."

"I 'spect, Smoke, they's a long line of folks ahead of you thinkin' the same thing."

Saturday, they went to the trading post on Mud Lake.

Walt drove the wagon, with Alice by his side, and Doreen, all prettied up, and Micky sitting on boxes in the back of the wagon.

Doreen was a looker, no doubt about that, and a flirty thing, too. Smoke did his best to avoid her sliding glances. The heat coming out of her eyes could fry an egg. Although Smoke didn't think kitchen cooking was what she had on her mind.

Cheyenne, Winchester across his saddle horn, rode on one side of the wagon, Smoke on the other.

As they rode and rattled up to the big store, Cheyenne pointed out the two fresh graves out back of the building.

Doreen and Alice and Micky went into the store part of the building to shop, and Smoke, Walt, and Cheyenne went into the bar to have a beer.

"Not you agin!" the barkeep moaned, as Smoke stepped inside.

"I'm peaceful," Smoke grinned at him.

"Haw! You won't be when some of them no-count hardcases from the Bar V show up. Just don't wreck my damn place," he warned.

"Why don't you just shut up and get us a bottle," Cheyenne told him. "You prattle on like a scared old woman."

The bartender looked at the skinny old mountain man with the wicked look in his eyes and shut his mouth. He placed a bottle on the bar and several shot glasses. Smoke pushed the shot glass away and ordered a beer.

Cheyenne downed one quick belt and poured another, taking the shot glass and moving to the far end of the bar where he could watch the door. He had left his Winchester in the saddle boot. If anything happened in the barroom, he would rely on the old Colt with the worn handles hanging low on his right side. Or on the Bowie knife sheathed on his left side. Or on the .44 derringer in his boot. Or anything else he could get his hands on. If it just had to be, the old mountain man would pick up a porcupine to use as a weapon and damn the needles.

Micky had a bottle of sarsaparilla and was sitting on a bench in front of the store. Coming to town was quite an outing for the boy.

Alice and Doreen were oohhing and aahhing over some new dress material in the store.

Two farmers were sitting at a table, nursing mugs of beer, talking quietly. They finished their drinks and left. A fat man, a drummer from the looks of him, was sitting alone at a table next to a window. He kept shifting his eyes to Smoke, stealing fast sly glances.

"Say!" he finally spoke. "Aren't you Smoke Jensen, the gunfighter?"

Smoke cut his eyes. "I'm Smoke Jensen."

"Well, I'll just be hornswoggled! I just read a big article on you in the *Gazette*. The writer said you've killed more'un five hundred men."

"Not quite that many," Smoke corrected.

"Kilt two right in here a few days back," the barkeep said with a grin. "This is my place. I'm Bendel." He pointed. "Kilt 'em right over yonder. They's buried out back."

"You don't say!" the drummer bobbed his head up and down. "I'm from St. Louis myself. I got the finest line of women's underthings and unmentionables on the market today, I do."

"How kin you sell 'um if you cain't mention 'um?" Cheyenne asked him.

The drummer looked startled for a moment, then burst out laughing. "Oh, that's a good one. I'll have to remember that." He stared at the old mountain man. "Are you somebody famous?"

"I have been a time or two," Cheyenne grumbled.

"That's Cheyenne O'Malley," Smoke informed the drummer.

"No kidding! You once fought off a hundred hostile savages."

"More like fifteen," Cheyenne told him. "And they wasn't savages or hostile. They was just mad at me 'cause I bedded down with the chief's oldest daughter. She was due to marry the war chief who led the band who come after me. Never could make no sense out of that. I enjoyed it and so did she. I went back about ten years later and looked her up. Sorry I did that. She was about the size of a tipi. Hit me up side the head with a rock and called me all sorts of vile names. Damned if I didn't have to fight the same bunch all over again. But this time that war chief was mad 'cause I hadn't toted her off ten years back. I don't think they got along too well."

"That's incredible!" the drummer said.

Cheyenne belched. "Damn squaw follered me from the Sun River all the way over to the Bitterroot. Hollerin' and cussin' and raisin' hell. I finally lost her around Lolo Pass. Things like that tend to take some of the joy out of messin' with wimmin."

"What stories I'll have to tell when I get back to St. Louis!" He looked out the window. "Bunch of riders coming."

Smoke walked to the batwings and looked out. "Gunhands," he said.

"Is there going to be a Wild West shoot-out?" the drummer questioned.

"I hope not."

"Oh, that would be so exhilarating!"

"Not for them that gits shot," Cheyenne said, slipping the hammer thong from his pistol. "All they git is plugged."

Half a dozen Bar V hands began crowding into the barroom. They pulled up short and fell silent when they saw Smoke.

Smoke knew two of them. Blackjack Morgan and Gus Fall. The others might well be hell on wheels with a short gun, but they just hadn't made a name for themselves as yet. And if they decided to brace Smoke Jensen and Cheyenne O'Malley, the only name they were going to get would be carved on their gravestones.

"Jensen," Blackjack said, walking past him, his spurs jingling.

Smoke nodded his head.

Gus stopped by the bar and stared at Smoke. He shifted his chew around in his mouth and spat toward a spittoon near Smoke's boot. He missed the cuspidor, the tobacco juice striking Smoke's boot.

Gus grinned at him. "You can get the boy out front to come lick it off."

His grin was wiped off his face in a bloody smear as Smoke swung the beer mug, hitting Gus's jaw and knocking a couple of teeth slap out of his mouth. Gus was propelled backward, his boots slipping on the fresh-mopped floor. He slammed through the batwings, tearing one off, and fell into the dusty street, on his back, out cold.

Micky sat on the bench and stared, mouth open, eyes wide.

Smoke tossed the handle of the mug onto the plank. "Another beer, please."

"There wasn't no call to do that," one of the young so-called gunslicks told Smoke. "'Sides, Gus is my friend. I feel obliged to take up for him."

Cheyenne laid the barrel of his Colt against the young man's head and he dropped to the floor like a rock.

One of the young man's buddies thought it was a dandy time to grab for iron. He changed his mind as Cheyenne eared back the hammer on his Colt and put those cold old eyes on the kid.

"Boy," Cheyenne warned him, "I'll blow a hole in your gawddamn belly a horse could ride through."

"That's Cheyenne O'Malley!" the drummer blurted out as warning.

The young man's face turned gray and shiny with sweat. He let his eyes slide away from the eyes of death staring at him from the face of the mountain man. Slowly, very slowly, he let his hands drop to his sides, as far away from the butts of his guns as humanly possible. He would have grabbed the boards on the floor if his reach had been long enough.

Cheyenne eased the hammer down and holstered the Colt. He turned his attentions back to his shot glass.

"See about Gus," Blackjack told one of the men. He cut his eyes to Smoke. "You're right touchy today, Smoke. Who twisted your tail?"

"Two-bit gunhands have a tendency to annoy me." Smoke lifted his fresh mug of beer with his left hand and took a sip.

"When Gus gets up from the dirt, he's gonna kill you, Smoke."

"He'll try." Smoke turned his back to the gunfighter and sipped his beer.

Blackjack moved to a table and sat down, ordering a bottle.

The drummer was scribbling frantically in a notebook; he wanted to be sure to get all this down. He might write a book about this.

Gus was helped back into the barroom, his mouth bloody and his eyes wild with hate and fury. Smoke turned to watch him, his right hand by his side.

Gus shook himself away from the men on each side of him and faced Smoke. He was so mad he was trembling.

"Gus," Blackjack warned. "Back off, son. This is not the time."

"Go to hell!" Gus said, without taking his eyes off of Smoke.

"You better do what he says, boy," Cheyenne told him. "You're just about to step off into where the waters is deep and dark."

"You go to hell, too, old man!"

Cheyenne shrugged his shoulders. "Nobody can ever say I didn't try to warn you about the currents."

"You ready, Jensen?" Gus asked.

"I'm not finished with my beer, Gus. I would suggest you get you a cool one and calm down some."

"You, by God, don't tell me what to do, Smoke."

"I'm just trying to save your life, Gus."

Gus cussed him. "Here or in the street, Jensen?"

"It doesn't make a damn bit of difference to me, Gus." Smoke sat his beer mug down on the plank.

Gus reached for his guns.

5

Smoke's left-hand Colt roared and bucked as his cross-draw flashed.

The slugs hit Gus in the chest and belly, doubling him over. He stumbled back and grabbed onto a table's edge for support. He finally managed to drag iron just as Smoke fired again, the .44 slug slamming into his chest. The light began to fade around him as the men in the barroom took on a ghostly appearance, drifting into double images as the sounds of the pale rider grew louder in his ears.

Gus looked down at his hands. What had happened to his guns? His hands were empty. But he had drawn them. He was sure of that.

Gus sat down heavily in a chair and the legs broke under the sudden weight, spilling him to the floor. The last thing he would hear was the sounds of the pale rider's horse galloping closer. And finally, the feel of that cold and bony hand reaching down to touch his shoulder.

"Did anybody even see Jensen draw?" the drummer asked, his voice filled with awe. "Jesus God, I didn't."

The young man whom Cheyenne had bopped on the noggin with the barrel of his Colt finally sat up and moaned, both hands to his head. "What happened?" he asked.

47

"Gus finally saw the critter," Blackjack told him.

The young man looked up into the cold eyes of Smoke Jensen. Right then, and unfortunately for him, only for a very brief moment, did the old homeplace farm back in Minnesota pull at him slightly.

The young man who had just recently taken to calling himself the Pecos Kid pushed those thoughts out of his head and began to think about how he could kill Smoke Jensen. Yeah . . . the man who killed Smoke Jensen would be famous all over the world. He'd have fame and money and all the women anybody could ever want. So he very wrongly thought.

Smoke stared down at him from the bar. His words momentarily chilled the Pecos Kid. "Put it out of your head, kid. Don't even think about it."

Smoke turned and Walt and Cheyenne followed him out of the bar and into the general store.

When Smoke was well out of earshot, Pecos said, "I bet I could take him."

Blackjack just shook his head in disgust.

It appeared that the bitterly cold and long winter had finally given way to spring as the warming winds began to blow. The syringa began to bloom, as did the balsam and lupine, and the marsh marigold and blue columbine lent their hues and fragrances to the cacophony of color. Harrison had ridden to the store by the lake and came back with bad news.

"That Clint Perkins done struck agin, Mr. Walt. This time he killed a man over on the Little Malad. Some big landowner over thataway."

Walt kicked at a rock and cussed.

"And that ain't all. Jud Vale—had to be him—done upped the ante on Smoke's head. Five thousand dollars to the man who kills him."

Smoke had walked up, listening. The news came as no surprise to him.

Walt looked at him. "Jud knows that with you out of the picture this whole operation would fold. Me and Cheyenne and Dolittle and Harrison could hold on for a time, but not for long. Maybe it's time for me to sell out and move on; take Doreen and Mickey with me and the old woman and just get gone."

"Is that what you want to do, Walt?"

"Hell, no!" There was considerable heat in the man's voice.

"Then don't. But here's what we can do: round up the rest of your herds and sell off the older stuff. That would take some strain off the range. We could use the boys to drive them to the railhead at Preston. Me and Cheyenne would stay here on the place with you to make sure Jud's men don't burn the house down."

Walt thought for a moment, then nodded his head. "All right, let's do 'er."

Leaving Cheyenne in charge of the roundup, Smoke saddled up and headed for the nearest telegraph office to find a buyer for the cattle. He did not take the normally traveled roads or trails, but instead cut across country, blazing his own trail.

Smoke wasn't worried about the men Jud Vale had hired. Most of them were stand-up, look-you-in-eye gunfighters. They had a reputation to defend or to build, and back-shooters they were not. It was the bounty hunters that Smoke knew would be coming in who worried him.

That scum had no scruples or morals or anything that even remotely resembled those attributes.

And they would be coming in once that five thousand dollar ante on his head was spread about the country; that would not take long to accomplish.

He made the ride to the wire office with no trouble, and sent wires out until he found a buyer who knew him and was interested in the cattle. He made arrangements over the wires to meet the shipment at the railhead with a bankdraft.

He walked over to the hotel and checked in, then got himself a bath and a shave and changed clothes while his range clothing was being washed, dried, and ironed. Then he headed for a cafe for a meal.

Smoke was a handsome, striking-looking man, tall and muscular, and he turned many a female head as he strode up the boardwalk, spurs jingling. And he caused many a man to step back as he passed, for even though Smoke did not know it, and would have scoffed at it if someone had told him so, there was clear and present danger in those cold brown eyes. And by the way he wore his guns, there was no denying that he was very comfortable with those Colts, and knew how to use them. And more importantly, would use them.

He had changed into dark pin-stripe trousers over his polished boots, a white shirt with black string tie, and a leather vest.

He decided to have a beer before he ate his lunch and pushed open the batwings of the saloon, stepping inside.

The bounty hunters and the gunfighter locked eyes.

John Wills, Dave Bennett, Shorty Watson, and Lefty Cassett were sharing a bottle and playing poker.

Smoke told the barkeep he wanted a beer and walked over to their table, pulling out a chair and sitting down. "Deal me in, boys."

"You got a lot of brass on your butt, Jensen," Lefty told him. "Who the hell invited you?"

"You're hurting my feelings, Lefty. Makes me think I smell bad. And to think I just spent good money to have a bath and a shave."

"Very funny, Smoke," Wills said. "Notice how we're all laughing."

"I can see that. You boys gonna deal me in or not?"

"Closed game, Jensen," Shorty told him. "Just like you're gonna be soon. Closed. Like in a box."

They thought that was funny. Hysterically so. Smoke smiled with their laughter. They stopped laughing when they heard the almost inaudible click of a hammer being eared back.

"Is the joke over so soon?" Smoke asked, an innocent expression on his face. "Keep your hands where I can see them, boys."

"You can't shoot us like this, Jensen," Wills said, a very hopeful note in his voice. "That'd be murder!"

"And you law-abiding boys certainly don't hold with murder, now, do you?" Smoke's voice was low-pitched and deadly.

Lefty softly cursed Smoke.

"Boys," Smoke told them, as he tapped the barrel of his Colt on Shorty's knee, that action bringing a sheen of sweat on the man's face. "I'm going to have myself a nice quiet drink and then I'm going to the cafe for something to eat. While I'm having my drink, you boys finish yours. While I'm in the cafe, I'd better see you scum ride out of town and don't come back while I'm here."

"And if we don't?" Dave Bennett challenged.

"I'll come out of the cafe with both hands full of Colts and one thing on my mind: killing all four of you."

Wills swallowed hard and said, "This ain't like you, Smoke. You've usually had to be pushed into a gunfight."

"I came out here for a vacation. Soon as I crossed over into Idaho Territory, folks started pushing me. Now I'm pushing back. Keep another thought in mind, boys: if you ride out of here heading east, I'll know what side you're on."

"And . . . ?" Shorty asked.

"I will officially declare open season on bounty hunters."

Smoke holstered his Colt, much to the relief of all lthe men around the table. He stood up, turned his back to the men, and walked to the bar, ordering a drink.

Lefty exhaled slowly. "We got some talkin' to do, boys. We cross the Bear headin' east. This here job ain't gonna be no cakewalk."

"I say we take him as a group," Wills said. "Winner take it all."

"Here and now?" Shorty asked, doubt in his voice. "Standin' up and lookin' at him?"

"Hell, no! We'll ambush him. But we're gonna wait. The ante is sure to go up as Jensen puts more and more punk gunslingers into the ground. We'll just lay back and let them reputation-huntin' gunhands get kilt. Then we'll make our move."

Smoke sat at a table by a window, eating his meal, and watched the bounty hunters ride out of town, heading west. The move was not unexpected and didn't fool him one bit. He'd bet a sack of gold nuggets that Wills and his bunch would get a couple of miles out of town and then swing around and double back, try to get ahead of him and maybe set up an ambush. For sure they were going to head east where the trouble was, and the blood money was waiting for the man or men who killed Smoke Jensen.

Right then and there, over his apple pie and third cup of coffee—for Smoke was a coffee-drinking man—he made up his mind that he was in this fracus to stay, come Hell, Jud Vale, or that hot-eyed Doreen.

Smoke Jensen just did not like to be pushed.

Smoke left before dawn the following morning. He rode straight south out of town and did not turn east until he came to a canyon very close to the Utah line. He built a hat-sized fire and cooked his supper, then mounted up and rode until dusk before finding a place to bed down for the night. The bounty hunters might find him, but Smoke was going to make it as difficult as possible for them.

He was back in the saddle again before dawn, and did not stop to boil coffee until the sun had bubbled its way up into the sky and he'd found a place that was easily defended.

He crossed the Wasatch Range and pointed Dagger's nose north, keeping on the west side of Bear Lake. He was on home range by late afternoon.

"Any trouble?" Cheyenne asked in the barn.

"None. But I did run into four bounty hunters."

"More than that drifted in the last couple of days. And Jud Vale is hirin' more guns. I think the no-count is gonna hit the herd and to hell with whether the boys gits hurt."

Smoke smiled. At the wire office he had sent and received more than one telegraph. He handed a copy to Cheyenne. The man read it and his leathery face crinkled in a smile.

Received your wire stop Would be delighted to accompany the boys on a cattle drive stop Expect me at the ranch in three days stop.

It was signed by the editor of the Montpelier paper.

"Tomorrow morning, I'll ride over to the trading post and tack this to the wall," Smoke said. "Jud will have it in his hands within hours. Then we'll see how he reacts to this news."

"Son of a bitch!" Jud shouted. Then he tore the wire to small bits, flinging the paper to the floor and kicking at the shreds. "Damn that Smoke Jensen to Hell!"

"This shore changes the plans," Jason said.

With a long sigh, Jud nodded his head. "Tell the boys to

relax. We can't hit the herd with a damn newspaper man along. Public opinion would crucify me. The territorial governor would have this place swarming with U.S. Marshals if just one of those damn kids got hurt and it was reported."

"But they might not have a ranch to come back to," Jason said with a wicked smile.

"Yeah," Jud said softly. "You damn right!"

"You boys take 'er easy," Walt told the gathering in dawn's first light. "Ten miles a day is fine with me."

The editor of the newspaper had brought three men with him, a cub reporter from back East and two tough-looking men from his church. The men were heavily armed and ready for trouble.

Smoke knew there would be no trouble against the herd on this run. Jud was arrogant and perhaps crazy in the head, but he wasn't stupid. Smoke expected the drive to make it through with only the normal mishaps that took place on any cattle drive.

But he was equally certain the ranch would be attacked.

They stood and watched as the men and boys began moving the cattle out, the cattle setting their own pace.

After the dust had settled, Smoke began his preparations for the attack he was sure was forthcoming.

Cheyenne would stay in and defend the bunkhouse. The old mountain man and gunfighter had loaded up several rifles and half a dozen pistols. He had plenty of food prepared by the ladies and a couple of barrels of water to use against fire should it come to that.

Before the drive began, Smoke had fortified the horses' stalls with extra boards. The stalls were as safe from bullets as they could make them.

Both Alice and Doreen could handle a rifle or pistol as well, or better, than the average man. They would stay in the house with Walt and Micky.

Smoke would station himself in the loft of the barn. He had placed loaded rifles and shotguns at both ends of the building, and he had plenty of food and water to last out any siege.

Now all they had to do was wait, and sometimes that was harder than the actual battle.

The next move was up to Jud Vale and his men.

Probably forty or more men to wage war against an old rancher, his wife, a young woman, her eight-year-old son, three old men, a group of boys whose average age was twelve, and one gunfighter.

Smoke had to laugh and question the bravery of those who rode with Jud Vale.

Just before dark, Smoke did a once-around of the buildings, looking in first on those in the house.

"We're set, Smoke," the rancher told him. "We've got Micky in the basement, guardin' the potatoes and the canned goods."

Smoke grinned and nodded. "No bullet can reach him down there, for sure." He noticed that both Alice and Doreen had changed into men's britches, so they could get around faster. Doreen did things to those jeans that the manufacturer never dreamed of.

She noticed the direction his eyes were taking and smiled at him.

"I got to go," Smoke muttered, and left the house.

In the bunkhouse, Cheyenne waved him toward the coffeepot. "I went over to the house about an hour ago," the old mountain man said. "Both them wimmin was prancin' around in men's britches. I never seen the like. This goes on, wimmin'll be votin' 'fore long and that'll be the ruination of the country." He was reflective for a moment. "Not that I ever voted that much myself. Quit altogether about a year after I cast my vote for Millard Fillmore. But, hell, anybody can make a mistake. I was gonna vote for that Abe Lincoln. But by the time I made up my mind and got to where I could vote, somebody had done up and shot him. Plumb disheartenin'. Damn shore ruined Abe's night out, too. You much on votin', Smoke?"

"I wasn't until I married Sally. Kind of hard to find a ballot box at Brown's Hole."

"For a fact. Fort Misery, we used to call it. But I 'spect Preacher told you that."

"Yes, he did."

"Ol' Warhoss is still kickin'. He's got to be eighty-five if he's a day. But them Injuns is takin' right good care of him. And I understand they's some old gunslingers and mountain men got together and in the process of building a retirement home for us old coots."

"That's my understanding."

"Won't that be grand! I'll have to go check that out—if I ever live to be old, that is."

Smoke laughed at him and walked back to the barn.

It was full dark when he crawled into the loft and made himself comfortable at the east end of the barn. He figured that was the direction from which the attack would most likely come.

Before taking his position, he watched the lamps go out in both the house and the bunkhouse as the defenders made ready for war.

Smoke settled down and waited.

6

Arrogant! Smoke thought, as he heard the sounds of hooves drumming on the road. Jud is so sure of himself that he just rides right up the road to the gate.

He heard the gates being torn down and then the wild screams of the hired guns as they galloped up the road toward the house.

Smoke quickly shifted positions and sighted a man under the hunter's moon that illuminated the night sky. He took up slack on the trigger and the butt-plate slammed his shoulder. A saddle emptied just as gunfire from the house and bunkhouse roared, shattering the night and emptying half a dozen more saddles.

He heard Jud's voice, hollering for his men to fall back to the ridges.

Smoke fired again, and saw a man jerk in the saddle. He managed to stay on his horse, but one arm was hanging useless and flopping by his side.

The attackers had been able to fire no more than half a dozen shots before they were beaten back.

One man struggled to his boots in the road and began staggering and lurching toward the gates. The defenders held their fire and let him go. Just before he reached the gates, he collapsed face down in the hard-packed dirt and did not move.

That sight must have done it for the riders. Someone shouted, "Hell with this! The luck ain't with us this night."

The attackers rode off, heading back for the friendlier range of the Bar V. They left their dead and wounded behind them.

Smoke and the others waited a reasonable length of time, to see if it was a trick, and then slowly and cautiously gathered in the yard.

Smoke and Cheyenne roamed about, checking on the men sprawled on the ground.

They found several alive. "What do we do with those still alive?" Cheyenne questioned.

"Patch them up and get word to Jud to come and get them," Smoke told him. "Maybe pile them in a wagon and send them back to Jud. We'll see." He was kneeling down beside a man who was alive, but not for long. He had been shot in the center of the chest.

"He'll never quit, Jensen," the dying man gasped. "Vale's a crazy man."

"Why is he doing it?"

The man ignored that. "As long as he's got a dime in his jeans he'll hire fighting men."

"Why?" Smoke persisted.

"King. To be king. Wants to control everything from the state line to Preston. Everything and everybody."

"Shut up, Slim!" another wounded man growled, mercenary and loyal to the gun right to the end.

"You go to hell, Lassiter!" Slim told him. He cut his eyes to Smoke. The light was slowly fading from them. "Vale's got gunhands comin' in on the train. This is shapin' up to be the biggest range war in . . . the state. He'll overpower you just by . . . numbers, Jensen. And he's just about reached . . . the point where he don't give a damn if the kids git hurt."

Slim groaned and closed his eyes. He did not open them again.

Smoke rose to his boots and took the blanket that Doreen handed him, spreading it over the dead gunfighter. Cheyenne had taken all the guns and ammo from the dead and wounded men. They would be added to the arsenal of the Box T. Smoke felt sure they would be needed before all this was over.

He knelt down beside Lassiter. The man had a bullet-burn on the side of his head and a slight shoulder wound. Painful but not serious. "I ought to call the U.S. Marshals in here and file charges against all of you, Lassiter . . ."

The gunfighter sneered at him.

". . . But that would take weeks and we'd have to keep you prisoner and look at your ugly face every day. It just isn't worth it."

"You better kill me, Jensen," Lassiter warned. "Davidson was a friend of mine."

"You should choose your friends more carefully, Lassiter. No, I'm not going to kill you. Not like this, anyway. Not at this time."

"Then you're a damn fool, Jensen!"

"Maybe. But I can sleep at night, and I don't make war against kids and women and old people."

"Who gives a damn what happens to a bunch of snot-nose brats!"

Smoke was a hard man in a harsh time and environment, and he had killed many, many men. But he had to shake his head at the cold-blooded callousness of Lassiter.

"Back away and let me finish him," Cheyenne said, walking up. "We got it to do sooner or later."

Doreen stood looking at it all through wide and scared eyes.

Smoke had no doubts about the old mountain man's ability to do just what he suggested. And he knew the old man was right: they would have it to do sooner or later.

But he just couldn't kill the wounded man that way.

He shook his head. "Get him patched up, Doreen. We'll put him in a wagon."

He walked over to where a young man lay, gut shot. The young gunfighter, no more than a couple of years out of boyhood, lay with both hands clutching his belly. The blood seeped darkly through his fingers, glistening wetly under the light of the hunter's moon.

"You got a mamma you want me to write, boy?"

He shook his head, wincing with the painful movement. "They throwed me out of the house a long time ago. I wasn't about to spend the rest of my life . . . sloppin' hogs and milkin' cows."

"Beats what you got now," Smoke coldy and bluntly informed him.

The young man cussed him. Smoke watched as his right hand slipped toward his large belt buckle. Smoke reached down and pulled a derringer from behind the buckle before the gunhand could reach it. The young gunfighter cursed him even more.

"How much was Jud Vale paying you, boy?"

"A hundred a month and found!" He moaned the words as the pain reached higher levels in his bullet-shattered belly.

"Maybe you can buy something in Hell."

"They'll kill you, Jensen! This is one fight you ain't gonna win. Your reputation . . . ain't gonna hep you none this time around. Jud Vale's better than you. His real name is . . . is . . ."

"Shet your mouth, you bastard!" Lassiter shouted at the young man.

But the admonition fell on dead ears. The young gunny's eyes rolled back in his head as his soul went winging to a fiery, smoky eternity. His boot heels and spurs drummed and jangled against the ground and then he was still.

Smoke walked over to Walt. "How long has Jud been in this area, Walt?"

"'Bout twenty-five years. He just appeared one day with that damn Jason fellow."

"He doesn't look that old to me."

"He's older than he looks. But he's one hell of a man still. Don't sell him short none. I'd peg him in his late forties. He might be fifty even. Hard to tell with a man like that."

"No idea where he came from?" Smoke got the strong impression that Walt was lying. But why?

"Not a clue."

Cheyenne walked up, hearing the last of the conversation. "He come up here by way of Texas," the old mountain man told them "But I doubt he was Texas born. I 'member when he got here. Like all them hands of his, I think he's runnin' from the law somewheres."

"And you would guess . . . ?"

Cheyenne shrugged. "Back East. But that's just a guess. It'd be hard to read his backtrail after all these years."

"What's the count on those still alive, Cheyenne?"

"Four dead and three wounded. None of them hurt too bad."

"Can one of them drive a wagon?"

"Oh, yeah."

"Let's hitch up a team and get them on their way. We'll pile the dead in with them."

"Beats the hell outta diggin' a hole," Cheyenne said with a wicked grin.

Walt, Smoke, and Cheyenne took turns standing guard that night, but as it turned out, they could have all slept soundly, for Jud Vale and his so-called fighting men had had quite enough of the Box T for this go-around.

"Four dead," Walt said, holding a cup of coffee in his

hands, warming them against the early morning chill.

"They'll be more," Smoke told him. "This battle is just getting started. Now I'm afraid that some of the kids are going to be hurt."

"I don't think that even Jud Vale would do that. Not deliberately. One of those kids gets hurt, the whole area would turn agin him, and he knows it. But they might catch a bullet that was meant for one of us."

"The kids desperately need the money for their families," Smoke concluded. "I think what I'll do is ride around the area and speak to the mothers and fathers about it. Lay it on the line. Whatever they say, that's it."

Walt spoke around the stem of his pipe, "With most of the herd gone, we could do without the younger ones. Whatever the parents say, Smoke."

Smoke began seeking out and questioning the parents early the next morning, riding first to Little Chuckie's house; if that's what the shack could be called. It wasn't that his parents were rawhiders, they were just having a tough time getting the farm operation going—with Jud Vale and his men no small part of that struggle.

"It would really be a blow to Chuckie's pride iffen you was to send him home, Mr. Smoke," the father said. His wife nodded her head in agreement. "The boy is right proud of being able to bring in some money this summer. We'll leave it up to him."

Smoke rode over to the parents of Matthew, the frail little boy with the thick glasses. He got the same message as before. The parents were not unconcerned about their children; it was simply that this was still the raw frontier, and one grew up and pulled his or her weight from the git-go. It was called survival.

Smoke spent that day and most of another day talking

with the parents of the boys. The message he got, albeit worded differently came out to mean the same thing: it was up to the boys whether to stay or leave.

Smoke drifted on over to the railhead, arriving there about the same time as the herd. He watched through hard, chilly eyes, as the passenger car spewed forth a dozen or more booted, spurred, and two-gunned men. Smoke did not need a telegraph wire to tell him that these were the men the kid had told him about before he died in the front yard of the Box T spread.

Jud Vale was going for the brass ring this time, for Smoke recognized many of the newly arrived hired guns.

He watched as Gimpy Bonner limped off the train and made his way back to the horse cars. Gimpy was deadly quick and had no backup on him. He had a horse shot out from under him years back and the horse rolled on his leg, breaking it in several places, leaving him with a permanent limp.

Shorty DePaul, all five feet five inches of him followed Gimpy. Short he may be, but those guns of his, and his ability to use them made him as tall as the next man.

The editor of the Montpelier newspaper had walked over to stand by Smoke's side and watch the gunfighters leave the train. "Who is that one?" he asked.

"Scott Johnson. From down Arizona way. That stocky fellow with him is called Yates. Right behind them is De Grazia and Jake Hube. They work as a team; they'll shoot you front or back. Doesn't make any difference to them."

"Looks like Jud Vale is pulling out all the stops, doesn't it?"

"For a fact," Smoke said, as he watched two gunfighters named Becket and Pike step out of the car.

Jaeger, the German immigrant turned gunfighter, stepped down right behind them. Molino was right behind him.

Smoke ticked the names off to the editor.

Chato Di Peso, the much feared and very dangerous New Mexico bounty hunter stepped down, hitching at his gun belt as he walked.

There were several young punks, with fancy guns and silver adorned gun belts tagging with the better known gunnies. Smoke counted them out as two-bit never-would-be's with no sand in them.

"I think," the editor said, "that I shall inform the governor of this gathering of trash."

"Go ahead. But it won't do any good."

"Why?" the man asked indignantly.

"There isn't a man over there who is wanted for anything that I know of. And there is no law against hiring tough men to work for you."

"There is going to be a bloodbath around the Bear, Mr. Jensen."

"Yes. And the only way I know to avoid it is for Walt and Alice Burden to turn tail and run; just give up their holdings to a madman and leave the country. Would you want to see them do that, Mr. Argood?"

"No," the editor replied quickly. "I would not. Is there a joker in this deck, Smoke?"

Smoke smiled. "Yes. And his name is Clint Perkins. He's an unknown. Have you ever seen him?"

"No. Few people have over the years. Or at least, if they have, they aren't talking. But I can tell you that many still look upon him as some sort of Robin Hood."

"But you don't."

Argood snorted in disgust. "He's no better than a common outlaw. And personally, from what I know about him, I think he's insane."

"Is he headquartered in this area?"

"No one knows. He's a mystery man. And a master of disguises." He looked at the most famous gunfighter in the West. "You think he'll show up here?"

"I think so. This is just too good for him to miss." He didn't know how much the editor knew, so he chose his words carefully. "I think there is a lot of hate in the man; all bottled up and ready to explode. When it does, it's going to get very interesting."

"That, young man," Argood said drily, "is one way of putting it."

7

Smoke took the bank draft from the cattle buyer and tucked it safely away in a money belt around his waist. He had a letter from Walt giving him the authority to endorse the draft and deposit it in the bank over in Malad City, a wild, rip-roaring town with a history of murder, lynchings, and stage holdups. But the Overland Stage Company —whose run stopped at Malad City—had a good record of foiling holdups, so Walt's money would be reasonably safe after being deposited.

Smoke told Dolittle and Harrison to keep the boys close until he got back.

He crossed the Bear and headed for the wide-open town of Malad City. The town was named by French trappers, who, after becoming sick from gorging on beaver meat, named the town Malade, thinking the area unhealthy.

Smoke had a hunch that with the news of Jud Vale's hiring of gun hands now so widespread, Malad City would be crawling with guns for hire stopping for liquid refreshments—and a fling with the hurdy-gurdy girls—as they made their way to the Bar V. And he also wondered if the ante on his head had been upped past the five thousand dollar mark.

It wouldn't surprise him a bit.

As he rode, Smoke tried to put some more reason behind what Jud Vale was doing. Or was what Walt had told him the sum total of it all? Smoke concluded that Walt was probably right in his assessment of the situation. If Vale could get his hands on the Box T, he would then have the largest spread in the state, and would certainly be a powerful man, a man to reckon with.

On this trip, Smoke stayed with the main road leading to Malad City, and a sorry road it was.

He met several groups of men, riding in twos and threes, all looking like hardcases, and all heading east. They either did not recognize him, or did not want to brace him with such short backup.

Since he had been late getting away from the railhead, Smoke made camp just to the south of Oxford Peak, the snow-capped mountain thrusting up more than a mile and a half into the air. He was boiling his coffee and frying his bacon when he heard the faint sounds of hooves approaching his camp from out of the fast falling dusk, the rider coming from the north.

"Hello, the fire! I'm friendly."

"Then come on in and light and sit. Coffee's almost fit to drink."

Smoke saw the young man's hair sticking out from under his hat before he saw anything else. Flame red. He'd bet the young rider was called Rusty. The man's outfit was old, but well-cared for, and Smoke liked the way the young rider saw to his horse's needs before he took care of his own. He carefully rubbed the animal down with handfuls of grass and saw that it was watered and picketed on good graze. Smoke also noticed that the redhead's gun was tied down—which might not mean anything, or everything.

As he approached the fire, tin cup and plate in his left hand, his grin was genuine and his handshake firm and quick.

"Sure am glad to see a friendly face. Most of the hombres

I been seein' the past couple of days all looked like they could eat a porcupine and not feel the quills!"

Smoke filled his coffee cup without comment.

"My folks dubbed me Clarence, but nobody calls me that. Just Rusty."

"I guessed right at first glance." Smoke speared some bacon out of the pan and handed a hunk of bread to Rusty.

"Much obliged." He let his eyes drift over Smoke's rig, noting the two guns, one butt-forward.

"You ridin' east like all them others?" Smoke asked.

"West for a day, then I'll do a turnaround back to the Bear. Any work over yonder?"

"I'm lookin' for hands."

"You shore found one. My poke's as flat as a sit-on pancake."

"Might be dangerous signin' on with me."

Rusty's eyes narrowed. "What kind of work you got in mind, mister-whatever-your-name-is?"

"Punching cows. Fixing fence. Cleaning out water-holes. Cowboy work. You up to it?"

"Shore! That's what I been doin' since I was big enough to sit a saddle. What's the danger you talkin' about?"

Smoke sipped his coffee before replying. "Big rancher who is about half nuts is trying to run the old man and woman who own the spread off their land. They hit us the other night. We emptied seven saddles."

"How many is us?"

"You talking about hands?"

"Yep."

"Three old men who are about seventy and a handful of kids, average age twelve."

Rusty looked dead at him. "Are you serious?"

"As a crutch."

"What're you payin'?"

"A hundred a month and found."

"A hundred a month! Shoot, man! You just hired

yourself a hand."

"Those are fighting wages, Rusty."

"I kinda figured they was. But I got to tell you, I ain't never hired out my gun."

"Can you use it?"

"Oh, yeah. I reckon I'm as good as the next man. I've drug iron a time or two."

"Any family?"

"Ma and Pa died years back. I got some cousins somewhere that I ain't never seen."

"Just curious. I want to know who to notify if you catch one."

"Just plant me where I fall, I reckon. And make sure my horse is taken care of. He's a good one."

"I'm heading over to Malad City. Then we'll head back to the Box T."

"Sounds good to me. You got a name?"

"Doesn't everyone?"

"You are a most exasperatin' feller! You 'shamed of your handle?"

"No."

Rusty cussed and then ate his bacon, mopping the grease out of his tin plate with bread. He poured another cup of coffee, rolled a cigarette, and leaned back. "You a gunfighter?"

"Some say I am."

"You look familiar to me. I seen you somewheres before. On a wanted poster, maybe?"

"No. I'm not wanted. I own a ranch down Colorado way. The Sugarloaf. I'm just helping out an old couple. I don't like to see folks shoved around."

"Right nice of you. I kinda get riled up some myself when somebody tries to roll over other folks. You gonna tell me your name?"

Smoke smiled faintly. "I tell you my name, you might not come to work."

"For a hundred a month and found? You could tell me your name was Satan and I wouldn't back away."

"All right," Smoke replied. "Come to think of it, you just might be riding into a corner of Hell after all." He left it at that.

Smoke and Rusty reached Malad City at mid-morning, just as the town was catching its breath after a wild and raucous night. Things had been reasonably quiet the previous night, with only one killing.

"Don't never ask nobody for directions in this place," Rusty told him. "When they laid out these streets, they just tossed a handful of sticks on the ground for a blueprint . . . and then followed it."

They stabled their horses and Smoke pointed out a cafe, telling Rusty he'd meet him there in a few minutes. He took care of Walt's bank draft and walked the boardwalk to the cafe. He saw several gunslicks he knew by name and a dozen more who had the hardcase brand stamped all over them. And a half-dozen punks who were looking for a reputation, but more than likely would find a grave to hold their swagger long before they found a reputation.

Smoke Jensen had been elusive for over a decade, surfacing outside of his ranch in Colorado only briefly. Many people knew his name but could not put a face to it, unless they had memorized the covers of the many penny dreadfuls, most of which were rarely accurate.

He received many a furtive glance as he walked toward the cafe, for danger clung to him; it was an aura that made many strong and brave men step aside until he had passed.

Smoke was scarcely into his thirties, just now approaching the prime years of his life, but he was already a living legend, and not just west of the Mississippi. Had he elected to cut notches into the handles of his Colts after each kill, he would have gone through half a dozen sets and still not have any handles left. But only tinhorns did that.

He opened the door to the cafe and stepped in, the good smells of cooking making him realize how hungry he was. Rusty was already working on his first plate of bacon and eggs and fried potatoes—and the first of several pots of coffee.

The redhead pushed out a chair with his boot and Smoke sat down.

"Been several folks wonderin' who you are," the newly hired puncher said. "Most I heard come to the conclusion that you was a lawman of some sort."

"I've worn a badge a time or two," Smoke admitted, then called out his order to the counterman. He picked up his cup and allowed the waitress to fill it.

She met his eyes. "I seen you two or three years back," she spoke the words softly. "You be careful in this town. It's filled up with hired guns, all of them just burnin' to kill you."

"I appreciate that."

She nodded and walked back into the kitchen.

Rusty's freckled face screwed up with disgust. "Seems like ever'body knows who you are but me!"

Smoke sugared his coffee and stirred. "The name is Jensen."

The redhead's fork froze midway to his mouth. "*Smoke Jensen?*" he finally managed to say.

"That's it. Now close your mouth before a bug decides to fly in there."

Rusty filled his mouth with food and then closed it. "Boy, I sure know how to pick 'em," he muttered. "I'm beginnin' to wonder if a hundred a month is enough."

"And found," Smoke reminded him.

"Food ain't too tasty with a bellyful of lead," the puncher said mournfully. But there was a definite twinkle in his eyes.

"You didn't sign a contract," Smoke reminded him.

71

"Feel free to ride."

"Naw! Hell, I'll stick around. I ain't never ridden with such highfalutin' company before. Might be interestin'.''

"I'm not looking for trouble, Rusty. After we eat our meal, I plan on saddling up and riding out."

"That must be why you walk around with them hammer thongs off your guns."

Smoke grinned. "I just believe in being a very cautious man, that's all."

"Right. With your name, you damn well better be."

The two men cleaned their plates, Rusty eating two plates of food without apology, then finished off another pot of coffee. Not as strong as they liked it, but it would do. Then they leaned back, rolled cigarettes, and lit up. The cafe was gradually filling with the lunch crowd, all of the diners giving the two men short and cautious looks as they took their seats.

Then the door opened and four hardcases stepped inside.

Bob Garner and Montana Slim were the only two that Smoke recognized. The other two were unknown to him. But Garner and Montana Slim were quite enough to face on a full stomach.

Or an empty belly for that matter.

Slim's eyes widened as they settled on Smoke and recognition set in. Then he grinned, his hands close to the butts of his guns.

But the humor—if that's what it was—did not reach his killer eyes.

"We done got the hotshot all bottled up, boys," Slim announced, in a too-loud voice. "And some funny lookin' pup with him."

"This dog's got teeth, partner," Rusty told him. "An' I ain't been a pup in a long time."

"Little puppy dog done got up on his hind legs, boys," Garner said with a nasty grin. "I just might have to find

72

me a stick and whup his tail back between his legs. What'd you boys think about that?"

"I wouldn't try it," the redhead warned. His quietly spoken words had steel behind them. "You just might find that stick stickin' out of a part of you that you didn't figure on."

Several of the men in the cafe laughed at that.

Several more men in the cafe softly pushed back their chairs and took their leave before the lead they knew was coming started flying.

And a stray bullet doesn't give a damn who it hits.

"You got a fat mouth, red on the head," Slim told Rusty.

"You wearin' a gun, ugly face?" Rusty popped right back at him.

Slim's face turned as red as Rusty's hair. "In here or outside?" He challenged the soft-voiced but hard-talking puncher.

"It don't make a damn to me."

The counterman came up with a sawed-off shotgun, pointed right at Slim's belly. "You hardcases ain't gonna shoot up this place," he informed them, earing back both hammers. "So this is my way of tellin' you to take your guns and your big mouths and your quarrel out into the street. And I mean lak raht now!"

Slim nodded then looked at Smoke and Rusty. "We'll meet you boys at the south edge of town. That is, if you've got the belly for it."

"We'll be there," Smoke told him, finishing his cigarette and stubbing it out. "Watching our backs all the way."

Bob Garner spun around, red from the neck up and his ugly face turning even uglier. "What the hell does that mean, Jensen?"

"It means, Garner, that I think you're all a bunch of back shooting cowards!"

"Git outta here!" the counterman hollered. "Afore I

turn loose both of these barrels!"

The four hired guns and bounty hunters stomped out of the cafe. Smoke poured another cup of coffee and Rusty did the same. They sugared and stirred and sipped.

"How do we handle this?" Rusty asked, his voice low so that only Smoke could hear. "And what's this about them bein' back-shooters?"

"They're not back-shooters. I just said that to make sure they wouldn't try it. It's a matter of pride for them now. Some of their own kind would shoot them if they tried to set up an ambush."

They both looked up as the waitress set two thick slices of apple pie on the table before them.

"On the house, boys," the counterman said. "I ain't never had nobody as famous as Smoke Jensen come in my place afore."

The men nodded their thanks and fell to eating the pie, chasing it down with gulps of coffee. Around them, men were beginning to place wagers on the outcome of the impending gunfight. Most of the bets went to Smoke and the red-headed cowboy with him.

Their pie and coffee finished, Smoke and Rusty pushed back their chairs, settled their hats on their heads, and stood up, hitching at their gun belts.

"Good luck, boys!" the waitress called, as they were stepping out the door and onto the boardwalk.

The street that had been bustling with people when Smoke entered the cafe was now barren of human life as the two men began their lonely walk toward the edge of town. The word had been quickly passed among the townspeople that lead was about to fly.

A dog looked up from its midday doze and wagged its tail, its eyes seeming to say: you leave me alone and I'll do the same for you.

They walked past the animal, their spurs softly jingling. They stayed in the shadows of the buildings until coming to the very edge of town.

"I got a hunch that Slim and Bob will stay together," Smoke said. "So we play it like that. I'll take Montana Slim and Bob Garner. You handle the other two. I don't know them; they might be fast as lightning."

"I ain't all that fast," Rusty conceded. "But I don't hardly ever miss."

"That's the main thing. Many so-called fast guns usually put the first bullet into the dirt. There they are, Rusty. I got a hunch they'll want to jaw a little first; work up some courage. We'll let them. You ready?"

"As I'll ever be."

The men stepped off into the dirt of the street and began the short walk toward destiny.

8

The hired guns and bounty hunters had positioned themselves by a falling-down old barn, obviously one of the first structures to be built in the town. And it was just as obvious that the men had done so with a plan in mind. Smart, Smoke thought.

"After the first rounds are fired," Smoke told Rusty. "Any left standing are going to dive for the protection of that old barn. You hit the ground behind that log pile and I'll take the back of the building." His words were spoken low, so only Rusty could hear.

But the hired guns could see his lips moving. "What the hell are you two whisperin' about?" Montana called. "You workin' up some sort of sneaky play?"

"Neither one of us need sneaky plays to deal with scum like you," Smoke called, his voice easily carrying the distance.

Montana Slim cursed them both, loud and long.

All four of the men Smoke and Rusty faced were wearing two six guns, low and tied down.

"Most men can't use but one gun at a time. And some of them can't use that one very well," Smoke pointed out as the gunfighter and the cowboy continued their shortening the distance to death.

76

"And you . . . ?"

"I'm the exception," Smoke said without a single note of bragging. He was simply telling the truth.

There was about fifty feet between them when Smoke halted the parade.

"All right, Montana," Smoke called. "You made your brags back at the cafe. Now let's see if you've got the sand to back it up."

"Ten thousand on your head, Jensen!" Bob Garner called out. "We'll live nice on that money."

"You have to collect it first, Garner," Smoke tossed that reminder out to him.

Garner's laugh was full of confidence.

Ten thousand, Smoke mused. Surely it can't go much higher than that.

But then, after a second's thought, he changed his mind, realizing that perhaps there was no limit to Jud Vale's obsessions with being king.

"Ten thousand!" Rusty muttered. "Man, I am choppin' in some high cotton, Smoke. Somebody is shore scared of you."

Smoke did not reply, nor did his eyes leave Montana Slim. It was as he had thought, Slim and Garner were partners and were staying together. Rusty would have to deal with the two bounty hunters—if that's what they were.

Smoke could hear faint rustlings on the boardwalks behind them. He knew that the crowds were gathering to watch the show. It was a dangerous sport for spectators, and many an onlooker had caught a stray bullet. But entertainment was scarce in western towns; many folks packed picnic lunches and would drive a wagon for a hundred miles, bringing the entire family to make an all-day event out of a public hanging.

"I'm tired of all this jawing, Slim," Smoke told him. "And I really don't want a killing. Why don't you boys just get on your horses and ride out of here?"

There was something unnerving about Smoke, something that shook even a hardened gunfighter like Montana Slim. He was just so damned sure of himself. Maybe he ought to be, Montana admitted silently. He's put more than a hundred men in the ground and there he stands, lookin' at me.

But Montana Slim knew he had backed himself into a corner with only two ways out: either walk away victorious, or be propped up in front of the undertaking parlor on a board for all the folks to see.

"And I'm just damn tarred of your mouth, Jensen," Montana yelled. "Grab iron!" His hands flashed to his guns.

Montana thought he heard Smoke say, "All right, Slim." Then he felt twin hammer-blows slam into his chest as his knees began to buckle. Out of the corner of his eyes, the light fading fast, he saw Bob Garner run into the old barn. Montana Slim, the veteran and victor of half a hundred gunfights, lifted his hands and looked at them.

They were empty! Jensen had been so fast he hadn't even grabbed iron. But that was . . . impossible! That thought was his last as he pitched forward into the dust, dead.

Rusty had taken his time and placed his shots well. One bounty hunter was down on his belly, his blood staining the dirt from two bullet holes in his belly, and the other so-called gunfighter was holding up his one good arm in surrender; his other arm, his shooting arm, was broken at the elbow and hanging at a very queer angle.

Smoke was off and running between the old barn and another building which looked to be in just as bad a shape as the barn. He quickly reloaded as he ran.

A bullet whammed into a corral post and Smoke dropped to his belly, scooting behind an old watering trough. He caught a glimpse of a red and white checkered shirt and snapped off a shot. He didn't think he hit

Garner, but the slug came close enough to bring a yelp of surprise from the man.

Smoke triggered off five more rounds then holstered that Colt, drawing his left-hand pistol just as Garner ran briefly into view.

Smoke dusted him from side to side, spinning the man around and holding him there long enough for Smoke to take careful aim and put another slug into the man's chest. Bob Garner went down slowly and didn't get up.

It was over.

For this go-around anyway.

Smoke reloaded both guns and walked over to where he'd seen Garner fall. The gunny was lying on his back, very close to death.

It was not a pretty sight. Of course, Garner hadn't been very pretty to start with.

Smoke squatted down beside the man. There was not much life left in him.

And much of what life remained was spent in cussing Smoke.

Smoke waited until the dying man coughed up blood and tried to catch his breath. "Anybody you want me to write, Bob?"

A funny look came into the gunfighter's eyes. He shook his head. "Best . . . if the wife . . . just don't never see me agin. I ain't . . . been much of a husband or . . . father."

"Any money you got you want me to send them?"

"Spent it last . . . night on the . . . whoors."

Rusty walked up and stood listening.

"I'll swap your guns for a buryin', Bob," Smoke assured him.

"Right kind . . . of you. See you . . . boys in Hell!" Bob Garner closed his eyes and died.

Rusty was quiet as they rode out of Malad City that

afternoon. The dead gunman had, for the moment, taken the fight out of those remaining in the town. They stood on the boardwalk and watched Smoke and Rusty clear town. Most would continue on toward the Bar V. But there were some, mostly older and wiser, who would elect to seek another trouble spot where they could ply their deadly trade. It was not that they were cowards, far from it. They simply knew Smoke Jensen's reputation and their own capabilities and limitations.

"Mean right up to the end," Rusty finally broke his silence.

"What are you talking about?"

"Garner. What makes a man like that, Smoke?"

"Some folks back East and in the cities are claiming it comes from bad rearing."

"Huh!" Rusty summed up his opinion of that. "I ain't disputin' your word, Smoke, but I just don't believe in that at all. I been on my own for years. And my pa was a mighty mean man. He liked to whup up us boys and girls. Didn't make no difference to him. My older sister run off when I was just a little shaver. I heard she was doin' good out in California. My other brother died from a beatin' Pa give him. Hell, Pa knocked me unconscious with his fists or with a chunk of stovewood more'un once. And I ain't never stole nothin' in my life, or rode the hootowl trail or done nothin' much that was ag'in the law. And nobody could have had a worser home life than me. So them folks that think what you just said don't know a pot of beans from a pile of cow droppin's."

Smoke grinned. "I had to be a man grown just after my thirteenth birthday, working a hardscrabble farm back in Missouri and looking after my sick mother. Wasn't ever enough food; just enough to keep body and soul together. So I know what you mean, Rusty. And no, I don't believe those so-called experts either.

"What makes men like Montana Slim and Bob Garner

and all the rest be what they are?" He shook his head. "I think they were born to it, Rusty. They could have had all the advantages in the world and they would have turned out bad. A different kind of bad, maybe, but bad just the same."

"What do you mean, a different kind of bad?"

"Oh, they might have been bankers cheating old ladies or grocers cheating people and being mean-spirited folks. That type of thing."

Rusty thought about that for a mile or so. "You know, Smoke. You're right. There sure are a lot of mean minded and mean-spirited people in this world. Why, I know a few people who was born into money, and come from nice parents. Kind parents. But their kids would steal the pennies off'n a dead man's eyes."

"That's what I mean, Rusty. Born to it. I call it the bad seed theory."

Rusty settled into the bunkhouse with the old men and the kids. Smoke had taken to sleeping in a room out in the barn.

And Doreen stopped batting her eyes at Smoke and seemed to be quite taken with Rusty—much to the relief of Smoke. She got to getting all gussied up and swishing around him until it was embarrassing for all the others around them. Rusty, he just grinned like an egg-suckin' dog and stood around in sort of a daze.

There had been no trouble from Jud Vale or his men during the time Smoke had been gone.

But gunfighters kept drifting into the area, in groups of twos and threes. Pretty soon, Smoke thought, Jud Vale was going to have his own private army. And he was going to have to make his move pretty quick, for he was paying out a lot of money for all his hired guns to sit around and do nothing. While many of the bounty hunters and hired guns could work cattle, Smoke had a hunch that damn few

81

were going to. Most of them were just downright lazy.

On a bright, sunshiny morning, Smoke lined the boys up and laid it on the line to them, telling them what their parents had said, and leaving the final decision up to the young cowpunchers.

The boys huddled together for a time, and then Jamie stepped out of the group and faced Smoke.

"I allow as to how we'll stay, Mr. Smoke," the boy said. "We got to have the money to help out at home. And it ain't as if we never faced outlaws and the likes of Jud Vale before, 'cause we all have. I figure it like this, and you tell me if it don't meet with your approval and we'll work something else out."

Smoke waited, as did the other adults.

Jamie took a deep breath. "You see, sir, me and Alan and Cecil and two or three of the others, well, we know more about Jud Vale than you do, we think. We know it won't make no difference to him whether it's a grown man or a boy—not when it comes to standing in his way when he's a-goin' after something he wants. Like this ranch and Miss Doreen. So we went ag'in your orders and each of us stuck a pistol in our saddlebags."

Smoke sighed. He couldn't really blame the boys. He would have done the same thing had he been in their position. Smoke had been toting a pistol since he was thirteen. A Navy .36 caliber that had been given him back in '63 by the as yet unknown Confederate guerrilla fighter name of Jesse James.

"'Way we all figure it, Mr. Smoke, it's gonna be comin' down to the nut-cuttin' right shortly. And it ain't fair for no one to ask us to ride unarmed when we might catch a bullet at any moment. I reckon that's all I got to say, Mr. Smoke."

Smoke towered over the boy, staring down at him. Finally, and with a sigh, Smoke nodded his head. "All right, Jamie. I fear for your lives, but I can't ask you to disarm yourselves. I been packing a pistol since I was just a boy. But I have to ask you all to show me that you know how to use those guns."

"That's fair, sir," Jamie agreed. "When do you want us to do that?"

"Nothing like right now."

Cheyenne took one group of boys, Rusty took another, and Smoke took the third.

But damned if Smoke was going to have ten-year-olds packing pistols. Any boy under the age of twelve would stay close to the house and work in the yard or in the barn or corral The boys packing iron would be Jamie, Matthew, Ralph, Leroy, Cecil, Alan, Rolly, Pat, and Oscar.

The frail Matthew, thick glasses and all, surprised Smoke. The boy was a born gun hand, the pistol seeming to be a natural extension of his arm. And his aim was deadly true. Even Jamie took a backseat to Matthew. Smoke had held the very strong suspicion that Matt had been secretly practicing his draw and firing for some time. He asked him about it.

"Yes, sir," the boy said, blushing. "Whenever I could scrape up a few pennies to buy ammo, I been ridin' out far from the house and workin' at my draw."

"It's a natural talent you have, Matt. But it's not one your ma and pa will look upon with favor. You know that, don't you?"

"Yes, sir. I reckon that's right. But if a feller's got a knack for something, he ought to polish on it, shouldn't he?"

Should he? Smoke silently pondered, staring down at the frail boy packing the short-barreled sheriff's model Peacemaker. Should he? What would I be doing now if I had not discovered and polished my talent for weapons?

How many graves have I filled because of my quickness with a gun? And did this boy have enough sand in him to live with a gun by his side and not use it recklessly?

But can I stop him? Should I stop him? This was still the frontier, and it was filled with hard, tough, and often cruel men. Men like Jud Vale and his hired guns.

"Yes, Matt," Smoke said slowly. "Yes. Conditions being what they are, I guess you should polish it. As long as there are men like Jud Vale around, and with us being miles from the nearest law, I guess you should. But use that gun wisely, boy. If the law can handle it, let them. If you're pushed into a corner, then it's all up to you. I reckon that's the way it's always been and I suppose that's the way it's always going to be."

"I ain't smart like no grownup," Matt said. "But that's the way I think, too."

Matt turned, drew, cocked, and fired. All in one smooth quiet motion, the bullet striking true. Smoke experienced a hard push of memory, winging him back in years. Back to when he was a boy, traveling with Preacher. Back to his first real gunfight with white men.

Preacher and the boy, Smoke, had stopped in a rip-roaring mining camp just west of the Needle Mountains. It would soon be named Rico.

They had bought their supplies and were just about to leave when two rough-looking and unshaven men stepped into the combination trading post and barroom.

"Who owns that horse out yonder?" one demanded, trouble plain in his voice. "The one with the SJ brand?"

The boy Smoke laid his purchases on the counter and slowly turned. "I do."

"Which way'd you ride in from, boy?"

Preacher had slipped to his right, his left hand covering the hammer of his Henry rifle, concealing the click as he thumbed the hammer back.

Smoke's hands were at his sides; his left hand just inches

from his left hand gun. "Who wants to know—and why?"

No one in the room said a word.

"Don't sass me, boy!" the bigger and uglier of the two said. "My name's Pike, and I say you come through my camp yesterday and stole my dust!"

Smoke smiled grimly. "You're a damn liar!"

Pike grined, an ugly peeling back of the lips, exposing blackened rotting stumps of teeth. His right hand was hovering close to the butt of his pistol. "Why you smart-mouthed little punk. I think I'll just shoot your damned ears off."

"Why don't you try. I'm sure tired of hearing you shoot off your mouth," Smoke told him, no fear in his voice.

Pike looked confused for a moment. This kid didn't seem to be at all afraid of him. Odd. Pike was as big and strong as he was ugly. And he had been a loud-mouth bully all his life. People just didn't talk to him like this kid was doing. "I think I'll just kill you for that, kid."

Smoke laughed at him.

Pike and partner reached for their guns.

Four shots thundered in the low-ceilinged room. Four shots so closely spaced they seemed as one thunderous roaring. Dust and bird's nest droppings fell from the ceiling. Pike and friend were slammed out through the open doorway. One fell off the rough porch, dying in the dirt street. Pike, with two holes in his chest, died with his back against a support post, his eyes wide staring in disbelief that the kid, any kid, could be so fast. Neither man had managed to clear leather before the death blows hammered them into the hot, yawning, smoking gates of Hell.

All eyes in the black powder-filled and dusty barroom moved to the young man standing by the bar, a Colt in each hand.

"Good God!" a man whispered the words in awe. "I never even seen the draw!"

Preacher had moved the muzzle of his Henry to cover the men at the tables. The bartender put his hands slowly on the bar, indicating that he wanted no trouble.

"We'll be leaving now," Smoke said, holstering his Colts and picking up his purchases from the counter. He walked out the door without looking back.

Outside, Smoke stepped over the sprawled, dead legs of Pike and walked past his dead friend.

"What are we 'posed to do with the bodies?" a man asked Preacher.

"Bury 'em."

"What's that kid's name?" another called.

"Smoke Jensen."

Smoke brought himself back to the present, standing and watching Matt shoot. The boy turned with a smile on his lips, waiting for approval from the most famous gunfighter in all the West.

"You'll do to ride the river with, Matt," Smoke told him.

Smoke walked back to his room in the barn, his thoughts still lingering back over the years—long and bloody years. He tried to recall the year he'd killed that trash over at Rico. 1868, he thought it was.

He'd have to watch Matt, and watch him carefully.

He looked up as Cheyenne entered the room, his wise old eyes still startled at the speed of the young boy.

"Cheyenne, take the boy under your wing, just like Preacher did me. Teach him what Preacher taught me. He's going to need all the help he can get, I'm thinking."

Cheyenne nodded. "First time one of them so-called gunslicks of Jud Vale tries to draw down on that boy and gets plugged in the brisket, the boy is gonna be legend. Like another young man I do seem to recall from some years back."

Smoke nodded. "Yeah, I've been recalling it myself. Matthew's sure got the speed and the eye, Cheyenne. But I don't think it's God-given. I think it's passed up from Hell!"

"Mayhaps you be right. I have thought the same thing myself more'un a time or two. Now then, Jamie ain't real fast, but he's shore enuff a good shot. And Leroy is a fine rifle shot but ain't worth a puma's poot with a short gun.

Damn near shot hisself in the foot awhile ago."

"How about the others?"

Rusty walked in, hearing the last. "They'll do, Smoke. They ain't no burnin' firebrands with short guns, but they generally hit what they aim at. I been teachin' them to take their time and aim, even though the lead might be flyin' around them."

"Good advice. Sometimes hard to follow though," he said the last with a grin.

"I heard that," Rusty returned the grin. "Been there myself a time or two."

Cheyenne poured a cup of coffee from the ever-present battered old pot and squatted down on the rough board floor. "I been doin' some head-figurin' whilst you was gone, Smoke. Jud's got hisself a regular army now. I figure he's got nearabouts thirty gunslicks recent hired on the payroll. That ain't countin' his regular hands, which is about fifteen on any given day. That comes to about fifty men ag'in us. And that ain't countin' the bounty hunters snoopin' and a-salivatin' around the countryside, lookin' for a shot at you."

"Yeah, we were lucky the other night. Jud won't be fool enough to try that move again. But it bothers me about the boys carrying guns."

"They've had 'em in they saddlebags all along. And you can bet that whilst they was out of our sight, they was haulin' 'em out and showin' 'em around. Bet, too, that Jud Vale's had snoopers out lookin' us over through spy glasses and seen them boys with the guns."

"I hadn't thought of that, Cheyenne. You're right." He glanced at Rusty. "Think you can do a day's work without your mind on Doreen?"

Rusty grinned. "That woman can walk into a room and raise the temperature fifteen degrees."

"Do we have to tell you what to do to cool it off?" Cheyenne grinned at him.

The flush on Rusty's face was a pretty fair match with his hair. He mumbled something about having to see to his horse and left the room while Cheyenne and Smoke had a good laugh at his expense.

The days began to drift together, each one bringing with it the promise of full summer. And still Jud Vale made no more moves against the ranch. Smoke couldn't figure out what he was waiting on. Then an idea came to him.

"Is Mr. Argood Mormon?" he asked Walt.

"Big time Mormon. Big worker in the church. It's just about time for him to take his annual trip down into Utah. Church meeting of some sort."

"That's what I figured," Smoke said.

"Figured what?" Cheyenne asked.

"That's what he's waiting on. For the editor of the paper to be gone. No news would be reported if Argood was not around to cover it. And you can bet that Vale will create some incident around Montpelier to keep that young reporter busy while he's striking at the ranch."

"You may be right," Walt said, touching a match to the tobacco in his pipe. "He's sorry, but smart."

"It's time for another run into the village for supplies. I'll take two of the boys with me. I want to leave as many defenders behind as possible. We'll pull out in the morning."

Leroy drove the wagon, Smoke and Matthew rode beside the wagon as it bumped and bounced along the narrow, rutted road toward the trading post. Smoke knew he was taking a chance bringing Matt along, but the boy needed some personal things for himself and wanted to buy his ma a present with money he'd earned himself. Smoke had not asked Matthew to stow his pistol in the saddlebags. The gun had become a natural part of the boy—a feeling that Smoke knew only too well.

But Smoke had talked hard to the boy just before leaving. "Matt, I want you to realize that out here, once you strap a gun on, there are those who won't give a damn how young you are. The only thing they're going to see is that hogleg on your hip. If any of Jud Vale's hired guns are at the post, they're going to taunt you; try to pull you into a fight. And because the West is what it is, I won't interfere unless they gang up on you."

"I understand, Mr. Smoke," the boy had replied solemnly.

"You won't reconsider and stay at the ranch?"

"I reckon not, sir."

"Very well."

Smoke breathed a sigh of relief as they approached the post. Only a couple of horses were tied at the hitch rail, and he recognized them as beglonging to some area cattlemen, men whose holdings were so far to the west of Jud Vale's spread that they really had little to fear from the man and his obsessions—so far.

Smoke felt that they might be able to pick up the supplies and get away safely. At least he hoped so. But he wasn't going to put any money on it. Once again, doubts assailed him. He could have ordered Matt to stay behind at the ranch. But the boy had earned his money and had a right to spend it. Matt was not a slave to the Box T; he could come and go as he pleased.

Smoke swung down from the saddle and looped the reins around the hitchrail, Matt doing the same. Out of the corner of his eyes, Smoke watched the boy slip the hammer thong from his pistol. Cheyenne had drilled that into the boy's head. With a sigh, Smoke stepped up onto the porch. He handed Leroy the supply list and told Matt to stay with his friend. Smoke turned away and stepped into the saloon for a cool beer.

The barkeep eyeballed him dubiously as he pushed open the batwings.

"You agin! My stars and garters. I was in the hopes you'd left the country!"

Smoke grinned at the man. "It's me in the flesh. Pull me a cool one."

Drawing the brew, the barkeep said, "Did my eyes deceive me or did I really see that four-eyed kid wearing a gun?"

"You saw it."

The barkeep snorted in disgust. "Some of Jud Vale's men is liable to take that thing off'n him and spank his butt with it!"

"I'd hate to be the one who tried it," Smoke told the man.

"They might decide to do it in a bunch."

"Then if that happens I reckon I'll just have to step in."

"Naturally," the barkeep said mournfully. "And I just had new tables and benches built."

Smoke sipped his beer and kept his eyes on the outside, as best he could through the dirty, dusty, and fly-specked window.

One of the two cattlemen broke the short silence. "Why don't you just ride on outta here, Jensen? Jud Vale will settle down if you was to leave."

"You really believe that?" Smoke had turned, his back to the plank that served as a bar.

"That's what he told us," the other cattleman said. He had noticed that the hammer thongs had been slipped from Smoke's Colts.

Matt was sitting quietly on a bench in front of the store, minding his own business and sipping a bottle of sarsaparilla. Leroy was still inside the store, picking out the supplies from the list Alice and Doreen had given him. Smoke wished that Matt had stayed inside the store. He reflected sourly that people in Hell wished for ice water, for all the good it did them.

"Jud Vale is good decent man," the cattleman said.

"He's gonna bring changes to this area. Good changes. Progress and all that."

Smoke smiled grimly. He wondered if these men really believed that or had Jud bought them off with more than just words?

"Yeah," the other rancher said. "And if that little snip Doreen had any sense, she'd grab ahold of the offer Jud's handed her. She could live like a queen in that big mansion of hisn."

"She doesn't love him."

"Love!" the other said contemptuously. "Hell's fire, man! What's that got to do with anything?"

"Yeah," his drinking buddy agreed. "Love ain't got nothin' to do with livin' well. All a woman's got to do is perform her wifely duties when the lantern is turned off and keep her mouth shut 'cept when she's told to talk. And I'll tell you something else, gunfighter: you best get shut of them snot-nosed squatters' brats you hired to work on the Box T."

His buddy gave him a dark look and the cattleman shut his mouth.

"Is that a threat or a warning?" Smoke asked.

"Tain't no threat, gunfighter," the man said, his mind quickly working through the murk the alcohol had caused, as he realized just who he was talking to. "Jist a fact, is all. Jist lak 'at four-eyed little turd rode in with you with a man's iron strapped on. I've a good notion to go out there and take it away from him. But you'd stick up for him, wouldn't you?"

"No," Smoke surprised them both by stating. "Not as long as it stayed one on one. But I'd leave that boy alone if I was you."

The cattleman muttered something that Smoke could not make out. His buddy said, "He ain't gonna bother that boy, Jensen. That's just whiskey talk."

"Why did he say to get rid of the boys?"

"I don't know," the man said, then fell silent.

Smoke sipped his beer and ignored the drunk and near drunk cattlemen. He had thought all along that the age of the boys would make no difference to Jud Vale—when the man decided to make his move. In a way, he was glad the boys had taken to carrying guns.

He walked to the door that opened into the store, looking in. Leroy was still buying supplies. The boy caught his eye.

"It's gonna be a few more minutes, Mr. Smoke. Miss Alice and Miss Doreen really gave me a long list."

"Take your time, Leroy. I'll have another beer."

"Yes, sir."

Smoke walked back to the bar and ordered a refill. "And pull it from a new barrel," he told the barkeep. "That last one was flat."

The barkeep grinned. "Cain't blame a man for tryin' to drain the barrel, now, can you?" He pulled a fresh brew. "This one's on the house, Mr. Jensen."

Smoke nodded his thanks and leaned against the plank. He had a bad feeling about this day. One he just could not shake. At the sounds of hard-ridden horses he knew his premonition was about to turn into reality.

Four Bar V riders came to a halt in an unnecessary cloud of dust, fogging everybody and everything in a brief dust storm. Smoke silently cursed as he recognized one of the riders as a man called Smith. Smith had a shallow-made reputation as a gunslinger; but Smoke knew there wasn't much to the man. He was a bully who picked his fights, fists, and guns very carefully.

"Wal, lookie here!" Smith hollered, spotting Matt sitting on the bench, a disgusted look on his young face as he brushed the dust from his clothing. "Would you boys just take a look at that little piss-ant with the big iron strapped on!"

Smoke forced himself to stay put. He had warned Matt.

Warned him several times. Smoke would not interfere unless the Bar V riders tried something in a bunch. As long as it was one on one, with both parties armed, it was an unwritten code that the fight was fair. It was not always a fair code, but that was the way it was.

Leroy heard the commotion and went out the back door to the wagon, getting his Winchester and jacking a round in the chamber of the carbine, easing down the hammer. He reentered the store and moved to the open doorway, staying concealed from the Bar V riders.

He had been getting something extra for Miss Alice. Some candles. She was going to surprise Matthew with a birthday cake. Tomorrow was his birthday. His fourteenth.

If he lives through this, Leroy added that to his thoughts.

Then his thoughts turned grim as he gripped the Winchester. Matthew would live through it. One way or the other. It was time for everybody in this section of the state to stand up to Mr. Jud Vale. And if it had to begin right here and now? . . . Well, let it come.

The Winchester he carried was a hand-me-down from somebody. His dad never said where he'd got it. It was a .44-40 that some owner had sawed the barrel off to make into a saddle gun. It was several inches shorter than the short .44 carbine. It kicked something fierce, but when that bullet hit, it packed a wallop, especially at short range.

Leroy had never shot a man before—and didn't especially want to now, but if his friend Matt got into it with that trash from the Bar V . . . well, there was a first time for everything. He wished he could have had his first time with a girl before having to kill a man. But if wishes were horses then nobody would have to walk, would they? He inched closer to the door and settled down, waiting.

"Yes, siree!" Smith said. "I think we ought to get us a bottle of whiskey and hold the little craphead down and pour it in him. Since he's totin' a man's gun, he ought to have hisself a man's drink."

Matt wisely ignored the bully's comments. He had finished brushing himself off and then calmly wiped the neck of his soda pop bottle on his shirt sleeve and proceeded to take a big swig.

"Hey, piss-ant!" Smith hollered. "I'm talkin' to you, pig farmer's boy!"

"I'm not deaf," Matthew said softly. "Do you eat bacon, mister?"

"Haw?"

"I said do you eat bacon?"

"Why . . . hell, yes, I eat bacon. Don't ever body?"

"Where do you think it comes from—grown on trees?"

"Are you gettin' sassy with me, punk?"

"No, sir," Matthew replied respectfully. "I was just curious. If you enjoy eating bacon, why do you make fun of those people who raise the hogs?"

Smith—no mental giant anyway one wanted to view it—wore a look of bewilderment on his face. "I don't think I lak you very much, four-eyes. As a matter of fact, I *know* I don't lak you."

"That's a shame. I have nothing against you, mister."

"Let's take his pants down and make him ride back home buck-assed nekkid!" another Bar V hand suggested.

The four men all agreed that would be a great idea. They made some crude remarks about what they might find when they shucked Matt's jeans. And what they might do if one of them could find a corncob.

"No way," Smoke muttered, as he stepped away from the bar.

The two cattlemen suddenly looked very sorry, sober, and sick.

The barkeep shook his head in disgust at the Bar V hand's suggestion.

Leroy earred back the hammer on the .44-.40.

Matt set his soda pop bottle on the bench and stood up, his right hand hanging by his side.

"Well, now!" Smith said, surprise in his voice. "The little piggy's done gone and thought hisself to be all growed up."

"I'll get the corncob, Smith," a Bar V hand said.

"You'll get a bullet," Matt told him, his quiet words stopping the man and turning him around.

"You threatenin' me, pig-boy?" the hand challenged.

"Aren't you threatening me?" Matt countered.

Leroy stepped to a dusty window and pulled the Winchester to his shoulder, sighting in one of the V hands.

Smoke moved closer to the batwings.

"Why, you little turd-faced punk!" the Bar V hand hissed at the boy. "I think I'll just kill you!"

"You have it to do," Matt said softly.

The Bar V riders spread out, all of them grinning, seconds away from a killing.

10

Smoke pushed open the batwings and stepped out onto the porch. "I'll take these two so-called gunslicks on the right, Matthew."

"And I've got that ugly, skinny, bow-legged one on the far left in rifle sights!" Leroy called from inside the store.

"I guess that leaves you and me, doesn't it?" Matt told Smith.

The Bar V riders looked sick at the appearance of Smoke Jensen. This was not something they had counted on.

"You got no call to interfere in this, Jensen!" Smith hollered. "This ain't none of your concern."

"It is when four of you gang up on one boy, you sorry piece of buffalo droppings." Smoke then proceeded to hang a cussing on the Bar V riders, and having been jerked up, so to speak, by the old mountain man, Preacher, Smoke could let the cuss words fly when he had a mind to. And today was one of those days.

The riders took it for a time, and then pride got the best of them.

"I've had it, Jensen!" one yelled at him. "You don't cuss me like some saddle bum!"

"Then make your play, damn you!" Smoke lost his temper and started to push.

The puncher held his hands away from his side. "No way, Jensen. I ain't no match for you with guns. But I'll tear your damned head off with my fists if you've got the belly for it."

"I'll take you up on that, partner. Whatever your name is."

"Larry Noonan."

"Oh, yeah!" Smoke said, his voice filled with scorn. "I know enough about you to know you're a yellow little two-bit punk. You killed an unarmed sheepherder. Shot him in the back, so I recall reading on the dodger."

Noonan flushed but did not deny the damning charges.

"I still got something to settle with this loud-mouthed, sassy pig-farmer's kid!" Smith said. "You gonna interfere with that, Jensen?"

"No. I'm as aware as you concerning a fair shoot out between two armed men. In this case a man and a boy. But I'll kill any of your buddies who try to step in."

"You ready, punk?" Smith sneered at the boy.

Matt had stepped to the edge of the porch. Smoke glanced at him. There was no fear to be seen about the boy. His face was impassive and his hands were steady. He stared at Smith through his thick spectacles.

"Too bad, boy," Smith tried to rattle Matt. "You got about ten seconds left to live."

"I have a whole lifetime ahead of me, Mr. Smith. Let's just say this is payback time for you."

"Huh?"

"Don't you remember that time you and those other hooligans rode your horses over my mother's garden? Ruined it. We didn't eat very good that winter, Mr. Smith. It was too late to replant. I remember it very well."

"You gonna bawl about it, kid?" Smith sneered at him.

"No, sir. But I am going to kill you."

Smith stared at the boy while something crawled slowly across his face. He wanted to brush away the invisible sensation, for he knew what it was. Fear.

"My baby sister died that winter, Mr. Smith. I won't say it was all because of what you done, even though you did kill our milk cow. She needed milk bad. You had a hand in her dying."

Smith said nothing. There wasn't very much left to say.

"Goddamn nesters should have stayed out this area," Smoke heard one of the cattlemen in the bar say.

Smoke ignored him for the time being. The man had his own conscience to live with. Providing he had one at all.

"Are you ready, Mr. Smith?" Matthew asked, very politely.

"Smith," one of the Bar V hands spoke softly. "Back away. I don't like this. The kid's too damn sure of hisself."

"I ain't backin' up for no damn snot-nose pig farmer's whelp!" He stared at Matt. "All right, boy. You've made your brags. Now do something 'sides talk!"

"After you, Mr. Smith."

Smith hesitated. Something was terribly, awfully wrong here. He'd seen any number of two bit, show-off, would-be gunhands in his time. At the last minute, they always backed down. And even before they backed down, they were nervous, their voices shrill, faces shiny with the sweat of fear. But not this kid. Kid, hell! He was just a *boy*— barely in his teens.

"My little sister suffered, Mr. Smith. I don't think I'll ever forget that."

"Shut your mouth, damn you!" Smith screamed. "Draw, you punk!"

Matt waited, waited in his worn-out, low-heeled farmer's boots. In his faded and patched old jeans and carefully mother-mended shirt. His eyes were calm behind his thick glasses.

Smith jerked iron. He just managed to clear leather as Matt's pistol belched and roared smoke and sparks. The first slug hit him in the belly, spinning him around in the

99

dirt. The second slug struck him in the side and knocked him down to one knee. The expression on his face was one of utter disbelief that this could be happening to him. The third slug hit him in the face, entering between nose and upper lip and making one Godawful mess. Smith trembled once and died.

The three remaining Bar V hands stood in open-mouthed shock, all of them knowing they were not nearly as fast as this fresh-faced, as-yet-to-shave farmer's kid standing on the porch of the store, and all of them so very, very glad they had not tried to brace him.

Leroy stepped out of the store, his short-barreled .44-.40, hammer back, in his hands. The barrel of the carbine was pointed straight and rock-steady at the belly of a Bar V hand.

"I'm out of this, kid!" the hand said quickly.

"You interfere in the fight between Mr. Smoke and Noonan and you'll be out of it forever," Leroy told him, his young voice holding hard steel.

Matt had quickly reloaded and holstered the Peacemaker. His calm eyes, magnified behind the thick glasses, looked at the other Bar V hand.

"That goes for me, too, kid!" the hand said.

"Mr. Smoke?" Matt said.

"Matt?"

"If you'll excuse me for a minute, I got to go behind the building and throw up!"

"Go on, Matt."

The boy ran from the porch.

"I done the same thing my first man," a Bar V rider admitted. "It ain't nothin' to be 'shamed of." He didn't know what else to do with his hands—only wanting to keep them as far away from his pistol as possible—so he stuck them into the back pockets of his jeans.

Noonan looked at the bulk of Smoke Jensen and swallowed hard. "Come on, boys!" he urged, panic in his voice. "They's three of us. We can take them two."

The Bar V rider with his hands in his back pockets told Noonan what he could do with his suggestion, together with the same corncob they had originally had in mind for Matthew.

"That goes double for me," the remaining Bar V rider added. "You wanted to fight Jensen, you just go right ahead, Noonan." He removed his gun belt and hung it on his saddle horn.

The other hand thought that was a dandy idea, and did the same. Leroy shifted the muzzle of the .44-.40 to Noonan's belly and the man let his gunbelt fall.

The shopkeeper, his wife, the barkeep, and the two cattlemen had walked out on the porch, to stand and stare. The body of Smith was, for the moment, being ignored. Matt walked around from behind the building, wiping his mouth with his shirt sleeve.

Smoke took off his guns and laid them on the bench. He stepped off the porch, walked up to Noonan, and knocked the puncher down in the dirt with one very quick and unexpected hard left hook.

Noonan rolled and came to his boots, the side of his jaw beginning to bruise from the blow. He shook his head, clearing it of stars and chirping birdies, and backed up, lifting his fists.

He swung at Smoke. Smoke ducked the punch and busted the cowboy in the belly with a hard right. Noonan whoofed out air just as Smoke came around with another left which connected on the man's ear, spinning him around and seriously impairing his hearing for a few moments.

Just as Noonan regained his balance, Smoke stepped in and blasted him in the mouth with another straight right punch. Noonan's boots left the dirt and he sat down hard on his butt, his mouth bloody.

Smoke backed up. He wasn't even breathing hard;

101

hadn't even worked up a sweat yet.

Noonan wisely sat on the ground. He took another good long look at the gunfighter who stood above him, his fists balled, hanging at his sides, waiting. Smoke looked awesome. A big man, six feet or more, with a massive barrel chest and shoulders and arms that were packed with hard muscle.

Noonan came off the ground in a rush, a long-bladed knife in his right hand.

Smoke slipped the first swing of the knife, bending down as he parried the thrust, his left hand scooping up dust from the road. When Noonan closed with him, Smoke tossed the dirt into the man's eyes, momentarily blinding the man.

Smoke kicked the man on the knee, bringing a howl of pain. Smoke hit the man twice in the face, a left and a right. The knife dropped from his hand just as Smoke's right hand clamped down on the man's fingers. Smoke bore down, using all his strength. Noonan began screaming as the bones in his fingers were crushed, the crunching sounds causing all the spectators to wince.

Still holding onto Noonan's now ruined hand, Smoke began battering the man's face with short, hard, chopping blows from his left fist. Within a minute, the man's face had been turned into a bloody, misshapen mask. His nose was flattened, his lips smashed into bloody pulp, several teeth knocked out of his mouth. Both eyes were beaten closed.

Smoke let him drop to the dirt. Noonan was unconscious.

Smoke walked to the horse trough and washed his face and hands and buckled his gun belt around his lean waist. He looked up at Leroy.

"All the supplies loaded, Leroy?"

"Just about, sir."

"I'll get right on that, Mr. Jensen!" the store owner said.

He and his wife rushed back into the store.

Smoke looked at the now completely sober cattlemen. They were standing on the porch, faces pale under the tan, staring at the crippled Noonan.

Smoke pointed first at Smith, then to Noonan. "When you men decide to take a stand in this issue," Smoke told them, "I would suggest that both of you keep this sight fresh in your minds."

Smoke turned and swung into the saddle.

The news of the gunfight between the seasoned Smith and the nester's kid, and the short but brutally crippling fight between Smoke and Noonan spread like unchecked wildfire throughout the southeastern corner of Idaho. Noonan would never regain the use of his right hand. The so-called badman drifted out of the country, sucking on a bottle of laudanum to ease the pain. He would drift far away, change his name, and work the remainder of his life as a cowboy with a crippled hand, his true identity hidden forever, even to the grave.

Jud Vale had been oddly silent after the shooting and the beating at the trading post. Smoke had a hunch all that would abruptly change as soon as Editor Argood left on his journey to Utah. And that was just about a week away.

At Smoke's suggestion, the ranch house and the bunkhouse had been fortified against both attack and against siege—Smoke suspected the latter would be tried, with Jud Vale's marksmen in carefully placed positions attempting to pick off the defenders one by one.

The remaining Box T herd had been moved to safer pastures; a huge valley with good grass and water, difficult for rustlers to get the cattle clear without being seen.

On a warm bright late spring morning, Smoke walked around the compound, inspecting the work that had been done. He could not think of anything else they could do.

And Smoke was growing restless. Edgy, might be a better word for it. Calm it might be—for now—but he knew their position was lousy, and if Jud would just do a little thinking and planning, logically instead of emotionally, and then turn his rabid dogs loose, there was no way that Smoke and the defenders could hold back a well-planned and well-executed attack against them.

So what to do?

Cutting down the odds would certainly help. Perhaps a little night work? Like headhunting?

Smoke smiled a warrior's smile, thinking: Why not?

He remembered Preacher's words: "You'll always be a fighter, boy—a warrior. You'll take the quiet home life for a time, then the itch will git to where you cain't jist sit at home and scratch it. And then you'll head for the high lonesome, lookin' for trouble. And knowin' you, boy, you'll find it."

Smoke rounded up Cheyenne and Rusty and took them to one side. "I'll be gone for a couple of days, maybe longer. I don't like the odds, so I think I'll do something about them."

"You crave some company?" Cheyenne asked.

Smoke shook his head. "No. This is something that's best left to one man. I'll be pulling out at dusk."

"You going to tell Walt and the wimmin what you're up to?" the old gunfighter asked.

"I'll tell Walt. If he wants to let the women in on it, that's up to him."

"If anybody can pull it off, you can, son. You had the best teacher in the world in Preacher."

Smoke certainly agreed with that last sentence. There had been no finer night fighter in the world than Preacher. "I'll start getting my gear together. Rusty, fix me up with a packet of food enough to last two days."

The cowboy nodded and walked away. Smoke turned

back to Cheyenne. "My horse is too well known. Put a rope on that steeldust for me, will you? He's mean as hell but he's mountain bred and quick as lightning and can go all day and still have bottom left."

"He's a good one. I'll dob him for you."

Smoke filled up all the loops in his gunbelt and filled up a bandoleer, slinging that around his shoulder. He slipped another box of .44's into his saddlebags and made sure his moccasins were tucked into the leather. He would soon slip out of his boots and into the moccasins when it was time for the night stalking to begin. He sat down on his bunk and began putting a finer edge on his Bowie knife. That done, he walked to a stone building behind the barn and opened the locked door with a key he had found in a cabinet in the storeroom. He had a hunch what he would find, and his hunch was correct.

He filled a small sack with sticks of dynamite and caps and fuses. He might not be able to cut the head off the snake, but he was sure intending to tweak its tail.

■■

Smoke talked to Jamie and Matthew before he pulled out into the night.

"Tell the boys to ride carefully and keep a sharp eye out. I'm going into the lion's den, and there is no telling what Jud Vale will have his men do in retaliation after I'm through."

"There used to be a lot more farmers in this area than there is now, Mr. Smoke," Jamie said. "Women and girls has been tooken and misused by Vale and his riders. Men has been tarred and feathered and horsewhipped and killed. Killed outright if they was lucky. A deputy sheriff come in here once. He just disappeared. There ain't been no more lawmen come around the Bear. Jud Vale is pure trash, Mr. Smoke. Trash livin' in a big fancy house, with servants and such as that. When he can get them to stay, that is. He fancies young women all around, to wait on him. And he abuses them in ways we heard that would make you sick to your stomach, so they leave as soon as they can get a way out. You cain't tell us nothin' about Jud Vale and what he might decide to do."

"The more I hear about this man the more I think the best thing to do would be to just go in and chop his head off, so to speak," Smoke said.

"Ain't gonna be that easy, Mr. Smoke. Not even for you. Jud ain't never alone. He's got half a dozen bodyguards with him all the time. Men that have been with him for years, my pa says."

"We'll see, boys. We'll see. I might not be able to do much more than rattle the bars on his cage this time around. But, by God, he will know that his territory has been violated."

Walt came out to the barn just moments before Smoke was to pull out. "Clint Perkins is in the area, Smoke. Don't ask me how I know—I can't explain the feelings I get when he's close. I just know. You be careful."

"Whose side is he on, Walt?"

"His own," the old rancher said bluntly. "He's like a goose; wakes up in a new world every day. I always knew he was about half nuts. Now I think he's gone slap dab crazy."

Smoke led the steeldust out of the barn and swung into the saddle. "I'll see you in two or three days, Walt."

"Be careful, boy."

Smoke rode slowly away from the ranch and into the night. He fought shy of the roads and well-traveled trails as he worked his way toward the range of the Bar V. Editor Argood had told him that there was not one single person on the Bar V payroll that was worth the gunpowder it would take to blow their brains out. To a man, Argood said, they were bullies and trash and petty criminals and all wanted by the law somewhere. The people in the area put up with them because Jud Vale kept them all on a tight leash. Jud had forbidden them to enter Montpelier, restricting their carousing to a few small towns and trading posts in the area around the Bar V range.

All in all, Smoke concluded as he rode through the night, a snake pit could best describe the Bar V . . . and that included the owner.

With a tight smile on his face, Smoke thought that the

next couple of days and nights should prove to be quite interesting.

Before leaving the Box T, Smoke had taken tape and silenced anything that might jingle. Only the clop of the steeldust's hooves and the occasional creak of saddle leather could be heard. By midnight, he was on Bar V range. He would ride for a while, then dismount and stand listening for several moments. He began passing bunched and sleeping cattle and slipped his rope free, knowing he would soon make contact with a night herder. If his luck held, the night herder would think him one of the Bar V riders—at least long enough for Smoke to dab a loop over the man and cause a little mischief.

He rode parallel to a series of ridges for a few moments, before finding a pass that would, hopefully, take them to the flats on the other side. He let the steeldust set his own pace and pick his way through the night. On the flats, reined up in the opening of the draw, Smoke spotted the night herder as the man worked his way around the herd, riding slowly so as not to spook the cattle, which was an easily done job. The cattle had, as usual, risen about midnight, grazed for a few moments, and then settled back down.

As the night herder passed Smoke's position, the gunfighter let the loop fly and jerked the rider out of the saddle. The man hit the ground hard, knocking the wind out of him. Smoke was off and running as the loop settled and he further silenced the herder by a hard right fist to the side of the man's jaw. He then tied him up, using cut-off sections from the Bar V rider's own rope. He gagged the man with a dirty bandana taken from the man's equally dirty neck and then squatted down beside him, waiting for him to regain consciousness.

The man's eyes opened and widened as he recognized

who he was looking at.

"You want to live?" Smoke asked softly.

The man nodded his head up and down vigorously.

"You know who I am?"

The rider nodded.

Smoke took out his long-bladed knife and laid the cold sharp steel against the man's throat. "I've a good notion to cut your throat and just have done with it."

The Bar V man made desperate choking sounds behind the gag, being careful not to move his head for fear the sharp blade would slice him.

"On second thought," Smoke told him, "I think I'll just strip you and tie you between two steers and then stampede the herd."

More frantic choking sounds.

"Unless you agree to ride out and never show your face in this part of the state again."

The muffled sound from behind the gag were definitely in agreement with Smoke's last remarks.

Smoke very slowly moved the knife point, just scraping the man's unshaven jaw, and the Bar V night herder looked like he was developing the first stages of a heart attack. With one flick of his wrist, Smoke cut the gag from the man's mouth.

"Oh, Jesus!" the rider softly moaned.

Smoke grabbed him by the hair and jerked his head back, exposing the softness of throat. He laid the blade against the man's skin and the sharp odor of urine filled the night.

"If I see you again, I'll kill you," Smoke told him.

"Mr. Jensen, if you was to cut me aloose, I'll be two counties away come the dawn."

Smoke cut his bonds and stood up. "Ride. Ride like you've never ridden before. Forget your warbag back at the bunkhouse. Just get clear of this area."

"I'm gone, mister!"

The cowboy staggered to his boots and ran to his horse and swung into the saddle, wet drawers and all, and was gone into the night, heading west. Smoke had not disarmed the cowboy, but the man made no moves toward his six gun. The night became quiet as the rider got the hell gone from Smoke Jensen.

Smoke removed his spurs and stashed them in a saddlebag. Back in the saddle, he guided the steeldust out to the edge of the herd and began making the night herder's rounds, working in a slow, rough circle. He soon spotted another night rider.

Smoke rode up to the man and just as the rider realized he was not looking at a Bar V hand, Smoke leaned over and knocked him clear out of the saddle. He was on the ground and standing over the man as the cowboy came up, fighting mad and cussing to beat sixty. He reached for his gun and Smoke knocked it out of his hand then proceeded to beat the man to an unconscious bloody pulp. Smoke tossed him belly-down across the man's saddle, tied him securely, and slapped the horse on the rump, knowing the animal would head straight for the corral.

Smiling, Smoke swung back into the saddle and went in search of more night herders.

Long before first light, he had cleared the Bar V range of nighthawks. He had sent three packing, riding hell-bent for leather toward a more hospitable climate, and had either whipped with his fists or clubbed over the head four more, tying them across their saddles and sending the horses racing back to the corral, jumping and bucking under the strange load.

Smoke headed for the high country and some food and sleep. He was still smiling as he plopped his hat over his eyes and leaned back, his saddle for a pillow. The sun was just coming up. He was less than a mile from Jud Vale's mansion.

*   *   *

Jud Vale threw his hat on the ground and stomped around, cussing and hollering. "Get him!" he finally screamed, his face beet-red, spittle spraying over his lips. "Put a rope on him and drag that bastard back here! Ten thousand dollars to the man who brings him in, dead of alive! *Ride*, dammit!"

Forty riders hit their saddles and left the ranch complex in a cloud of dust, which was exactly what Smoke planned on them doing. He knew they would not expect him to be within ten miles of Jud Vale's mansion, much less standing on a brush-covered ridge overlooking the estate.

Smoke had carefully picketed the steeldust over good graze and a small pool of collected water—water enough for a couple of days. If Smoke did not return, the steeldust could break free with little trouble and head back to Box T range.

Smoke took his time studying the ranch layout through field glasses, including ways to reach it and ways to get out once there. Jud had chosen his building site carefully, including a little creek that ran some three hundred yards behind the out of place mansion.

Smoke removed his boots and slipped on moccasins. He carefully checked his guns, wiping them free of any dust they might have collected. He removed his Winchester from the boot and checked it, making sure it was loaded full up. He patted the steeldust on the neck and spoke to it for a moment, then he started to move out.

Movement on the other side of the creek halted him. He squatted down and watched. He was sure he had seen movement. Or had he? He waited. There! He'd been right. Somebody, or something, was sure enough down there. He went back to his saddlebags and got his field glasses.

He moved several hundred yards closer to the mansion, adjusted the glasses for range and once more settled down to wait. Then he picked out the shape of a man. It startled him as the face of the man came into view. It was almost like looking into a mirror. There was some difference, of

111

course, but the facial features of the man were startlingly similar to Smoke's own.

Clint Perkins. It had to be. But what the devil was he up to?

He watched as the man left the creek and ran to one of several privies behind the house. The privies surprised Smoke. He thought Jud would have installed some of those new fangled indoor water closets he'd seen back East.

Clint began working his way closer to the mansion, finally ducking into a shed not far from the back porch. The call of a meadowlark drifted to Smoke, and Smoke could tell the call was not real. Within a moment, a young woman stepped out onto the porch, shaking out a small rug.

Someone must have said something from inside the house, for the girl turned her head. Smoke could see her lips move in reply. She had an angry expression on her face. Her reply must have satisfied the questioner for she moved off the porch and walked toward an outhouse.

She angled toward the privy just behind the shed; that move would effectively block the view of anyone watching from the house, but not from the ridge and Smoke's magnified eyes.

The girl did not go into the outhouse. But she did disappear from view. So the shed either had a back door or a couple of loosened boards. Clint Perkins, the so-called Robin Hood of the West either had him a girlfriend, or was planning to rescue the lady from the sweaty evil clutches of Jud Vale. Probably a combination of both, Smoke thought. This Clint Perkins, as it was turning out, was quite the ladies' man.

Smoke wondered just how many starry-eyed women Clint had loved and left and how many woods' colts this dubious Robin Hood had in his back trail?

After only a few moments, a man wearing two guns

belted around his waist stepped onto the porch and, judging from the expression on his face, started yelling. The girl appeared, seeming to come from out of the privy. And from the expression on her face, she seemed to be yelling at the man. When she reached the porch, the man slapped her, staggering her, only the railing preventing her from falling off the porch. He grabbed her by the arm and hurried her into the house, slamming the door behind them.

Interesting, Smoke thought. Then he wondered how many more young ladies Jud Vale was keeping against their will in the huge mansion?

Smoke settled back in a more comfortable position, his back to a tree, his hat on the ground beside him and waited and watched. This might prove to be a very interesting morning.

And Smoke might not have to do anything for a change. Except enjoy the show.

12

Smoke shifted his attentions to the front of the mansion as Jud Vale stepped out onto the porch with a cup of coffee in his hand and took a chair. Smoke envied him that cup of coffee, for a fact. His had been a cold camp the night before, and he sorely missed his usual full pot of hot, strong, black cowboy coffee upon waking up.

He contended himself by chewing on a biscuit sandwich made with fried salt pork and chasing it down with sips of water from his canteen.

The girl Smoke had seen meeting with Clint Perkins came out onto the porch and began talking to Jud, gesturing with her hands.

Jud shook his head a couple of times and then, with an angry expression on his face, pointed toward the door. The girl, her shoulders slumped in defeat, walked back inside the house.

Jud stood up and hollered something; Smoke could see his lips move but could not make out the words. Three men stepped out of a bunkhouse and walked toward the house. Three more men, with the girl in tow, quite unwillingly, Smoke noted, by the way one held onto her arm, came out of the mansion to stand by Jud on the porch.

The man holding onto the girl nodded his head and the three went back into the mansion. Shifting his glasses, Smoke watched as Clint ran the short distance from shed to back porch and then disappeared into the mansion.

Gong to get interesting very soon, Smoke thought.

Jud's horse was saddled and led to the porch, and Jud and three of his bodyguards rode off. Smoke finished his biscuit and salt meat and waited for something to start popping.

It wasn't long in coming.

One man was suddenly hurled through a side window, the side of his head bloody. Gunfire shattered the early morning quiet and one of Jud's bodyguards came staggering out onto the back porch. He fell over the railing and lay still.

More gunfire came from within the house and the third bodyguard fell out of the front door, on his back, on the porch. The front of his shirt was bloody.

Wisps of smoke began leaking out of an open window in the rear of the house as Clint and the girl ran out the back door and toward the creek. Several moments later, Smoke watched as two horses pounded away, the girl riding astride. They topped a hill and were gone.

"Robin Hood strikes again," Smoke muttered, as he took out another biscuit and settled back, just as Jud Vale and his bodyguards came galloping back to the ranch.

The fire had been confined to the kitchen and had been extinguished in a few minutes. Jud was talking to the man who had been bashed on the noggin and tossed out the side window.

"So it wasn't Jensen all along," Jud said, standing up, his face tight with anger. "It was that damn Clint Perkins!"

"They look enough alike to be brothers," Jason

reminded his boss. "Be easy to mistake them in the dark."

"Maybe they're brothers?" a hand suggested. "And Smoke Jensen come in here to help him out?"

But Jud Vale rejected that on the spot. He'd been in the West for some years when the stories about Smoke Jensen first began surfacing. Jud knew that Jensen's father had died and the mountain man, Preacher, took care of the boy's raising after that. Smoke had always been a loner, with no family to speak of, certainly no brother.

He shook his head. "No. He doesn't have a brother. Not anymore. His brother was killed in the war. Tortured and killed by a group headed by three men who later moved into Idaho. Jensen killed them all and detroyed the town."

"Then what's he doin' here, Boss?" Jason asked.

"Exactly what he said he was dong," Jud replied, bitterness in his voice. "He was just seeing the country when we braced him. That got his back up, and he stayed." Jud shrugged. "We brought it on ourselves."

"And we do what about it?" a gunslinger asked.

"Kill him."

A Bar V hand had gotten close to Smoke's hiding place while taking a shortcut to a search area. He now found himself flat on the ground looking up into the cold eyes of Smoke Jensen, with a knife blade across his throat. There were any number of questions he wanted to ask, but wisely kept his mouth shut, figuring if Jensen wanted him to talk, he'd tell him so.

"Who is in the house besides Jud Vale and his men?" Smoke asked.

"Nobody! I swear it!"

"The girl who got away—who is she?"

"Susie somebody-or-another. Nester's kid from over Wyoming Territory."

"She was the only servant?" Smoke moved the razor-sharp knife blade and the man cringed in fear.

"If that's what you want to call what she done. Yeah. She cain't cook and don't clean house. It's like a boar's nest in that house. There was two more girls. One run off—never seen her agin, and Jud kilt the other. But it was an accident, Jud said. He broke her neck whilst they were messin' around. You know."

"Sounds like a nice gentle fellow, this Jud Vale does."

The hand didn't know how to respond to that, so he kept his mouth closed.

"What's Clint Perkins's beef with Jud?"

"Lord, man, I don't know! 'Ceptin' that Perkins is crazy, I reckon. He hates rich folks, I do know that."

Smoke stared hard at the man. The Bar V hand was scared and sweating, even though the day was cloudy and cool, threatening rain. "Where are you wanted?"

The hand hesitated. Smoke moved the big blade. That loosened his mouth. "Kansas!" He blurted out.

"What for?"

"I robbed a store. I was down on my luck and needed some cash."

Smoke grabbed him by the hair and jerked his head back, exposing his throat even more. "Tell it all!"

"Nebraska! I robbed a bank, kilt a teller! You gonna turn me in?"

"Not if you level with me."

"Anything you want. Jist anything at all, Mr. Jensen. You want me to git down and howl lak a dog, you jist say so."

"Is there any puncher on Vale's payroll who isn't wanted by the law?"

"Lord, no! Jud laks to hire people on the hoot owl trail. He's got more control over 'em. They's more outlaws down yonder than at Robber's Roost."

"And Jud Vale wants to be king of this part of the state?"

"Mister Jensen, he *is* king!"

117

"Uneasy lies the head that wears a crown."

"Huh?"

"Shakespeare wrote that."

"I ain't never heard of him. What outfit does he ride for?"

"Forget it." Smoke stuffed a gag into the man's mouth and tied him to a tree. He picked up his rifle and began making his way toward the creek that ran behind the mansion of Jud Vale. He wasn't worried about being spotted by any ranch hands; there weren't any hands left on the ranch, except those gunslingers and bodyguards in the house with Jud. Every hand, including the cook, was out looking for Clint Perkins and the girl. According to the tied-up and gagged Bar V hand, no one believed Smoke was within thirty miles of the mansion. And by this time, there wouldn't be a puncher, bounty hunter, or hired gun within ten miles of the ranch.

The day had turned cloudy along with the coolness, and any gunfire would be muffled by the humidity, not carrying nearly as far as on a fair, sunshiny day.

Smoke followed the creek to the rear of the house and then made his way to a pile of wood stacked behind the great two-story mansion. He poked his rifle through a good-sized crack in the stack and let a few shots bang.

The first shot tore through the kitchen wall and ricocheted upward, shattering a chandelier in the fancy dining room and sending bits of glass and coal oil from the expensive lamps spraying. Jud Vale and his men hit the floor, yelling and cussing. The second .44 round whined off the polished wood of the dining room table and stopped in the china hutch, destroying several plates and cups. The third round bounced off a kettle in the kitchen and whined wickedly around the stove before rolling across the floor and coming to rest about three inches from Jud Vale's nose.

The men began crawling across the floor, toward the rear of the house. Smoke anticipated that move, and lowered the muzzle of the Winchester, letting it bang.

"Somebody get around to the side of the house!" Jud yelled. "Try to get him in a crossfire."

But Smoke was off and running, coming to rest behind the gazebo in the side yard. He saw the bodyguard come chugging around the corner and knocked a leg out from under him. Dragging his limb, the man crawled back around to the front of the mansion.

Jud and his men moved to the side of the house, but by this time, Smoke had again changed locations, back to the rear of the house. He decided he'd pressed his luck enough for this day, and took a stick of dynamite out of his pocket, capping and fusing the thunder stick. He lit it and let it fly and was heading for the creek before the sputtering stick landed.

The charge landed on the ground and rolled under the porch. When it blew, it tore the whole porch off the rear of the house and busted most of the windows in the back of the mansion.

Smoke stopped at the creek bank long enough to empty his rifle into the back of the house and then ran toward the ridge and his horse.

Inside the mansion, their hearing momentarily impaired from the booming of the giant stick, Jud and his men hugged the floor until the rifle fire stopped. Their ears ringing, the men crawled to their knees.

"That wasn't Clint Perkins," Jud said, his voice seeming to come out of a well. "That was Smoke Jensen. Bet on it!"

Chuckling, Smoke cut the Bar V hand loose, laid the barrel of his pistol on the back of the man's head, insuring that he would be out for some time to come, and mounted up, riding off.

He had a full day of headhunting to do.

The hand Smoke had busted on the noggin finally found

his horse and rode back to the mansion, a lump on his noggin the size of a hen's egg.

"Jensen," he told Jud.

"Which way did he ride out?"

"Don't know. He busted me on the head. I just now come to my senses. I don't know how long I've been out."

Jud cussed and stomped and paced up and down behind the mansion and the ruined porch. He fought to keep his anger under control and managed it.

"Get the boys in," he told Jason. "Jensen was raised by Preacher. Probably the best Injun fighter the West ever seen. He's gone headhunting, bet on it. If the boys stay out, he'll do us some more damage. Get them back here, pronto."

Jason looked confused. "Jesus, Boss. How? They're scattered all forty miles."

Jud Vale sat down on a stump and cussed. Smoke Jensen planned all this, he concluded. He didn't know how, or even the why of it, but it was all Smoke Jensen's fault. He convinced himself of that. Damn Smoke Jensen to the pits of Hellfire!

Jud again calmed himself and did a little mental figuring. As of last evening, he had 18 hands on the payroll. He had hired 25 men at fighting wages—God knows they hadn't earned a penny of it—and he was giving another 15 or 20 men—he forgot the exact number—money just to hang around. Three riders had deserted him last night, thanks to that damn Clint Perkins; or had it been Perkins? And two more had been so badly beaten they were out of it for several days. Maybe a week. So savagely mauled that they hadn't even been able to leave the bunkhouse when Perkins and then Jensen attacked the house. He had lost two of his most trusted men to the guns of Perkins. Jensen had busted the leg of another. And a third had his head busted open.

"Damn!" he muttered. He looked up at Jason. "You boys stick close to home. I reckon them forty-odd men out in the field can deal with Smoke Jensen."

A gunslick whose Christian name was Wilber Hammersmith—his friends called him Hammer—thought a damn puma had done jumped onto his back, knocking him from the saddle. Then he looked up into the eyes of Smoke Jensen, sitting on top of him, and suddenly felt an urgent need to relieve his bladder.

He cut his eyes as Jensen balled his right hand into a huge fist. "Aw, hell, man!" he managed to say before his whole head exploded in pain.

And speaking of his head . . . when he finally awakened, he had a whale of a headache, his whole world was upside down, and his head was unnaturally cold.

Hammer figured out why his world was upside down. It wasn't the world—it was him! Jensen had taken Hammer's rope and strung him upside down from a tall limb. After stripping him down to his long handles and taking his boots and socks and guns.

But how come his head was so cold? He had always been right proud of his blond hair. He finally managed to get his hands free and to his head.

He screamed as if he'd been mortally wounded, the sound echoing around the hills and ridges.

That damn Smoke Jensen had taken his knife and shaved his head!

"Halp!" Hammersmith started hollering as he swayed in the breeze at the end of the rope. His own rope. "I'm a-gonna kill you, Jensen!" Hammersmith squalled. "Damn your eyes, you heathen! This ain't right. Halp!"

Buck Wall thought he heard someone hollering. He pulled up and listened. Yep. Someone was sure hollering all right. Coming from over that next ridge, he thought. He eased over that way and found the source of all the noise.

"Boy," he said to Hammer. "How come you got

yourself all tied up like that there?"

"Cut me down, damnit!" Hammer squalled.

"All right, all right." Buck was in the process of dismounting when the loop settled over his shoulders and he felt himself jerked from the stirrups. He landed heavily on the rocky ground.

Then Smoke Jensen was all over him, fists flying. The last thing Buck recalled, for a few moments, was that getting the living hell beat out of you was not a very pleasant experience.

When he woke up, his world was also upside down. And his clothes were gone, right down to his socks and boots and guns. And there was not a horse to be seen anywhere.

"Hammer," he managed to speak through battered lips. "The next time you get in trouble, I wish you would please keep your mouth shet!"

"Halp!" Hammer hollered.

"Will you stop that! You're makin' my head hurt!"

"Halp!"

"Who said that?" Hammer asked.

"Well, it damn shore wasn't me!"

By twisting around, they could just see a newly hired gunny name of Ben Lewis. Someone—Jensen for sure—had peeled him buck naked and tied him backwards in the saddle. And from the looks of him, he'd been sitting in that saddle for some time. Looked worn to a frazzle.

"I'm a-gonna kill that crummy Smoke Jensen!" Ben hollered.

"Yeah," Buck said drily. "Right. Shore you are. Me, too. But furst I'd like to get shut of this damn tree limb!"

13

The hired guns and bounty hunters and would-be toughs began drifting back to the ranch one by one, and they were a sorry sight to behold. Jud Vale sat on the front porch sipping whiskey and viewed the unfolding scene with disgust in his eyes.

Glen Regan, the punk who fancied himself fast with a gun was the first back. Hooting it. Naked, except for his fancy silver conchoed gun belt, all the shells shucked out of the loops. He wore his empty holsters in strategic locations.

"Plumb pitiful," Jud said mournfully.

"What do you want done with him, Boss?" Jason asked.

"Get him out of my sight. And, Jason? Get ready for a lot more of the same. Jensen's playing games."

Barstow, the no-good from Colorado way was the next to come limping in. Barefoot and clad only in a bush he had uprooted. Jensen hadn't even left him his guns. Jud just pointed to the bunkhouse and poured another drink.

Three of Jud's own regular hands came staggering in about fifteen minutes later. They were drawerless and had been tied together in such a way so they had to move in a circle to get anywhere. They were so dizzy they fell down in a heap in the front yard.

Jud looked at the pile of struggling flesh in his front yard. "Jason?"

"Boss?"

"Get me a headache powder, will you?"

"I believe I'll join you," the foreman said. "But it cain't get much worse than this."

"Don't bet on it."

Jaeger, the German gunhand, came in riding his own horse and wearing clothes. But he had a bloody bandage tied around his big head and a very grim expression on his broad face. "Jensen shoot ear off," he said, and rode on toward the bunkhouse.

"Least he left you your britches," Jud told him.

"I vould ratter have mein ear!" the German called.

The bounty hunter, John Wills, came riding in without his clothes, his hands tied to the saddle horn. But Smoke had neatly wrapped him up, from neck to waist and both his legs, in poison ivy. He was already breaking out and swelling.

Jud pointed to the bunkhouse. "Ointment in the cabinet over yonder," he said with a sigh.

Hammersmith and Buck had found their horses and came riding in with Ben Lewis, the last two in their birthday suits. No guns or rifles. Jensen was going to have quite a collection before this was over.

Of course, Jud knew what he was doing: arming the kids to the teeth.

"I don't want to hear it," Jud told the three, and pointed to the bunkhouse.

It just got worse. But the numbers were fewer. Hazelhurst came in draped over his saddle. His partner explained. "He wanted to make a fight of it. Stupid thing to do with Jensen. I figured my life was worth more than my britches and guns. Jensen said the shirts and jeans was gonna have to be altered some—and shore washed—but the kids would have work clothes a-plenty."

124

"Get a shovel and some boys and plant Hazelhurst," Jud told him, a weary note to his voice.

Vale got up and walked into the house, closing the door behind him. He just did not want to see any more of this.

Smoke stampeded the Bar V horses that night. He jerked down the corral bars and tossed a stick of dynamite outside the corral so no horses would be hurt—just scared half to death.

It was a move that no one expected. After the damage he had done all that day, all thought he would head back to the Box T.

Smoke put an end to those thoughts by emptying his six guns into the bunkhouse, then grabbing two more hung on the saddle horn and blasting away at the mansion, sending Jud Vale jumping out of bed, skinning his knee, banging his big toe on the chiffonier and ultimately falling down his own fancy curving stairs. In his long handles.

"You son of a bitch!" Jud hollered, holding his aching head where he'd banged it on his way down the stairs, head over butt. "I'll get you, Jensen. I swear by my mother's grave—I'll kill you for this!"

But Smoke was smiling as he crossed over the series of ridges that would lead him out of Bar V range, leading a Bar V pack horse carrying clothes and guns.

"Don't you look like the cat who licked the cream," Cheyenne told him when Smoke rolled out of bed and walked outside to wash and shave.

When Smoke had finished telling him what he'd done, the old mountain man and gunfighter was cackling and slapping his knee.

"By God, I'll just bet that was some sight to see! I'd have

give a month's wages to seen 'er."

"Well, it was fun," Smoke admitted with a smile. "Most of it. But there is no telling what Jud will do in retaliation."

"And Clint Perkins come up and stole the girl away, huh?"

"Yes." Walt and Rusty had walked up, to stand listening. "He's a tough one. Don't ever sell him short on courage. He's got his share and more of that."

Smoke had collected thirty pistols and fifteen rifles and more than five hundred rounds of .44 and .45 caliber ammunition. He distributed the weapons and ammo and gave Alice and Doreen the clothes to wash and alter for the boys. He had tossed the boots in a pile in the barn for the boys to prowl through.

"Argood has gone to Utah," Walt told him. "Be gone for a month or more."

"Then Jud will throw everything he's got at us," Smoke said. "It'll be open warfare from this point on." He smiled. "And after what I did to the Bar V, I sure can't blame them."

With little else to do, Chuckie, Ed, Eli, Jimmy, Clark, and Buster busied themselves at the creek, picking up and carefully selecting rocks for the weapons they had been working on. The rocks they picked up were just the perfect size, round and smooth, flawless. They would fit well in the pockets of their slingshots. Maybe they couldn't carry guns around, but they could sure use those slingshots with deadly accuracy.

And the youngsters had just as carefully picked out the spots from which they would launch their small war when Jud Vale's men attacked the ranch. And it was there they stashed their carefully chosen hoard of rocks and spare slingshots, telling no one else about it.

But Cheyenne, wise and watchful old man that he was, had seen the boys scurrying about and became curious as to what they were up to. When he had satisfied his curiosity, he sat down and chuckled.

"Brave little lads," he muttered. And he knew just how deadly a slingshot could be in the hands of a boy with a steady eye. They might not kill anybody with those propelled little rocks, but they could spook some horses and cause some fearful bumps and dents in the head and some painful bruises in the flesh of any attacker.

"I do believe it's gonna get right interestin' around here," he quietly said to himself.

Matthew had been practicing daily with his Peacemaker. One hour a day, faithfully, every day, he practiced his draw. And with lots of ammo available, he could also practice his marksmanship.

The boy was a natural. Better than good, he was awesome in his ability with a short gun.

"I hate to see it," Smoke said to Cheyenne, after watching Matt practice.

"He'd a done it with or without us, Smoke," the old gunfighter said. "I allow as to how it was best that we was here to hep him along."

"Maybe you're right. But the West is slowly changing, Cheyenne. Perhaps not all for the better, but law and order is coming and fast guns will be a thing of the past before we know it."

"I'll never live to see it," the old man said flatly. "And for all the lawyers and judges with their fancy words, and handsewn duds, it's gonna be years afore all the West is tamed—maybe never. Matthew will be a growed-up man afore he'll be able to hang up his guns. And who knows, Smoke? Maybe he'll go on to become a fine lawman. There ain't a bad bone in the lad."

"I'm going to encourage him to do just that."

"I already been doin' that," Cheyenne said. "He seems

127

interested in it, for a fact."

Smoke's eyes came open out of sleep. Something, or somebody was in the barn. He looked out the open window without moving from his bunk. About three o'clock, he guessed.

He lay still, his right hand around the butt of a Colt. When the sound came again, Smoke eared back the hammer.

A soft chuckle came out of the darkness, just outside the open door to his room. "I didn't think I'd be able to get this far without you hearing me," the voice spoke.

"Perkins?" Smoke returned the whisper.

"Oh, my, yes. I've come to lend whatever assistance I can to this little war."

"I watched you the other day. From the ridges."

"Careless on my part, not seeing you. You're very, very good. As good as your reputation makes you out to be, I must admit."

Smoke felt that Perkins was not alone. All his senses were working overtime. "The girl with you?"

"Good guess, *compañero*."

With that correct useage, Smoke knew the man had spent some time below the border. "Going to leave her here?"

"I really have no choice in the matter. She'll be much safer with Walt and Alice."

"Why do you hate them so? They seem like good people to me."

"Oh, I don't hate them. Not at all. I know they think that, but it isn't true. There is a medical term for my mental condition, but I shan't bore you with ten-dollar words when a single word can sum it all up rather well. I'm crazy."

"You have good days and you have bad days."

"Umm. Gunfighter you may be, but you are not overcome with ignorance. Yes. That is correct."

"Have you sought help?"

"Oh, my, yes. But unfortunately, the field of psychiatry is still in its infancy, and the methods they use are really quite primitive. And they don't work," he added the last with a note of bitterness.

"There ought to be some coffee left in the pot. Help yourself."

"Thank you, but I'm afraid I must decline your kind offer. How is Micky?"

"He's a fine boy."

"Ah, good. Doreen thinks I deserted her out of pure callousness. That was not the case. When these twilight moods strike me, I can kill anybody who stands in my way, who speaks to me in a cross manner, or simply because of a wrong word. I would be sorry for it immediately afterward, but apologizing to a corpse is a rather futile gesture, don't you agree, Mr. Jensen?"

"I would think so, yes."

"Should our paths cross again, Mr. Jensen, and I have a rather obvious wild-eyed look about me, leave me alone. Depart the area immediately. It's for your own good, I assure you."

"I'll remember that."

Silence.

"Clint?"

But he was speaking to shadows. Clint Perkins had vanished as softly and silently as he had arrived.

"Susie?"

"I'm right here, Mr. Jensen."

Smoke rose from his bunk and dressed. Then he lit the lamp. Susie was perhaps eighteen—no more than that. A very pretty girl, she had a wide-eyed scared look on her pale face.

"You don't have to be afraid of me, Susie," Smoke told

129

her. "Come on. Let's go wake up the house and get you settled in."

Over coffee and bear sign, the story Susie told was one of horror, clearly indicating that Jud Vale was as nutty as a tree full of squirrels. She told of beatings, of being forced into Jud's bed—and into the bed of Jason when Jud was feeling magnanimous. And of being forced to do things, things about which no decent person should know. Walt looked sick and Alice and Doreen almost had an attack of the swooning vapors, both of them fanning themselves vigorously.

Cheyenne wore a very uncomfortable look on his leathery face. Rusty's face was red as a beet. Smoke had heard the boys gather around the windows, outside the house, but said nothing about it. They were getting an earful, no doubt about that. Dolittle and Harrison had not been awakened.

"Have you seen Jud kill other . . . slaves?" Smoke asked her.

"One. But half a dozen have just disappeared. I know where they're buried, though."

"Your parents?"

"Dead. I was on my way to California to stay with my uncle and aunt when outlaws robbed the train. They took me and sold me to Jud. If he finds out I'm here, he'll attack this ranch."

"He's going to do that anyway, girl," Walt told her. "Just relax. You'll be safe here with us. When this is over, we'll get you to California."

"How did Clint find out you were at the Bar V?" Smoke asked.

"How does he find out anything?" she countered. "He's like a ghost." She looked at Doreen. "And no, there was never anything between us. He's just been a good friend."

The look Doreen gave her silently stated that she

believed that about as much as she believed elephants wore pink tights and danced the can-can.

Susie met Doreen's eyes and accurately read the other woman's expression. She shrugged indifferently.

"Micky can sleep in with his mother," Alice said, stepping between the hot looks. "Susie, you take the boy's bedroom until we can fix up the other bedroom. Go on, dear. Walt's put fresh water in the basin and the towels are on the rack and the bedpan's clean. You get some sleep. We'll talk more in the morning."

"Good idea," Walt said, knocking the ashes from the bowl of his pipe and standing up. His wife joined him and they left the kitchen, Doreen and Susie following.

Smoke, Cheyenne, and Rusty sat around the table for a few more minutes, with Rusty and Cheyenne eating up every doughnut they could find.

"Near four-thirty," Smoke said, refilling his coffee cup. He was almost forced to break Rusty's hand as he reached for the last bear sign. "No point in going back to bed."

Rusty looked frantically around for another platter of doughnuts.

He found a fresh chocolate cake and his smile almost added new light to the room as he whacked off a hunk that would choke a bull.

"Growin' boy still," Cheyenne said with a grin. "Cut me a piece of that, too, Rusty."

"Smoke?"

"I'll pass, Rusty, thanks. I'm fixing to rustle me up some bacon and eggs before long."

"Fix some for me, too," the young puncher spoke around a mouthful of cake.

"Yeah. Me, too," Cheyenne said.

Smoke grined and shook his head at the two characters. Then he sobered when he thought of what Jud Vale might do in retaliation. And another matter had been nagging at

131

him off and on for a week or so.

"What you ruminatin' about?" Cheyenne asked.

"Jud Vale, for one thing."

"Just ride over and call him out and kill him. Me and Rusty and Walt will go with you."

"The odd thing is, Cheyenne, I don't want to kill him. He's not right in the head, and therefore he isn't responsible for what he's doing. It might come to a killing, but I hope it isn't me who has to do it."

Cheyenne thought about that for a moment. "And the other thing?"

Smoke sighed and finished his coffee. He nodded his head toward the outside. Rusty cut the lamps low and followed them. They walked over to the corral and Smoke pulled out the makings and built himself a cigarette.

"Walt has confided in me that he is a wealthy man," Smoke said. "Why doesn't he hire guns and let them bang it out with Jud's men?"

"I've pondered over that my very own self," Cheyenne admitted. "I can't come up with no firm answer."

Rusty looked startled for a moment. Then he shook his head in disbelief. He threw down his own cigarette and stomped it out, his spurs jingling with the movement. "I can't believe you two guys!" he finally blurted.

"What do you mean, you red-headed pup?" Cheyenne looked at him.

Rusty just laughed at him.

"I'll bust you up side your punkin head," Cheyenne told him, balling a hand into a fist and drawing it back.

"Whoa!" Rusty stepped back.

"You better explain yourself, Rusty. If you know something we need to know, spit it out."

"I didn't mean to laugh at neither of you. I just figured that you both knew."

"Knew what, you knothead?" Cheyenne growled at him.

Rusty looked at Smoke. "Soon as you told me I was workin' for the Box T, I figured the fire had done reached the grease. But it never dawned on me that Mr. Walt hadn't leveled with you. Hell . . ." He paused. "Well, maybe the old bunch has died out and the new bunch of folks in this area don't know. Jud Vale is Walt's kid brother!"

14

After recovering from his shock, Cheyenne said, "I been in and out of here for the last fifty years, Rusty. I ain't never heard that story."

"Rancher up in Montana told me some five or six years ago. Sorry, boys, I just figured you knew."

"So Clint is really Walt's nephew," Smoke spoke the words softly. "I wonder what surprises Doreen has in store for us?"

Rusty blushed.

"Not those surprises, Rusty! I wonder if she's kin to Walt and Alice?"

"Beats me. I done told you all I know."

"You shore this rancher wasn't just pullin' your leg?" Cheyenne questioned.

"I don't think so. We was sittin' around the fire one night during roundup, passin' a bottle around. Lemmie see if I can remember all, or most, of what was said." He rolled another cigarette, deep in thought while he was shaping and licking and lighting the tube. "Mr. Randolph—that was the rancher I was workin' for at the time—he said that Walt come out to this part of Idaho 'way back. The first white man to settle in this part of the territory."

"That much jibes with what Walt told me," Smoke confirmed.

"Mr. Randolph said that Walt had left a baby brother behind. I believe he said Ill-o-noise or O-hi-o or some of them faraway places like that. Said that Walt never really knew the kid all that good. He was in diapers when Walt left. The kid started gettin' into trouble right off the mark. Then as the kid got older, the trouble got worser. He's supposed to have raped and kilt a woman when he was 'bout fourteen or fifteen and had to flee, two steps ahead of the law."

"And Walt didn't know what was going on back home?"

"No way he could have. A thousand miles away like he was. Sure wasn't no letters bein' posted to this part of the territory. Mr. Randolph said that the kid turned to a life of crime—bad stuff. Robbin' and murderin' folks and abusin' women. He robbed a U.S. gold shipment, hundreds of thousands of dollars and him and his gang come out thisaways. Jason's been with him from the git-go, 'way Mr. Randolph told it. That gold was what set him up in the ranchin' business.

"Walt went to see the rancher one day, and was shook right down to his boots when Jud Vale—that's the name he took—started talkin' about where he was from. Walt started writin' letters to folks he figured was still alive back to home. He started puttin' two and two together and soon realized that Jud Vale was his baby brother.

"But he never let on to Jud. Not until about ten years ago, I reckon, maybe more than that. Mr. Randolph never did say; or if he did, I forgot. 'Way Mr. Randolph told it, Jud went into a screaming rage for some reason, and told Walt he would destroy him and take all the gold that Walt had found. Walt tried to tell his brother that there wasn't no more gold on the Box T, that the strike had been a fluke and had played out. But Jud wasn't havin' none of that."

"I wonder why Editor Argood didn't tell me all this?" Smoke questioned, his voice soft in the night.

"Well, he probably figured you knew already. Just like I done."

"And now you know it all," Walt's voice came from behind them.

The trio turned around to face the rancher.

"I wish you had told me," Smoke said.

"Shame. It was shame that prevented me from telling you."

Smoke swore an ugly streak. "You're lying, Walt. You've lied to me right from the start and I'm telling you now: clear the damned air and level with us!"

Walt came to the corral and hung his arms over the railing. He lit his pipe and sighed. "There isn't much else to clear. He's my brother, boys. Our blood is the same. I had him in rifle sights once and couldn't pull the trigger. I just couldn't kill him. Even knowing what trash he is— what he had turned into. I just couldn't do it. That's why, until recently, at least, I was just letting him run all over me. Then I got mad. I sent out word that I was hiring gunfighters." He laughed sourly. "But if I paid a hundred a month, Jud would pay two hundred. And so on. I had half a dozen. They left me and went to work for Jud. I hired some straight punchers. Jud and his men drove them off or killed them. I finally reached the point where I just didn't know what to do. I was confused, alone with the wife and Doreen and Micky. Scared for them and for myself. I'm not a young man. There is more than twenty years' difference between me and Jud Vale. His real name is Paul Burden. Then, Smoke, you showed up."

For the first time since arriving at the Box T, Smoke believed the man. "Doreen is no kin to you? No blood kin?"

"No."

"Walt, I've told Cheyenne that I don't want to kill Jud.

136

He needs killing, I'll be the first to admit that. He's a vile, loathsome person, for a fact. But I don't want to be the one to pull the trigger on him. And I won't unless he pushes me to it or gets caught up in gunfire while attacking this ranch. The man is insane. He needs to be confined in an asylum. For the rest of his life."

Walt's laugh was bitter. "You think I haven't tried to do that. I personally called on the territorial governor and informed him of Jud—without telling him that Jud was my brother. He sent people in to talk with Jud. Jud charmed them. He has that ability. Just like his son, Clint. And just like Clint, he can go off the beam into a raging, killing darkness at the smallest slight or word. Smoke, I don't know what else I can do. I have reached my wit's end in this matter."

Smoke felt an intense sorrow for the man. A grandson that wasn't his, and a blood brother who was a raging lunatic and invariably would have to be destroyed like a rabid dog was enough to fell all but the strongest of men.

"We'll work it out, Walt," Smoke assured him.

After Walt had returned to the house, Cheyenne asked, "Just how do you figure we're gonna work it out, Smoke?"

"I don't have any idea," Smoke admitted.

Susie slept late, it being almost noon when she walked out into the front yard. When the weather was good, the boys took their meals at a long setup table in the yard. When the weather was bad, they had to take shifts eating in the house.

Susie was amazed at the youth of the hands, and equally amazed at the ages of the old men. No one asked her to lend a hand with the cleaning up, she just fell to it as one by one the boys finished their nooning and got up, going back to work.

"Rider comin'," Cheyenne said, squinting his eyes.

"Who is it?" Rusty asked.

"Blackjack Morgan," Smoke told them. "You never know about Blackjack. Or Jackson, for that matter. They operate under a strange code."

Matthew had moved over from the table, to stand by the rose bushes planted in front of the house. The hammer thong was off his Peacemaker.

"You just steady down, boy," Smoke said. "Blackjack's not looking for trouble."

Blackjack reined up at the hitchrail and waited for an invite to dismount.

"Coffee's hot, Blackjack," Smoke told him. "You're welcome to a cup and something to eat if you're hungry."

Blackjack swung out of the saddle. "Neighborly of you, Smoke. Coffee sounds good." His eyes widened and he smiled. "Is them bear sign I spy?"

"Yes. Help yourself, Mr. . . . ah, Blackjack," Alice said.

"Thank you kindly, ma'am." He poured coffee and got a couple of doughnuts. He looked at Smoke. "But I got to say that this ain't what you'd call a social visit. At least not right off, it ain't."

"I didn't figure it was." Smoke moved to the table and sat down.

Blackjack munched on a doughnut and sipped his coffee. "That editor feller is gone to Utah. Won't be back for a month or more. And that youngster he hired to cover the news has recently got hisself a bad case of jitters. Didn't take much; just a little talkin' to, is all. He won't be comin' around here no more."

"We expected that."

Blackjack's eyes held a visible light of amusement as he looked around at the boys and the old men. "Damnedest outfit I ever did see. Pardon my language, ladies. These boys doin' a man's work. Drove that herd all the way to the railhead without a bobble. You boys is all right in my book. I brung a message from the Bar V," he said abruptly.

Smoke took a bite from a doughnut and waited.

"Jud Vale has done de-clared war on anybody ridin' for the Box T. Man, woman, or child. That don't set too well for a few of us. Me and Jackson, most especially. I don't believe in mistreatin' women or hurtin' no kid or dog. So, I ain't a-gonna do it. Neither is Jackson."

He finished his bear sign and wiped his mouth with the back of his hand. He drained his coffee cup and thanked Susie as she refilled it.

"But that's just two out of about forty-five . . . with more comin' in shortly. The odds is too high, Smoke. You can't win this one."

"These folks have no place else to go, Blackjack. So we have to win it."

"Figured you'd say that. You bein' who you is and all that."

Blackjack sipped his coffee. "Now I ain't got nothin' personal ag'in you, Smoke. But that ten thousand dollars that Jud's done hung on your scalp is just too good for me to walk away from. That money would get me a right nice spread down in Texas and I can hang these guns up."

"You ain't never gonna hang them guns up, Blackjack," Cheyenne told him. "You been around too long. You're one of the old breed. There's always gonna be some punk kid who wants to make hisself a rep."

"Not me, Cheyenne. I'm a-gonna change my name and bury myself down near the Barrillas. Me and Lassiter. We done talked it over. So me and Lassiter will be waitin' for you over at Preston, Smoke. That's the way it's got to be, and you know it."

Smoke nodded.

Blackjack cut his eyes to Matthew. "Git shut of that gun, boy. It ain't nothing but grief. You already got the stamp on you, but it ain't too late to shake it off. As young as you is, you kill another man, you're gonna be marked."

"I plan on becoming a lawman," Matt told him.

"Huh! That's even worse. Puttin' up with drunks and whoors and tin-horns and gamblers. It ain't no life." He smiled sadly. "O' course, my life ain't been all that great, neither." He stood up and smiled at the women. "Much obliged for the coffee and bear sign, ladies." Turning, he looked at Smoke. "Lassiter's just over the ridge. We're headin' for Preston. I 'spect we'll see you there, Smoke."

Blackjack Morgan walked to his horse and swung into the saddle. He rode off without looking back.

"Now that is interesting!" Walt said.

"Not really." Smoke began rolling a cigarette. "They're setting me up, that's all."

"You can bet on that!" Cheyenne agreed. "Blackjack and Lassiter will prob'ly have four or five men with them. Their plan is being the only ones standin' after the battle."

"That's the way I read it at first. Now I'm not so sure."

"What do you mean, son?" Walt asked.

"Jud wants me away from the ranch, probably figuring I'll take someone with me."

"And he'll hit the ranch when you're gone," Alice stated, a sick expression on her face.

"That's the way I see it."

"And if you don't go into Preston, Blackjack and them others will spread the word that Smoke Jensen has turned yeller," Cheyenne added that.

Smoke shrugged that off. "That kind of talk never bothered me, Cheyenne."

"Son, you can't face seven or eight men alone," Walt told him.

Smoke smiled. "I faced eighteen alone one time. I did take some lead. But I put them all down. Don't worry, Walt. I have no intention of riding into a setup. If I just stay put, that will probably make Blackjack and the others so mad they'll do something rash."

"Like what?" Rusty asked.

"Oh . . . like moving their ambush a lot closer than

Preston. Like over to the trading post."

"And you'd ride over there to face them?" Susie asked. "One man against seven or eight gunslingers?"

"I'd give it some serious thought," Smoke told her, pouring another cup of coffee.

"That man said that more gunfighters would be coming in shortly," Doreen said.

"I'm fresh out of ideas, Doreen. What do you want me to do, girl?"

"You could put the ranch up for sale. Advertise it in the paper, in papers all over the state. That would draw a lot of attention to our situation and maybe make Jud Vale back off."

"She's got a point, Walt," Smoke told him.

But the old rancher shook his head. "I been out here goin' on fifty years. Me and Alice fought Indians and outlaws, blizzards and droughts. We come close to packin' it in several times. This ain't one of them times. If you all was to leave—and I wouldn't blame you none if you was to pull out—I'm stayin'."

His wife moved to his side. *"We're* staying, Walt."

He put his arm around her waist and pulled her close.

The younger of the boys looked at each other, all thinking they had best head back to the creek as quickly as possible and gather up some more stones for their slingshots.

Matthew hitched up his gun belt.

"This here is a right good job of work," Dolittle said. "So me and Harrison is stayin' put. If I'm gonna die, I'd druther it be with food in my belly and some coins to jingle in my jeans."

"I'm stayin'," Cheyenne said.

"So are we!" the boys shouted as a unit.

Rusty shrugged his shoulders. "Count me in, too."

"That's settled," Smoke said. "Let's get back to work."

15

The sheriff rode out to the ranch two days after Blackjack Morgan had tossed down the challenge. He had three tough-looking deputies with him.

He told Walt to get his crew together. His adult crew.

Only Smoke, Cheyenne, and the women were close to the house. They sat at the long table in the front yard and talked.

"Lines bein' what they are," the sheriff said, "I ain't rightly sure this place is even in my jurisdiction. But I know damn well that Preston is. Excuse my language, ladies. And I ain't a-gonna have no gunfights in my town." He looked at Smoke. "I thank you for not ridin' in."

"I'm waiting for them to move it closer to the ranch."

The sheriff nodded his head. He waved his hand at the three deputies. "This is it, folks. You're lookin' at the law enforcement in this county . . . providing, that is, the Box T is even in my county. New lines was drawn up last year and it's still all confused. But that ain't the point. The point is that Jud Vale's done hired himself about sixty men, all drawin' fightin' wages, and there ain't a damn thing I can do about it. Oh, I could ride over to the Bar V and try to throw my badge around. But you all know how much good that would do. Jud's a charmer. He'd just tell me he was gettin' ready for roundup and hired all them men to punch cows."

He sighed. "Walt, there may still be warrants out on Jud back East. I know the story. And I've sent telegrams to them folks back yonder. The parents of the girl that Jud was supposed to have killed is dead. The lawmen who were in charge when it happened are gone. So that's a dead end. No help there."

"What you're trying to say, Sheriff," Smoke said, "is that we're on our own here."

"That's blunt put, Jensen. But yeah, that's just about it. You say that Jud attacked your ranch. Can you prove it in a court of law?"

"I doubt it," Walt admitted.

"There still ain't no laws about two growed-up men facin' each other over gun barrels. There will be someday, but that time ain't here yet. I talked to a man from the governor's office. The governor ain't got the manpower to step in and settle every dispute between ranchers. Territory is just too big. I've said what I come to say, Walt. I wanted to tell it to you face to face."

"I appreciate that."

"You've told us, Sheriff," Smoke said. "Now let me tell you."

The sheriff cut his eyes to the gunfighter.

"Just stay out of it," Smoke said flatly. "I roughed up a few and killed one the last time out. The next time I go headhunting, I'm going to leave bodies all over the range."

The sheriff flushed, but wisely kept his mouth shut.

"And that goes for me, too," Cheyenne said. "In spades. I'm gettin' tarred of all this dilly-dallyin' around. I'm an old man; I ain't got many years left me. So it don't make a damn to me if I check out now, just so long as I take a few, or a bunch, with me. And I plan on doing just that."

The sheriff stood up and his deputies followed suit. "I wish you luck." The lawmen walked to their horses and rode away.

"He's a good man, the sheriff is," Walt said. "I ain't takin' what he said nearabout as hard as you boys. Maybe I just understand the feelins around here better than you."

Smoke stared at the man. "What do you mean, Walt?"

"I've tried to tell you time and again, boy: folks around here is scared of Jud Vale. He's had them buffaloed for years, and it ain't got much better—if any better—since you come along. Man told me last time we went to the post that most of the bettin' money was with Jud and against you."

"You should have told him he was a fool."

"I did. Problem was, I don't know how convincing I sounded."

Walt and Alice, with Doreen and Susie right behind them, went back into the house. Smoke and Cheyenne walked to the corral and stood in silence for a few minutes.

"You changed your mind any 'bout just ridin' up to Jud and pluggin' him?" Cheyenne asked.

"No."

"Didn't figure so. Still think that would be the smart thing to do."

"You're probably right, Cheyenne. But it just isn't my style."

"You want me to do it? He ain't nothin' but a rattlesnake."

"No." Smoke looked off into the distance. "But it worries me about him declaring war on the women and the boys."

"It don't surprise me none," the old gunfighter said with a snort. "A rattlesnake don't give a damn who he strikes. Sometimes they'll just lay there on the trail still as death and watch you go past without even a short rattle. Next time you come by, they'll hit you. Jud Vale ain't got

144

no more sense than a rattler. And is just about as useless. Come to think of it, a rattler might be worth more. Least they kill rats and mice."

The old rounder limped off, toward the bunkhouse and a cup of coffee.

Smoke stood for a time by the corral, deep in thought. Maybe Cheyenne was right. Maybe he should just ride over to the Bar V, line up Jud Vale in rifle sights, and end it.

But Smoke knew he wouldn't do that. At least not yet.

But if one of the boys got hurt . . . ?

He shook his head. He didn't even like to think about that.

With his back to the corral rails, he watched the boys ride out, heading back to work; a gutsy bunch of kids.

Smoke wondered where Clint Perkins had gotten off to. The so-called Robin Hood of the West had not been heard from since he had rescued Susie from the Bar V. But Smoke had no doubts about his being near, waiting for that invisible trigger in his brain—always on half-cock—to fire his unstable mind into action.

Smoke went into the house, told Doreen to fix him a bait of food, and with the food-packet in his hand, went to the barn, saddling Dagger. Rusty had ridden in and was seeing to his horse.

"You headin' out?"

"Yes. Is the herd bunched?"

"And boxed."

"I want you and the others to stick close to the ranch. I don't know how long I'm going to be gone. Three days; maybe a week. However long it takes me to cut the odds down some."

"You goin' to face Blackjack and them others?"

"Probably. But it will be on my terms, not on theirs. Nobody has to leave the ranch. We're well-stocked with food; God knows we have enough guns and ammo to stand off a dozen attacks. Keep an eye on the boys, Rusty."

He swung into the saddle.

"I'll do it. You watch your back trail, Smoke."

"I've been doing that since I was fifteen years old," Smoke said with a smile.

He rode for the Bar V range, keeping to the timber and the brush, riding slow and stopping often to sit his saddle and listen. He marveled at the size of Jud's herds. The man was worth a fortune in beef alone; there wasn't a rancher anywhere who wouldn't be satisfied with these herds. Only Jud Vale wanted more. But then, Smoke concluded, Jud wanted everything.

Especially Doreen.

Smoke had warned her to stick very close to the ranch, and to stop wandering out into the meadows to pick wildflowers. Jud had made his brags that he would have Doreen, one way or the other. But whether Smoke's warnings had gotten through to the girl was something only time would prove out.

Smoke steered clear of Jud's mansion. What he wanted to see was whether anyone was working Jud's cattle, and after spending most of the afternoon carefully watching from the hills and ridges, he concluded that the cattle had been pretty much left on their own.

So Jud had pulled in all his hands. For what? An attack on the ranch? Maybe. But somehow he doubted that.

He had tried that once, with disastrous results. So if not an attack against the Box T . . . then what?

Smoke could come up with no reason for leaving the herd unguarded. Of course, Jud probably felt—and rightly so—that no one would have the nerve to rustle cattle from him, so his herds were safe.

So what was going on? And why had he not run into any of the Bar V hands this day? Odd. Very odd.

With about three hours of good light left and guessing

that he was a good ten miles—maybe more—from Jud's mansion, Smoke rode to near the top of a high ridge. Keeping in the timber, Smoke dismounted and took his field glasses, making his way to the top of the hill. There, on his belly and under cover, he began carefully sweeping the area.

Far in the distance, he picked up the small figures of men, some on foot, some on horseback. They were making a meticulous sweep of the area. Looking for what? Smoke silently questioned. Or for whom? Certainly not him. Jud knew he was at the Box T . . . or had been for days.

Had to be looking for Clint. That was all that Smoke could come up with. Had Clint pulled something over the past few days that Smoke did not know about? It was certainly possible.

Smoke studied the tiny figures of searching men through his field glasses. At least twenty-five or thirty. And that brought yet another thought to Smoke's mind: where were Jud's other hands and hired guns? That question made him uncomfortable.

He decided to get the hell gone from there.

He mounted up and rode toward the deep timber that lay to the east of the mansion, but still well on Bar V range. As he rode, he began seeing signs that this area had been searched and searched thoroughly. He reined up suddenly, knowing then where the other Bar V men were.

All around him, waiting to see if Clint—if that's who they were searching for—would double back.

Smoke found a place which offered deep cover and a good two days' graze and water for Dagger, picketed him, and slipped into moccasins. He filled any empty loops with .44's and taking his rifle, began Injuning his way through the brush and timber.

Smoke was under no illusions: these were dangerous men he was surrounded by, and after Smoke's initial attack against the ranch, and his making fools of the men,

147

they would be doubly alert, with more than one of them mad as hell and looking for blood.

Smoke's blood.

Making about as much noise as a drifting ghost, Smoke wormed his way under a pile of blown down brush and dead limbs—hoping that a rattlesnake had not made this spot his home—and settled in for a time.

As he waited, Smoke ran some questions through his mind: why the systematic search for Clint? Had the man staged another raid, or had Jud just decided to take out his enemies one at a time? Then Smoke rejected both ideas as another thought came to him.

Clint Perkins was a wanted man, a fugitive from justice. So what better way for Jud to show the people that he was a straight-up, honest, and law-abiding citizen than by killing or capturing the most wanted man in Southern Idaho. That would certainly swing public opinion in his favor.

And there was something else, too: after Clint was taken—and Smoke felt the man would not be taken alive, Jud simply could not risk that—Vale could, and probably would, charge that Walt and Alice and Doreen had been hiding the outlaw. That would further erode Walt's credibility with his neighbors.

Slick! Smoke thought, as his eyes continued to sweep the terrain from his hiding place. Jud Vale was beginning to think in a more rational way.

And that, Smoke reflected bitterly, was something he had not even considered Jud doing. He had been counting on the man to continue behaving in his usual emotional and irrational manner.

A stick popped not far from Smoke's hiding place. Smoke cut his eyes, not moving his head. That was no animal, for animals seldom stepped on sticks unless they were running in fear. And Smoke heard no follow-up sounds of any animal in panic.

He waited, motionless, his breathing very shallow and through his mouth to cut down even the slightest sound.

He saw the man move; a fatal mistake on the man's part, for movement attracts attention much faster than sound in any deadly game of hide or be killed.

The man was dressed in earth tones, blending in well with his surroundings. Smoke concluded that the man was a skilled woodsman, and the stick was the only mistake he had made.

It just took one mistake in this game, and the man had made his.

The manhunter moved closer, moving stealthily through the timber. As he drew closer, Smoke could make out his features. It was one of those he had seen stepping off the train some days before. A bounty hunter.

The man carried a Winchester in his hand, a bandoleer of cartridges slung over one shoulder. The manhunter stopped, tensed, and suddenly dropped to the ground.

Smoke watched through a small space in the pile of brush and dead limbs. What had the man seen? Or had his hunter's sixth sense alerted him of the unseen danger?

Probably the latter.

Now it was a game of wait and see.

Smoke waited. Several minutes passed. He could detect no other men, so the bounty hunter was probably working alone. But Smoke couldn't be certain of that, although he believed it to be true.

A bird flew into the timber, started to settle on a branch, then abruptly took once more to the air, its wings flapping furiously.

Smoke's smile was a grim one. Thank you, bird, he thought. Have a long and happy life.

He had yet to move his head. Only his cold hunter's eyes had shifted. Now they remained fixed on the dangerous brush where the bounty hunter lay.

The top of the brush moved ever so slightly, the

movement indicating the man was coming toward Smoke's location, making his way very cautiously.

Had he been spotted? Smoke didn't think so.

Smoke waited for several minutes, watching the slow movement of the man. He wanted him much closer; close enough to use his knife. He did not want to risk a shot; not knowing how many others were within earshot of his location.

Then the bounty hunter rose, all in one fluid motion. He was so close that Smoke could see the hard cruelty in his eyes.

The bounty hunter moved closer, pausing a few feet from the brush pile where Smoke lay.

Smoke exploded out of the brush, his knife in his hand.

16

The bounty hunter wheeled around, his eyes wide with panic, the rifle in his hands coming up. But Smoke's forward charge knocked the man sprawling, loosening his grip on the Winchester. The man opened his mouth to yell a warning. With one hard swing of the long-bladed knife, Smoke ended the life of the hunter.

He took the man's rifle, pistol, and ammo, and then dragged the body into the pile of brush. Smoke made his way back to Dagger, using a different route, stashed the weapons, patted the big stallion on the neck, and once more headed out into the woods.

This time out, he was going to show Jud Vale what he thought of a man who would declare war on women and young boys.

And he would write the message in blood.

Smoke stayed near the top of a ridge, working his way along, keeping to the brush and timber, not skylining himself. At the highest point of the ridge, Smoke bellied down and made his way to the crest.

A Bar V hand chose that time to stick his head up and look Smoke right in the eyes. Smoke recovered from his shock before the puncher and clobbered the cowboy right between the eyes with the butt of his Winchester, sending the man sprawling backward, his forehead bleeding.

Smoke was over the crest and on top of the hand before the man could recover. Smoke busted the man on the side of the jaw with the butt of the rifle and the hand's eyes rolled back in his head. He was out for a long time, with a broken jaw.

Smoke tossed the man's pistol into the brush and smashed the man's rifle useless against a tree trunk. He moved down the ridge, mad and on the warpath. A Bar V gunny spotted him and raised his rifle to fire. Smoke leveled his Winchester and shot the man in the belly, doubling him over and bringing a scream of pain.

Now the fire had reached the hot grease and the war was on.

The landscape seemed to erupt with ugly and very hostile gun hands as Smoke dived for cover just as unfriendly fire began zinging and popping and ricocheting all around him.

Jumping behind a fallen log, Smoke wriggled his way to the other end and rolled into a small depression in the earth. Below him, the Bar V gunnies were shouting and cussing.

Smoke leveled his Winchester and put an abrupt and permanent halt to one gunfighter's swearing. The .44 slug caught the man in the chest. The hand's rifle went flying as blood stained the front of his shirt.

Smoke lunged out of the depression and made the timber before the others could get him in gun sights; shooting uphill was just as tricky as shooting downhill.

On the crest of the ridge, in deep timber, Smoke settled in for the siege. He dusted one Bar V gunny's position, sending the man hugging the earth and losing his hat. Just for spite, knowing what value Western men put on their hats, Smoke lifted his rifle and knocked the hat spinning, ventilating the Stetson.

The gunny cussed Smoke, loud and long.

Smoke ducked down as the lead began whining wickedly all around him, bringing the thought to his mind that now would be just a dandy time to haul his ashes out of that particular location.

During a break in the firing, Smoke eased back, clearing the crest of the ridge, and began making his way west, working in a slow, careful semicircle until coming to a better, if temporary, area in which to work.

He lifted his Winchester, sighted in a foot sticking out from behind a large rock, and squeezed the trigger. The yowl of pain that followed told him he had taken another gunny out of the fight. The man was screaming in pain from his bullet-shattered ankle.

Another gunny, with more guts than sense, left his safe position to move to what he felt was a better one.

Smoke shot him, the bullet going in his left side and tearing out the right side, spinning the man like an out-of-balance top and dropping him to the hard, rocky ground. He did not move.

Smoke punched more .44's into his Winchester and made life miserable for a gunhand who was crouched behind a tree. The man decided to seek better cover and made a run for it. Smoke knocked a leg out from under him and the man rolled down the hill, hollering and cussing. He finally managed to break his downhill rolling by grabbing onto a small tree and painfully work his way behind it. Smoke let him be, and concentrated on the others.

But the fight was gone from this bunch. Smoke watched without firing as they began working their way down the hill, staying in cover, carrying and helping the wounded back out of range of Smoke's deadly rifle fire.

He left his position and worked his way back into deep timber, paralleling the gunnies' retreat, sensing from their urgency and the direction of their travel that they were heading for their horses. He was waiting for them when they reached the picket line.

Smoke shot one badman in the belly and dusted another gunhand before they all left in a confusing and disorderly retreat, some of them losing their weapons as they stumbled and ran away.

Smoke ran into the camp, grabbed up the fallen weapons, and stuck them in empty saddle boots. He grasped as many reins as he could, swung into a saddle, and led the horses back to where he had left Dagger. There, he tied and grouped the horses and headed back for Box T range.

All in all, it had been quite a profitable day.

It was late night before Smoke reached the ranch house. He put the horses into the corral, told the boys to strip the gear from them and clean and store the weapons. He switched horses and then filled a sack with dynamite and caps and fuses, and was back in the saddle, heading once more for Bar V range.

He made a cold camp, slept for a few hours, and was up about three in the morning. He checked his guns and then saddled up. With a grim smile on his lips, Smoke went headhunting under the stars.

About two miles from the main house, and not running into a single Bar V hand, Smoke moved several hundred head of cattle toward the direction of Jud's mansion and then tossed two sputtering sticks of dynamite near the bunched-up herd of Bar V cattle. The explosions sent them into a snorting, wild-eyed stampede heading straight for the mansion.

Smoke tagged along to see what other mischief he could get into this fine night.

The hard-running cattle hit the mansion grounds at full speed, demolishing several outhouses and destroying one corral. Smoke drove half a dozen of the frightened cattle into the mansion and then circled, tossing a stick of dynamite into a bunkhouse.

The charge of giant powder blew out one entire end of the bunkhouse and sent gun hands—in various stages of undress—rolling and running and crawling in all directions.

The dust kicked up from the wildly stampeding herd only added to the confusion, limiting visibility to only a few yards in any direction. Smoke's horse ran into one long handle-clad gun hand, knocking the man to the ground. The gun hand screamed as the horse's steel-shod hooves ripped flesh and cracked bone.

Jud Vale appeared on the balcony of the second floor of the mansion, clad only in his underwear. He was jumping up and down and screaming almost incoherently. "Somebody come up here and get this goddamn cow out of my bedroom!" he finally managed to squall.

With his six gun, Smoke put several slugs around Jud's bare feet. The man did a frantic little dance, and hollering to beat sixty, leaped back into the bedroom, obviously preferring the company of a smelly wild-eyed cow to the lead that was sending splinters into his tootsies.

A puncher grabbed onto Smoke's leg, trying to pull him out of the saddle. Smoke laid the barrel of his Colt against the man's head, splitting it wide open and dropping the man to the ground.

Hot lead came awfully close to Smoke's cheek and that convinced him that it was time to move. Riding bent low over his horse's neck, Smoke galloped around to the back of the house. Jud had just rebuilt the back porch and replaced all the windows at the rear of the house.

Smoke lit another fuse with the small can of burning punk and tossed the stick under the back porch.

Jud's wild cussing could just be heard over the confusion.

Smoke had cleared the creek and was heading into the starry darkness as the porch blew. The giant powder demolished the newly rebuilt porch and once more broke all the windows from the rear of the mighty mansion.

"Goddamn you, Jensen!" Jud's voice rang out over the dusty night. "I'll get you for this. I swear I'll get you! I'll stake you out over an anthill and let them eat your eyes. I'll . . ."

Laughing as Jud's voice faded, Smoke headed for the deep timber.

Dawn found him cutting fence wire and scattering Jud's cattle all to hell and gone. An hour later he had blown two dams and torn down several line shacks.

He looked up at the sounds of pounding hooves and cut his horse toward a long-deserted cabin and barn about half a mile away. The story was that the cabin and barn had belonged to a rancher and his wife. Jud had moved in and moved them out, after killing the rancher's son and badly wounding the rancher.

Smoke chanced a glance over his shoulder. There were ten or twelve riders coming hard at him, but still too far away for accurate shooting on their part.

As he rode toward the cabin, Smoke made his plans as he bent over the horse's neck, keeping a very low target. The cabin was built into a hill. The sod roof had long since become a living thing as the grass from the hill caught life and flourished.

Smoke dismounted at a run and threw open the door, leading the horse inside. He knelt in the open doorway and leveled his Winchester, clearing one saddle of a hired gun. The horse trotted on toward the cabin as the other gun hands veered off, left and right, seeking some sort of cover. They all knew how deadly Smoke was with any type of weapon.

Smoke grabbed the reins of the spooked pony, pulled the rifle from its boot, tore loose the canteen—that would give him three full canteens—and jerked off the saddlebags. He slapped the pony on the rump, sending it on its way.

Smoke slammed the door and dropped the old bar across it just as rifle shots began slugging into the logs of the cabin. He led the horse into the rear part of the house, as far out of harm's way as possible, gave it a hatful of water, and returned to the front of the cabin. If worse came to worst, he could pull grass from off the roof and feed the animal.

He smiled when he saw the kitchen. Luck was with him. Some of the Bar V hands had used the cabin as a line shack, and used it recently. Staying low, Smoke closed the still sturdy inside shutters—put there long ago against Indian attack—and tried the pump in the kitchen. Cold clear water gushed forth. He opened the cabinet. Cans of beans and peaches looked back at him. He selected a can of peaches and opened it with his knife, then ate the peaches and drank the juice.

"All the comforts of home," he muttered, then checked the Winchester he'd jerked from the boot of the riderless horse. It was full up.

He looked into the saddlebags of the hired gun who now rested face down on the ground. Several biscuits with salt meat, three boxes of .44's and a spare pistol and holster under one flap. Dirty underwear under the other flap. He kept the biscuits, the pistol, and the .44's.

Smoke moved to a gun port and looked out. He could see a man slowly working his way toward the house, but still too far off for a shot. Smoke let him come on.

He moved to the other side of the house just in time to see a man run from tree to tree. This one was well within range. Smoke earred the hammer back on his Winchester and waited. The gun hand broke cover and made a run for the corral. Smoke stopped him at midpoint, the .44 slug turning him around as it hit his side. Smoke didn't finish the man, choosing instead to let him lie on the ground and scream in pain. That would work on his buddies much more than a death shot.

Smoke sat down on the floor, his back to an overturned table as the lead really began to fly in his direction. He ate one of the salt meat biscuits and sipped water from his canteen and let the attackers expel all the ammunition they wanted to.

After a time, the hostile fire slacked off and then died. Smoke smiled a grim curving of the lips and moved to the window. He let out a long groan. He waited, and then groaned again.

"We got him!" a man shouted. "We really got the bassard this time!"

"Oh, yeah?" came the sarcasm-filled question. "And who wants to be the one to walk up and look inside the cabin to be sure?"

No one replied.

"That's what I figured," the man said.

Smoke removed the bar from the door and moved back to the overturned table laying his rifle on the floor, pulling his Colts and easing back the hammers. He waited. When they opened that door—and he figured they would come all bunched up for moral support—more than a few of them were going to be in for a very nasty surprise.

Once more, the outside air was filled with lead. Smoke waited.

"Hell, he's had it," a man called. "I'm goin' in."

"I'll go with you," another called, and several more added their agreement to that.

Smoke waited.

He heard the jingle of spurs as the hired guns and bounty hunters approached the cabin. Smoke had removed his boots and arranged them behind the table, placing them so it appeared he was lying dead, his body concealed behind the table. He slipped on moccasins and then stepped back into the shadows of another room.

The front door was pushed open with the barrel of a rifle.

"See anything?" a man asked.

"Hell, are you crazy? I ain't stickin' my head in yonder!"

"I see his boots," another said, looking through a gun slit. "He's all sprawled out and stone cold dead behind a table."

The room crowded with men.

Smoke opened fire, the Colts belching sparks and flame and death. He pulled the pistol he'd taken from the saddlebags and ended the lopsided gunfight. One lone gun hand tried to rise up and shoot him. Smoke shot him between the eyes. "Your mamma should have told you there'd be days like this," Smoke said.

He then counted the bodies. Six. He figured maybe three were left on the outside still alive, and that included the badly wounded man by the corral.

He reloaded and moved toward the open door, staying close to the log wall. "Come on, boys!" he shouted. "Come join the party."

"Hell with you, Jensen!" a man shouted. "They's always another day. We're gone!"

"Then ride, scumbag!"

The man cursed him. A moment later, the sounds of horses galloping away reached Smoke.

Smoke gathered up all the weapons and tied the rifles together. He found a bounty hunter's horse and stuffed the saddlebags full of pistols and gun belts, looping some over the saddle horn. He secured the rifles to the saddle and led the horse to the cabin. Shoving the dead out of the doorway, Smoke led his own horse outside and mounted up. He walked his horse over to the corral and looked down at the man lying on the ground. The man was dead. He left him there and rode out into the plain. The first man he'd shot out of the saddle was lying on the ground, on his back, his eyes open and staring at Smoke. His shirt front was covered with blood.

"You're a devil!" the man gasped.

"I've been called worse," Smoke acknowledged from the saddle.

"I ain't gonna make it, am I?"

"Not likely."

The man cussed him but made no attempt to reach for the pistol still in leather.

Smoke waited until the man stopped cussing and tried to catch his breath. "Anything you want me to do for you?"

"Fall out of the saddle dead!"

Jud Vale had hired hardcases, for sure. No give in them. "Would you really have shot one of those little boys over at the Box T?"

"Just as fast as I'd shoot you, Jensen."

"Then I don't think I'll turn my back to you."

"It wouldn't be a smart thing to do, for a fact."

Smoke sat his saddle for a few minutes. The gunny began to cough up blood. Twice he tried to pull his pistol. But the thong covered the hammer and he could not clear leather. The gunny died with a curse on his lips.

Smoke turned his horse and slowly rode toward Box T range.

17

Jud Vale pulled in his horns, so to speak. Even with his monumental ego and glaring arrogance, he was shocked to the bone at the havoc and carnage that Smoke Jensen had wreaked upon his possessions and hired guns. He had not believed it possible that one man could do so much.

A half dozen of his older and wiser hardcases drew their time and drifted out of Southeastern Idaho, wanting no more of Smoke Jensen. Had most of those who left known Jensen was involved in this matter, they would not have signed on in the first place.

Jud spent a lot of time on his front porch—while his back porch was being rebuilt, again—drinking coffee and wallowing in his festering anger. He had sent out the word that he was still hiring men at fighting wages, and men were drifting in. But even Jud Vale could see that most of them were trash and scum. That made no difference; he hired them anyway.

And then the gunfighter Barry Almond and his four brothers came riding up to the mansion. They were dressed in long dusters and were unshaven, with cruel eyes their hat brims could not conceal.

Jud sat on the porch staring at the men while Barry sat his saddle and met the man's eyes.

161

"I'm Barry Almond," the gun slick finally broke the silence.

"I know who you are."

"That ten thousand dollars still on Smoke Jensen's head?"

"It's still there."

"Me and my brothers come to claim it."

"I've heard that from fifty other men over the weeks," Jud snorted.

"This is the first time you've heard it from me, though."

Jud nodded his head in agreement with that. "All right, you're all on the payroll."

"I ain't punchin' no gawddamn cows," Barry bluntly told him.

The rancher laughed, but the short bark was void of humor. "Nobody else is either," Jud replied, the bitterness thick on his tongue. Ranch was going to hell in a bucket. "So what else is new?"

"We'll just drift around some."

"You do that." Jud poured another cup of coffee and watched the gunfighter brothers head for the long new bunkhouse which Jud had been forced to build because of the overflow of hired guns and because Jensen had destroyed one end of the other bunkhouse.

Jud silently cursed Smoke Jensen. It made him feel better. But not much.

On the day that Smoke accompanied the supply wagon to the trading post, Blackjack Morgan, Lassiter, and four bounty hunters headed for the post for a drink of whiskey. The men were in a bad mood and ready for a killing. Especially if it was Smoke Jensen or some of those snot-nosed brats on the Box T payroll. . . .

Clint Perkins lay on his ground sheet in his hidden camp and tried with all his might to fight the madness that once more began to slowly muddle his brain. He lost the battle. Clint stood up, pulled on his boots and buckled his gun belt around his waist. With a strange smile on his lips and an odd look in his eyes, he saddled up and went looking for trouble. . . .

Matthew and Cheyenne were moving some strays toward the huge box canyon that was the home for what was left of Walt's herds. The old gunfighter and the young boy had become good friends in a short time. . . .

Doreen slipped out the back door of the ranch house to go walking toward a meadow about a mile back of the house. She had seen some lovely wildflowers there and felt that a bunch of them would look very nice on the kitchen table. She didn't think Jud would be foolish enough to try anything in the daylight. . . .

Jud Vale and Jason and Jud's bodyguards chose that time to make a daylight foray into Box T country. They were heavily armed and one of Jud's men had a gunnysack filled with dynamite and caps and fuses. If they could get close enough to Walt's place, they intended to return in kind what Smoke had given them. Twice. And if some of those snot-nosed nester brats got killed . . . ? Big deal. It would serve them right and send a message to the rest of the nesters in what Jud considered to be his territory. . . .

Don Draper and Davy Street and half a dozen other Bar V hired guns had left the bunkhouse to see if they could cause some trouble for the nester brats working the Box T herd. They headed straight for the area where Matthew and Cheyenne were working. . . .

Rusty was about a mile from the box canyon, working alone. . . .

It was ten o'clock in the morning when all the ingredients that were needed to bring to a full boil what would turn out to be the bloodiest range war in all of

Idaho Territory's history were dropped into the cauldron.

Smoke stepped down from the saddle in front of the trading post/barroom, and slipped the leather thongs from the hammers of his guns. Walt went into the store to give the shopkeeper his order for supplies.

Doreen sat amid a wild profusion of flowers and began carefully picking out the most lovely and putting them into her basket.

Susie stepped out of the ranch house at Alice's request to go looking for Doreen. She waved Alan over and asked him if he'd seen her. The boy pointed to the meadow rising in wild and beautiful colors above the ranch, a good mile and a half away, he figured.

"She hadn't oughta get that far from the ranch alone," he added. "You want me to go fetch her, Miss Susie?"

"We'll both go, Alan." She looked at the gun belted around the boy's waist. "You really know how to use that thing?"

"Yes, ma'am. I sure do."

Susie hesitated for a moment. "Get a rifle, Alan. Just in case."

"Yes, ma'am. I'll be back in a couple of minutes."

Susie looked toward the meadow. She suddenly had a very bad feeling about this lovely day.

"Riders comin'," Cheyenne said, twisting in the saddle.

Matt turned and spotted the riders. He slipped the leather from the hammer of his six gun.

The movement did not escape the eyes of Cheyenne. "You just stay out of this, boy."

Rusty had seen Cheyenne and the boy working the strays. Then he saw a bunch of strays moving toward a coulee and went after them. Cheyenne and Matt were quickly lost from his sight as he followed the strays down into the deep coolness of the ravine.

"Boss!" one of Jud's bodyguards said, pulling up and pointing to the tiny figure sitting amid the wildflowers in the meadow.

Jud squinted his eyes and an evil smile turned his mouth. His lips were suddenly dry and he licked them as all sorts of wild, lustful and immoral thoughts, all involving Doreen and himself, raced feverishly around in his brain.

"Get her!" Jud ordered. "I'll have that woman. She'll come around. She'll learn to love me. I'll make her my queen!"

The bodyguards spurred their horses.

Doreen looked up at the sounds of pounding hooves, fear in her eyes. She jumped to her feet, her heart racing. She dropped the basket of wildflowers and began running just as Susie and Alan were beginning the long walk to the meadow.

Alan took stock of the situation quickly. He jerked Susie to the ground, knowing that he could not shoot—the distance was far too great. And there was no point in them being spotted and taken prisoner—or worse. At least for Susie.

All they could do was lie amid the flowers and watch.

Doreen ran for her life, screaming as she ran. Strong and hard hands jerked her off the ground and swung her across a saddle. She felt the horse turn and gallop back across the meadow. The horse slowed, then stopped, and she was dumped to the ground. She looked up into the hard eyes of Jud Vale.

"My queen," the rancher said. "You'll be my queen; you'll reign by my side. Together we'll rule this whole country."

"You're crazy!" Doreen hissed at him. "You're plumb loco!"

Jud laughed at her as his eyes roamed over her young body. "Hoist her up here, boys. I want me a handful of that woman."

Doreen began screaming.

Cheyenne had wheeled his horse to face the Bar V gun hands. The old gunfighter's face was hard, his eyes narrowed to obsidian slits. He looked straight at Don Draper. "What the hell are you and this bag of crap ridin' with you doin' on Box T range, Draper?"

"For a skinny old man, Cheyenne, you got a big fat mouth, you know that?"

"And for a punk, Draper, you're 'way over your head and outclassed facin' me, you know that?"

Draper flushed. "Anytime you're ready, Cheyenne. Then me and the boys will take that kid and have some fun with him."

"You'll visit the privy ever' day if you eat regular," Cheyenne popped back. "And you ought to, 'cause you shore full of it."

Draper's face darkened further at that remark. But still he hesitated, as did Davy Street. Cheyenne was known throughout the West as an old He-Coon who had never backed down from anybody or anything at anytime. If the truth be known. Cheyenne had killed as many men, or more, as Smoke Jensen or John Wesley or Rowdy Joe or Tom Horn—and maybe as many as all of them combined.

Old he might be, but Cheyenne was still a man not to be taken lightly.

It was an old man and a young lad that faced the eight Bar V gun hands that hot morning, but the smell of fear was coming from the so-called gun slicks, not from Cheyenne or Matthew.

"You're a fool, Cheyenne!" Draper spoke, stalling for time.

"Naw," the old gunfighter said, amused at the man's reluctance to drag iron, but at the same time worried about Matthew. "I'm just an old man who's lived a long, long time, that's all. Now I'm ready to see the varmint and rest for a time."

"We gonna kill you and this snot-nosed brat!" a

gun hand sneered at him, cutting his shifty eyes to the bespectacled Matthew.

The boy waited, his right hand close to his six gun.

"You might," Cheyenne admitted. "But they's gonna be a fearful toll taken on you boys whilst doin' it."

"You say!" the gun slick said.

"I say," Cheyenne replied calmly. He had faced this a hundred or more times, and he knew the time was now. This was the entire world. No one else existed. This little pocket was all there was. Time had stopped. Eternity was looking them all in the eyes.

"Now!" Davy yelled, grabbing for his gun.

Cheyenne drew, cocked, and fired, all in one smooth and practiced motion, blowing Davy out of the saddle, the slug taking the man in the center of the chest and knocking him backward.

Don jerked iron and fired, the slug striking Cheyenne in the side. Cheyenne leveled his long-barreled pistol and fired just as Matthew's Peacemaker barked. One slug struck Don in the belly, the other one took him in the chest, the bullet nicking his heart. He stayed in the saddle, one dead hand still holding onto the reins.

A Bar V gun blasted the smoky air, the bullet passing through Cheyenne's lungs. Cheyenne grinned a bloody smile and put a slug between the man's eyes as he was sliding from the saddle. The old gunfighter fell to the ground, on his knees just as Matthew put hot lead into the Bar V hand's stomach.

Cheyenne managed to lift his six gun and drill another hired gun before that pale rider came galloping up to touch him on the shoulder.

The old mountain man and gunfighter died on his knees, still wearing his hat and boots and holding onto his six gun.

Matthew was knocked out of the saddle by a slug that hit his left shoulder and tore out his back. But he held on to his Peacemaker and even though he had lost his glasses he could still see well enough to shoot. The boy leveled the Colt and shot the gun slick in the throat just as Rusty came galloping up, the reins in his teeth and both hands filled with guns.

When Rusty had emptied his Colts, only one Bar V man was left in the saddle and he was hard hit and fogging it back to more friendly range, just barely managing to stay in the saddle.

Rusty took one look at Cheyenne and cursed at the loss of a friend and another man who had helped in the uneasy settling of the West. Rusty hoisted Matthew back into the saddle, found his glasses for him, and tied Cheyenne across his saddle.

"All hell is gonna break loose now, boy," the redhead told the boy. He had inspected the boy's wound and found it to be very painful but not too serious. The bleeding was slow, indicating that no major artery or vein had been hit. Rusty plugged the holes with a torn handkerchief and stabilized the arm in a sling.

"Feels like to me it has broke loose," Matthew said, his voice grim and old for his age. He looked at Cheyenne. "He was my friend."

"He was my friend, too, boy. Let's ride."

Both Alan and Susie had raced back to the ranch compound, yelling as they ran. Alice started crying and Micky joined her.

The boys wanted to ride after the kidnappers and shoot it out and rescue Miss Doreen. Jamie yelled them into silence and literally had to slap some sense into a couple of them. They would wait for Mr. Smoke and that was that. There wasn't no point in going off half-cocked and getting killed.

*   *   *

"Oh, hell!" the barkeep moaned, as Smoke stepped into the saloon. "Not you agin!"

"If this keeps up I'm going to get the feeling that you don't like me," Smoke said with a grin. "But of course," he added, "you would be at the end of a very long list, I reckon."

Bendel shook his head. "That don't seem to worry you much." He returned the smile. "One thing about it, Mr. Jensen—with you around I don't never have to worry about bein' bored." He drew Smoke a mug of beer and set it down on the bar.

"I had hoped this place would not be filled up with Bar V riders."

"Stick around," the barkeep said mournfully. "It will be."

"We won't be here long. Just long enough to get supplies."

"I'm glad you didn't bring that four-eyed kid with you. That youngster is so calm he spooks me."

"He'll do to ride the river with, for sure." Smoke sipped his beer while he waited for Walt to finish with his supply ordering. They were making a trip a week to resupply, for with fifteen growing boys to feed, the food went fast. And Rusty was no slouch when it came to grub. He could eat up a whole apple pie all by himself if the girls didn't keep a good eye on him.

Smoke heard the sounds of horses coming up to the post and inwardly he tensed.

The barkeep cursed.

"What's the matter, Bendel?"

"Some of Jud Vale's hired guns ridin' up. A whole passel of 'em."

Smoke sighed. "One of these days I'm going to get to finish a beer in peace."

18

Doreen had been dumped into an upstairs bedroom. It wasn't long before Jud opened the door, his arms filled with boxes and a big grin on his broad face. He dumped the boxes on the bed.

"Them's the finest gowns and underthings all the way from Paris, France," he boasted. "Silks and satins and the like. And in that little box, they's a diamond and ruby thing you wear in your hair. I forget what it's called."

"Tiara?" she asked.

"Yeah! That's it, all right. I bought it all just for you, Doreen."

"But I don't want any of these things!"

Jud ignored that. Waved it away. Then he began to pout. "But I bought them just for you," he said, a sulky tone in his voice.

Doreen looked at the bulk of the man, lifting her eyes to his. She could plainly see the madness in his eyes; the same kind of madness she had refused—at first—to see in Clint's eyes. Clint Perkins, Jud Vale's own flesh and blood. And in that instant, she realized something else: that if she was going to survive, she had best humor Jud.

But that thought, or warning, flew right out the window as Jud opened more boxes. Grinning at her, he laid the gold and jewel-encrusted headpiece on the bed and shook out the garment. "See what I bought for myself, Queen Doreen. My, oh, my, won't we both look fine!"

Doreen couldn't help it. She burst out laughing and laughed until the tears were running down her cheeks.

"You stop that this minute!" Jud screamed like a petulant child.

But Doreen could not stop laughing. And her laughter became uncontrollable when Jud stamped his boot on the floor and began to jump up and down, behaving very much like a naughty boy caught with his hand in the cookie jar.

Her laughter almost put her on the floor. Where it failed, Jud's fist succeeded. "You're really not going to wear that on your head, are you?" she questioned, just as Jud swung a big fist.

Doreen got her reply as her head exploded in pain and she lost consciousness.

When Rusty brought Matthew in, the hysteria of the women vanished and they took over the doctoring of the boy while Rusty solemnly cut the body of Cheyenne loose and told Jamie and Leroy to get shovels and start digging. They'd wait and have the funeral in the morning. The body would keep that long.

What to do about Doreen?

Rusty didn't know. He looked at Alan. "Boy, could you positive say in a court of law that Jud took her?"

The boy looked at Susie. Both of them shook their heads. "No, sir," the boy replied. "We was too far off to say positive it was him."

"What are you getting at, Rusty?" Alice asked.

"He'll hide her if anybody gets within ten miles of that ranch. You can bet he'll have lookouts posted ever'where. He may be crazy, but he ain't stupid."

171

"So we wait for Smoke to come back?" Susie asked.

"That's all I know to do." Rusty would have liked to go charging into the mansion, both hands filled with Colts. But he was forced to put his anger and his feelings for Doreen aside and do his best to think logically, knowing that even if he should manage to reach the mansion without catching a slug, he would never breach the big house—not alive, and he would certainly be no good to Doreen dead. Or anybody else for that matter.

He would wait for Smoke to return.

Bendel looked out the dusty window. "Six of them, Mr. Jensen. I know two of them by name."

"Who are they?"

"Blackjack Morgan and Lassiter. But them others look just as tough."

Smoke signaled for another beer with his right hand as his left hand touched the butt of his left-hand Colt. Of late, he had been loading the Colts up full. You never knew when that extra round might save your life.

Boots and jingling spurs sounded on the porch of the trading post. The batwings squeaked open. Smoke did not turn around.

Blackjack paused at the bar and spoke to Smoke's back. "Well, well, boys. Look what we done come up on here. The famous gunfighter, Smoke Jensen. You reckon we ought to bow down or something like that?"

His friends laughed. Smoke did not acknowledge the presence of any of them. He sipped at his beer and spoke to Bendel. "I thought I just heard a jackass bray, Bendel. You certainly do have a very strange clientele."

Bendel got a sudden case of the jumps and moved to the end of the bar, carrying a couple of bottles of whiskey with him. He knew the drinking habits of Blackjack and Lassiter and could guess at the tastes of those with them. A

172

tray of shot glasses were bottom's up on a towel near the end of the bar.

"You callin' me a jackass?" Blackjack demanded in a loud voice.

Smoke slowly turned to face the man. "Why . . . it isn't a jackass, after all. It's Blackjack. Excuse me, Morgan. I must have been mistaken."

"That's the damnedest apology I ever heard," Lassiter said.

"Who said I was apologizing." Smoke cut his eyes to the gunfighter.

"What'll it be, boys?" Bendel hollered.

"We ain't deef," one of the bounty hunters said sourly. "Whiskey."

Blackjack still stood by the bar, facing Smoke. Smoke had noted that all the men wore their guns loose in leather, free of hammer thongs. And Blackjack wanted to try Smoke something awful; Smoke could read the challenge in the man's dark eyes.

"Don't do it, Blackjack," Smoke spoke the words softly, so softly that only Morgan could hear them. "It isn't worth it, friend."

"Don't give me orders, Jensen." Blackjack's returning words were equally soft, less than a whisper; a scant moving of the lips. "I want you before the Almond Brothers find you."

Smoke had heard of the Almond Brothers. A trashy bunch of no-goods that had drifted out of the Midwest some years back. A pack of back-shooting scum who would steal the pennies off a dead man's eyes. Jud was certainly scraping the bottom of the barrel by hiring that bunch.

"If they take me, Blackjack, it won't be facing me."

"They'll still have the ten thousand and you'll still be just as dead."

Smoke smiled and turned his back to the man.

"Don't you turn your backside to me!" Blackjack snarled, putting out his hand and dropping it to Smoke's shoulder, spinning the man around.

Smoke hit him with a left to the belly and followed that with a beer mug to the side of Blackjack's head, knocking the man to the floor.

Blackjack was up like a rubber ball, blood streaming down his cheek from the gash on his head. He swung a fist and Smoke ducked under it, again popping the man in the gut and bringing a grunt of pain.

Blackjack connected with a left to Smoke's head that backed him up. Blackjack was no stranger to brawls and he could punch.

Smoke faked him with a left and Blackjack took the bait, grinning and dropping his guard. Smoke punched through the hole and erased the grin, as he connected with a right to the mouth that smashed Blackjack's lips and loosened some teeth. Blackjack shook his head and came in swinging.

Smoke sidestepped and stuck out a boot, sending the man to the floor, clubbing him on the back of the neck as he went down.

With a curse, Blackjack got to his boots just in time to receive a left and right combination to both sides of his jaw that staggered and stunned the man. He fell back against the bar planking.

Smoke pinned him there and went to work, smashing at the man with big work-hardened fists. Smoke flattened Blackjack's nose and ruined his mouth. One of the man's ears was swollen and pulpy and the gunfighter's eyes were glazing over.

Smoke stepped back and let Blackjack fall to the floor. The man did not move.

Lassiter chose that time to stand up. "By God, Jensen, you'll not do that to another good man," and went for his piece.

Smoke shot him.

He drew, cocked, and fired in less than a heartbeat, his slug striking Lassiter in the belly and knocking him back against a table, splitting the wood right down the middle. Lassiter was drawing iron as he was falling and managed to get off one shot, which dead-centered the painting of a nude female hanging on the wall behind the bar.

"Why, you sorry son!" Bendel hollered. "I paid good money for that." He came up with a shotgun just as one of the bounty hunters was dragging iron.

Lassiter lifted his six gun as blood was leaking from his mouth.

Smoke shot him between the eyes just as Bendel's shotgun roared, the buckshot creating a terrible mess at close range. The torn-apart bounty hunter was literally lifted off his boots and flung across the room. He bounced off a wall and fell to the floor, lying still in a bloody mess. Two of his buddies cursed and then tossed good sense and caution to the gods of fate as they grabbed for their six guns.

Bendel gave one the other barrel just as Smoke shifted the muzzle of his Colt and let the .44 bang, the slug taking the second man in the chest and dropping him to his knees.

The lone bounty hunter left alive lifted his hands out from his body and held them wide apart to show that he was out of this affair.

Walt stuck his gray head into the gunsmoke-filled barroom. He held a six gun in his hand, the hammer earred back.

"It's over," Smoke told him, just as Blackjack moaned on the floor and tried to sit up.

Smoke jerked the man to his boots and spun him around, so he could see the carnage in the saloon.

Blackjack's eyes were swollen from the beating he'd just received, but he could see well enough to know that the best thing he could do would be to keep his mouth closed.

"Get on your horse and ride, Blackjack," Smoke told him. "And if you have any sense at all you'll keep going and not look back until you've cleared a couple of counties."

Blackjack broke his silence. "Lassiter was a pal of mine, Jensen."

"Was is right."

"I'll not let his death go unavenged."

"Then you're a fool. As crazy as Jud Vale." Smoke shoved him toward the batwings. "Get out of here, Blackjack. If you're in my sight ten seconds from now I'll kill you."

"And stay out of my saloon!" Bendel hollered. "All of you trash that work for the Bar V. I'm tellin' you now; pass the word: I'll kill the first one of you that pass through those batwings. I'm tired of this." He leveled his reloaded double-barrel, sawed-off express gun. "Move, damn you!"

Blackjack moved.

Smoke glanced at Walt. "Supplies loaded?"

"All on the wagon."

"Let's get back to the ranch. I suddenly got a bad feeling about this day."

Jackson took one look at Jud Vale and struggled to contain his laughter. At the same time he was fighting to keep from busting out laughing, he was making up his mind about the Bear Lake Fight, as it was being called by some.

Jackson was switching sides.

Jackson was a gunfighter, and a good one, but he had had a bad taste in his mouth about this fight right from the git-go. He just didn't think it was right to fight women and kids and old men. And now he had heard that Jud Vale and Old Walt were really brothers, and that didn't set well with him at all. He didn't have any trouble understanding how brothers could hate each other; he'd seen that many times before. But in this situation, there wasn't any reason for it. Come to think of it, there wasn't any reason for any of this, and there damn sure wasn't even one ounce of reason roaming around in Jud's crazy head.

And where in the hell did Jud come up with that costume he was struttin' around in?

Man looked like the fool he really was.

Time to go, Jackson concluded, just about the time the lone hand come staggering in from the gunfight with Cheyenne and the kid.

Jackson listened, then slowly walked to the bunkhouse to get his kit together. He rode out without being noticed. He headed for Box T range, but in a very roundabout way, going by the way of the trading post and stopping in for a drink of whiskey.

That longing for a drink of whiskey just about cost him his life: when he stepped into the saloon he was looking down the barrels of a sawed-off shotgun.

"Whoa!" Jackson said. "I'm friendly, Bendel!"

"Not if you're ridin' for the Bar V, you ain't."

"I quit 'um. Jud Vale is as crazy as a bessy-bug. All the wrappin' done come plumb off him." He grimaced, remembering the sight of Jud all dressed up in that silly-lookin' outfit. "In a manner of speakin', that is. I figured I'd toss my saddle on a Box T horse."

Bendel lowered the express gun. "They need some help, for a fact. Have a whiskey, on the house."

"Don't mind if I do. Smells like gunsmoke in here, Bendel."

Bendel told him what had gone down.

Jackson sipped his whiskey and mulled over that bit of information. He would have liked to seen Blackjack get the snot whipped out of him. If ever a man deserved a good butt-whippin', Morgan did. Him and Lassiter and those others with that grand plan to ambush Jensen. That hadn't set well with Jackson either, but by the time he'd learned of it, it had all blown over.

Jackson thanked Bendel for the whiskey, stepped into the general store for some tobacco and cartridges, then headed out for the Box T.

He was feeling better with every mile he put behind him.

19

"And I seen Jud sendin' men out in all directions," Jackson was wrapping it up for Smoke and Rusty and the others. "Ain't no way we're gonna bust Miss Doreen out of there with just two or three men and a handful of kids. I don't think her life is in no danger. Don't you ladies take this the wrong way now, 'cause I think a man doin' what Jud is gonna do against her will is wrong, but at least she'll be alive."

"And you say Jud has really gone around the bend?" Walt asked.

"Gone around the bend! Man, he is total loco. Walks around that big house with a gold crown on his head, all done up in diamonds and rubies and the like. And he wears a robe."

"You mean he's wearing something like a dressing gown?" Smoke asked.

"Hell, no! Excuse me, ladies. I mean one of them ear-mine robes that he had handsewn and all made up for him over in Russia."

"Ear-mine?" Alice questioned. "You mean ermine fur?"

"Yes'um. That's it. A white one. Comes all the way down to his ankles. He looks real stupid stompin' around the house in that robe, wearing a crown on his head, and cowboy boots on his feet. I'm tellin' y'all, it's gettin' to be awful weird around that place. Plumb spooky."

"Are the men laughing at him?" Walt asked.

"Not to his face. He's still totin' a gun strapped around his waist. And that makes him look even dumber."

"But still dangerous," Rusty added.

"Even more dangerous," Jackson told them. "'Cause you don't never know what a crazy man is goin' to do."

They all agreed with that.

Walt leaned back and scratched his head. "Well, let's come up with some way to get Doreen out of that nuthouse. Anybody want to start?"

Those seated around the table fell silent as they looked at one another. Smoke finally broke the silence.

"I'll gear up and leave tonight. We've got to know just where in the house she's located and how many men Jud has on guard and where they are. I'll find that out and then we can make some plans. But first we have to bury Cheyenne. Let's do it at sunset. That was his favorite time of day."

They all agreed that was a good suggestion.

"I just wish I knew if Doreen was all right," Alice sighed the words.

"She ain't all right, ma'am," Jackson said, a grim note to his statement. "But she ain't dead either."

They buried Cheyenne just as the sun was going down, with Walt reading from the Good Book. Alice and Susie and Micky cried, and some of the other boys looked like they were having a tough time of it keeping the tears back. All but Matthew. The boy stood with a grim look on his face. Smoke knew the look well. He could read revenge clear on the boy's face.

Smoke knew just how Matt felt. He'd been down that rocky path many times in his life.

After the words were read, one by one, they filed past the dark hole and tossed a handful of earth into the pit. The clods rattled against the rough pine box that Young Eli had built for Cheyenne that afternoon. Then each one of the other boys had solemnly driven a single nail into the coffin.

Moments after the funeral, Smoke saddled up and rode off into the gathering darkness. There was a hard look on his face. He was getting more than a little weary of Jud Vale and his hired guns.

Deep into Bar V range, about three miles from the mansion, he guessed, Smoke picketed his horse and slipped into moccasins, leaving his hat and taking his rifle. He had swung wide getting to the location where he had left his horse, taking a route that if he were in Jud's place, would post the least number of guards.

He worked his way toward the mansion, hoping to find the location of just one of the guards. He wanted to talk to one of Jud's men. Smoke didn't think it would take him long to get what information he needed . . . and it didn't.

The guard woke up with a raging headache from where Smoke had clubbed him on the back of the head. There was a bandana tied over his mouth and he was very cold from the waist down. He couldn't understand that. Then he realized his britches were gone. He cut his eyes and felt even colder fear clutch at his heart as he looked at Smoke Jensen, squatting a few feet away, clear in the moonlight, a big-bladed knife in his hand.

"I'm going to ask you a few questions," Smoke said, in a voice that made the hired gun want to go to the bushes to relieve himself something fierce. "And you're going to give me correct answers. You know who I am?"

The man nodded his head.

"You've heard the story about what I did to one of the

men who raped my first wife and then killed her and our baby son?"

The hired gun almost came unhinged. *Everybody* knew what Smoke Jensen had done to the gunfighter Canning. He had taken a knife—maybe the same damn knife Smoke was now holding—and turned Canning into a gelding, then cauterized the wound with a hot running iron.

The hired gun nodded his head vigorously.

"You wouldn't want me to do that to you, would you?"

The man made strangling, choking noises behind the bandana.

"I didn't think so." Smoke reached out with the point of the blade and the man almost had heart failure. He breathed a little easier as Smoke cut the gag loose.

"You yell, and it will be the last sound you'll ever make on this earth," Smoke warned him.

The hired gun nodded.

"What's your name?"

"Johns."

"I want the locations of all the guards. Quickly."

Johns told him. Quickly.

"What room is Doreen being held in?"

"Top floor. The room facin' the crick back of the house. The winders is all nailed shut so's she can't get out."

"Has any harm come to her?"

"No, sir. Jud hit her once, but that's all. He ain't messed with her in no way. He says he's savin' all that for when they get hitched up proper."

"And when is that going to be?"

"Don't know. And that's the truth."

"How many men does Jud have on his payroll?"

"I'd have to say close to a hundred now. He's got a regular army. But a lot of them is trash. They ain't gonna stand when it starts gettin' hot. I'd say he's got near'bouts seventy fighters. And hirin' more."

"Jud can't afford to pay that many men."

Johns sighed. "He can afford it. I'll tell you all I know. Then if you'll let me go, I'm gone to see the Pacific Ocean."

"You level with me and you can ride."

"Deal."

Smoke cut his bonds and told him to put his pants back on. And to wash his long handles the first chance he got. Smoke built a cigarette and tossed Johns the makings. The man lit up and inhaled, then started to talk.

"The ranch is just a front for Jud's other doings. He's into all sorts of things. Got hisself four or five gangs workin' all over two or three states, robbin' trains and stagecoaches and stealin' gold and cattle and you name it. I don't know all that he's got goin' for him, but I do know that he's a rich man, and that he's gone plumb crazy. A lot of his own men—not none of the ones that's been with him for years—is beginning to talk about doin' him in and takin' over. I been thinkin' about driftin'. So far I ain't kilt nobody that wasn't facin' me with a gun, and I ain't never stole much of nothin' in my life. A beef ever' now and then for something to eat, is all."

"Is he going to call his gangs in to help in this range war?"

Johns snubbed out his cigarette. "Smoke, there ain't no way of tellin' what that man is gonna do. He might have done sent for them for all I know. I'm tellin' you the man is crazy as a lizard."

"Anything else you can tell me?"

Johns thought for a moment. Then slowly shook his head. "I reckon not. Except for maybe to warn you to expect anything. Jud Vale has done turned crazy."

After Johns had ridden away, Smoke said, "All right, Clint, you can come in now."

A chuckle from the darkness. "You are very, very good,

Mr. Smoke Jensen. But I fear I must decline your kind invitation. I am in one of my moods and there is no telling what I might do."

"Jud has Doreen."

"I know. But now is not the time to attempt to mount a rescue. We are too few and Jud has too many. We will have to devise some sort of diversion to pull as many men as possible away from the ranch, and then no more than two or three go in to get her."

"Have you a plan?"

"Unfortunately, no. But I know Doreen very well. She is very, very bright. I am certain she has guessed that the key to her survival lies in her keeping a cool head about her. If Jud Vale wants her to be his queen, to parade about in fine gowns from Paris, France, that's what she'll do if that's what it takes to stay alive."

"Jud's own men—some of them—are talking mutiny. That might turn out bad for Doreen."

"Yes. I thought about that. I think we have a week or so before anything like that happens. Probably longer. It will take that long for Jud to pull in his various and far-flung gangs."

"If that's what he has in mind."

"He does. I've been on these ridges since early afternoon. He's sent riders out in all directions. I'm guessing that some of them are riding for the gangs."

"Then we'd damn well better do something before the odds against us get ridiculous."

"I'll let you know when I have a plan."

Smoke heard a whisper of cloth against brush, and knew that Clint Perkins was gone, slipping into the night.

Smoke sighed and shook his head. This had turned into one great big mess. The next time you think about a vacation, he thought sourly, try riding east instead of west.

Then he felt guilty for thinking that. His own children would be grown some day, and if they got into a jam that was not of their own doing, he hoped someone would be around to help them.

Someone like Smoke Jensen.

He rose to his moccasins and started back to his horse. This was one of the few times in his life that he felt helpless, and he had a hunch the feeling was going to get much worse until it bettered out.

If it ever did.

Matthew remained in bed, embarrassed by all the fuss being made over him, but enjoying it nonetheless. There were no signs of infection in his wound, and he seemed to be healing nicely and quickly.

Walt had ordered all the boys to stay close to the ranch. What cattle remained were bunched in the box canyon with plenty of graze and water and could take care of themselves for a time. The boys worked at turning the ranch compound into a fort.

Everybody knew that an attack, and it would be a big one, was inevitable. It was just a question of when.

Smoke and Rusty and Jackson went over everything they could think of.

"As far as weapons and ammo goes, we got enough to outfit a battalion of army," Jackson pointed out. He grinned. "I recognize a whole lot of them rifles and pistols from the Bar V boys."

"We've filled ever' water barrel we could tote in," Rusty said. "The house and barn and bunkhouse is fortified like none I ever seen. That was a good idea Jamie had about haulin' up big rocks and stackin' them window high around the house and bunkhouse. It'd take a lot of giant powder to do any damage."

Jackson rolled a cigarette, licked, and lit up. He glanced at Smoke. "You in deep thought, Smoke." He passed him the makings.

"Three reasonably young men—that's us. Three old men. Two women. One little boy, and fifteen young boys. That's all that's standing between maybe hundred or more hired guns, bounty hunters, outlaws, and a crazy man who walks around his mansion in an ermine robe with a jeweled crown on his head proclaiming himself to be king. I've been in some strange situations in my time, but this one has got to take the cake."

"How about ridin' into town and sendin' a wire to the governor?" Rusty suggested.

Smoke shook his head. "I discussed that with Walt. We both agreed we'd be wasting our time. The governor has made it clear that he doesn't have the manpower to do us any good down here. Reading between the lines of that remark, I'd have to say that the governor is not going to get involved. Why, is anybody's guess."

Jackson was thoughtful for a moment. "I know maybe half a dozen men I could get to come in here. If I could find them, that is."

"Yeah, that's my problem, too," Smoke said. "Louis Longmont would come in here in a flash, but I have no idea where to find him. For all I know, he might be in Europe. I have a hunch that all this is going to be over before any of us could locate and bring people in. Jud's got the jump on us in that respect."

"If we could just get Doreen free of that nuthouse of Jud's, we could sit back here and wait Jud out," Rusty reflected. "I think even if Jud sent all his men over here, we stand a pretty good chance of holding them off."

"Attacking us here will come," Smoke said. "I believe that. But only as a last resort. Jud's got Doreen; that's what he wanted most of all. His main concern now will be in keeping her."

"The thing to do, the way I see it," Jackson said, "is to try to think like Jud. But how in the blue blazes could anyone think like a crazy man?"

"You can't," Smoke nixed that. "I think his moods change, or could change, every day, maybe every hour. I believe he's so far around the bend that he's become totally unpredictable."

Rusty glanced at him. "You're sayin' that even Jud don't know what he's gonna do next?"

"That's right. And if you ever get a chance, look into the eyes of Clint Perkins. His and Jud's eyes are identical. They're both madmen."

"Then it's true that Jud is Clint's father?" Jackson asked.

"Yes. And Clint can be just as whacky as Jud. No telling what he'll do next. He doesn't even know."

"You think he still cares for Doreen?"

Smoke shrugged. "In a way, I suppose. But I think he's driven more out of hate for Jud than concern for Doreen. And that could get Doreen in trouble if Clint tries something on his own."

"How about contactin' the Army and seein' if they'll do something?" Rusty grabbed at straws.

Smoke shook his head. "There again, we'd have to go through the governor to get them. And for some reason, the governor, or more likely, someone in his office, is blocking all requests for help."

"Nearest Army unit is stationed up near that little ol' town some folks have taken to callin' Pocatello," Jackson said. "And there ain't no more than a handful of soldier boys garrisoned there."

"We seem to be just goin' around in circles," Rusty said bitterly. "Gettin' nowheres in a hurry."

Jackson allowed as to how that was the truth.

"Did you know that Matthew has Cheyenne's old Colt?" Rusty asked Smoke.

"No, I didn't. But it doesn't surprise me. The boy loved that old man. And everytime I look into his eyes I see revenge."

"I do know that feelin'," Jackson said. "The boy's a natural gun hand, Smoke. And there ain't nothin' none of us can do to slow him down. I knowed that the first time I seen him. I don't have to tell you that it's in the walk, the bearing, the eyes. He's gonna be hell on wheels, you mark my words."

Smoke slowly nodded his head. "I know. I saw it, too. It was like looking into a mirror and seeing myself years ago."

"I do know that feelin' myself," Jackson said drily. "I sometimes wish my daddy had taken the gun away from me and beat me over the head with it when I was a young'un. But it wouldn't have done no good. I had a fortune teller read my palm once. She told me I was a gunfighter. I was fourteen years old at the time. Rememberin' that still spooks me." Jackson touched the butts of his guns. "I think, Smoke, that when it's all said and done, we're gonna have to go in and fetch Miss Doreen."

"So do I, Jackson. But for now, all we can do is wait."

Rusty looked toward the direction of Bar V range. "I sure miss that girl. I surely do. I reckon I been smitten, and she feels the same way." He looked into the eyes of Smoke Jensen. "And I ain't waitin' very long."

20

Jud pounded the end of his staff on the floor and bellowed at his "subjects," as he had recently begun calling the assorted riffraff he had on his payroll.

"Bring the queen to my side!" he squalled.

Several of his bodyguards—he now had a dozen around him at all times—went upstairs to fetch the most unwilling Queen Doreen.

Jud had ordered all the furniture removed from one downstairs room in the mansion. All the furniture except for two huge padded chairs that were placed in the center of the room: his throne and Doreen's slightly smaller throne. Jud's "staff" was a thick piece of oak, about four feet long and weighing about twenty pounds, long enough and stout enough to fell a buffalo. Jud had read several books about how royalty dressed and behaved. Since he didn't have a goblet from which to drink his wine—wine being something royalty drank—he had found a quart jar, so he used that in place of a jewel-encrusted goblet. It was kind of hard to hold, but it was either that or a bucket, and a bucket wasn't very dignified. Jud had also stopped shaving and was growing a beard; that was something else that all male royalty of the time did. Or so he had read.

He had been informed that the sole survivor of the gunfight with Cheyenne, Matthew, and Rusty had died of his wounds. Jud waved that off with a mutter about serfs and the like. Since the gun slick who delivered the message had no idea what a serf was he couldn't take umbrage. He did think his boss looked like a plumb idiot; but as long as the good money kept coming, the gun hand didn't really care how Jud dressed. But he did figure that damn fur coat Jud wore was kind of hot for this time of the year.

Doreen was ushered in, all silks and satins and fancy shoes, with a jeweled crown on her head.

Jud pounded his staff on the floor and bellowed, "All rise for Queen Doreen!"

Since there weren't any chairs in the room except for the two thrones, that was an unnecessary command, but Jud thought it sounded regal so he did it anyway.

Highpockets left the "Crown Room" and walked up to Gimpy Bonner on the front porch. "The son of a bitch is crazy, Gimp!"

"I allow as to how you're right, Highpockets. But as long as the money keeps comin', I don't care if he walks around bare-butt nekkid and rides a camel."

"Now that would be a sight to see!"

King Jud and Queen Doreen held court for a few minutes, but since there was nobody with any complaints for Jud to hear and rule on it got sort of boring after a few moments.

"Would you like to stroll about the estate, my queen?" Jud asked.

"But of course," Doreen said with a smile. I might find a chance to cut and run away from you, you ninny! she was thinking behind her smile.

It was quite a sight to see. Jud in his cowboy boots and spurs, his six guns belted around his middle, wore a ankle-length ermine robe and toted his twenty-pound staff. Doreen had on a gown that would have been the envy of the Queen of England. As they strolled around the "estate," both were careful not to step in the many piles of horse droppings that littered the grounds.

"I wish you would do something about this . . . unpleasantness," Doreen said, pointing to a fresh pile of road apples.

"You're absolutely right, my queen." Jud told one of his bodyguards to order the mess cleaned up and keep it clean.

It did not take Doreen long to conclude that while Jud certainly was as crazy as a road lizard, he wasn't stupid. The bodyguards flanked them as they strolled, and there were guards in the front of them and in the back. Jud summed it all up with a strange smile on his face.

"There is no way you are going to escape, my queen. So put it out of your pretty head and just enjoy all the privileges you are being accorded. This is your home, for now and for always."

"Very well," Doreen spoke through tight lips. "I want my room redone and I want it done immediately. I hate the colors!"

"Uh . . . yes, dear."

"And I want satin or silk sheets. Those cotton sheets are just so shabby!"

"Right, my queen."

"I want my breakfast served to me in bed."

"Uh . . . of course, dear." Jud was beginning to wonder if having a woman around on a permanent basis was going to be worth all the trouble. He wondered if other kings had the same problem.

"And I want a party."

"A party!"

"Yes. A great big fancy ball." She was doing some fast thinking and hoping it would work. "And I want everybody in southeastern Idaho invited. We'll announce our engagement there."

Jud fell to his knees; unfortunately, one knee landed

squarely in a fresh pile of horse manure, but Jud appeared not to notice. "Oh, Doreen—do you really mean that?"

"Of course, I do. I'll start working on the invitation list immediately."

Jud kissed her hand. "I'm so happy, my queen!"

You won't be so happy when you see the guest list, Doreen thought. And on the night the ball is held, that's when I turn back into a pumpkin and get the hell away from you and this nuthouse!

"Bar V rider comin'," Jackson said. "And he's comin' up holdin' a white flag."

Jud had reluctantly agreed to invite Walt and Alice and Smoke and Rusty. He had done so after Doreen had pointed out that he had a hundred or so men on the ranch; what could Smoke do with all those guns around him?

Scott Johnson, the Arizona gun hand, handed Smoke several envelopes. "You lose, Jensen," he said with a nasty grin. "Miss Doreen and Jud is gonna announce their weddin' plans at this here shindig. And she said to tell you that that Shakyspear feller said it best when he was talkin' about friends, romans, and countrymen. Whatever the hell that means."

Scott turned his horse and rode off.

Smoke smiled, thankful that he had wintered that time with Preacher and all those books. He remembered the line well. I come to bury Caesar, not to praise him!

"Wipe that hound dog look off your face, Rusty," he told the man. "She's telling us to get her out of there and giving us a way to do it."

"Damned if I see how."

"Jud'll probably have men at the door friskin' certain people before they enter the mansion," Jackson said. "We won't be able to carry guns inside." He paused. "We, hell, I wasn't even invited!"

"You'll be going though," Smoke told him. "At least part of the way." He looked at the date on the invitation. "We've got a week to plan things out. First thing I've got to do is see who all was invited and who is planning to attend. I'm going to send Jamie and Leroy to poke around some." He looked at Rusty's long face. "Relax, Rusty. We'll get your sweetie back."

The governor was invited to the party. He sent word that he would not be able to attend. So did the general in charge of all federal troops in Idaho Territory. But Sheriff Brady said he wouldn't miss it for the world. And the young reporter from the Montpelier newspaper would attend. Most of the ranchers and a few of the farmers—Doreen had insisted the nesters be invited—agreed to attend the party.

Smoke had decided he would go in unarmed. When the time came to grab Doreen, he would bust a guard over the noggin with something—maybe the punch bowl if it came to that—take his guns and really liven up the party.

Smoke was going to stay close to the ranch until the night of the big event. He didn't want to put Doreen's rescue in jeopardy by running into any of the bounty hunters who were out looking for him. That could come later.

At the Bar V, Doreen had everybody there, from the cooks to the cowboys, running around the lower half of the territory, driving them about half-crazy, picking up this, that, and the other thing for the ball. She wanted them to be so tired come the night of the event that all they would want to do is lie down and sleep and to hell with the party. She didn't know if that would be the case, but it was worth a try.

Jud had ordered cases of champagne sent in, and as many different types of "finger foods," as Doreen called them, as could be found within three days' ride of the Bar V. Since no one in their right mind would work for Jud Vale, he was forced to use some of his own hired guns and cowboys to act as waiters. He bought them all brand new black suits, with white shirts and black string ties, and low quarter shoes and white gloves. There was a lot of bitching going on about that, but Jud told them either do it or haul their ashes.

Doreen had insisted upon a band, so Jud managed to round up a guitar player, a fiddle player, and someone to toot on a bugle. It was the best he could do on such short notice.

Jud was undecided as to what to wear to the gala event. Doreen said she would clean up his ermine robe—it had a few food and wine spots on it—and he could polish his crown and shine his boots and spurs. He would look so nice.

She wanted him to look like the fool he was so everyone there could see the real Jud Vale.

"Can I wear my guns, Doreen?" Jud asked.

"Oh, but of course, darling!" She had overheard him telling his men to frisk everyone. She hoped Smoke and Rusty would be able to arm themselves once inside the nuthouse.

Time was running out.

Smoke laid down the ground rules.

"Walt, when you get the signal from me, you take Alice and get gone from Jud's place. I'll wait about forty-five minutes before making my play. That'll give you time to get Alice to the west side of the creek. You wait there."

The rancher nodded his head in agreement.

"Jackson, you and Dolittle and Harrison will be stationed at the creek, our side of it, with rifles. Just as soon as we drop Doreen off, Alice and Doreen can take the buggy and hightail for the ranch. We'll hold off the men Jud is sure to send after us."

"Sounds good to me," Dolittle said. "I been cravin' some action."

"Yeah, me, too," Harrison agreed. "I may not be good for too much else, but I can damn sure still pull a trigger."

"And you can bet that Jud will have everybody that can ride a horse after you," Jackson warned. "He'll be killin' mad."

"We'll have a good fifteen to thirty minutes' start on him though," Smoke said. "After Doreen makes her little speech about being kidnapped, and me with a Colt stuck up Jud's nose, the sheriff will have to make some noises about law and order and all that. Of course, once I turn Jud loose and he hoofs it back to the mansion, he'll ignore anything the sheriff might have to say and come fogging after us."

"We might get some more people on our side by doing this," Walt mused aloud. "Maybe this will give some of the smaller ranchers and farmers the backbone to join us in fighting my brother."

"If this don't, nothing will," Rusty added. He looked at Smoke. "You got another plan if this one don't work?"

"No," Smoke admitted. "But I'm thinking this will work because it's so simple and it's something that Jud won't even suspect any of us trying. For a handful of us to kidnap the man right in front of all his men, at his very own engagement party is something that has to be unthinkable to him. At least that's what I'm hoping."

"I have to tell you, Smoke," Walt said. "Matthew says he's going to be a part of the action come the night of the party, whether we want him to be, or not."

Smoke took that news without even so much as a blink. "It doesn't surprise me, Walt. The boy has shed his youth and left it behind him. We've both seen it happen out here many times. It's a hard time in a hard land that's filled up with hard men. I was only about a year older than Matthew when I teamed up with Preacher. About two years older than him when I killed my first man, with a pistol that Jesse James gave me back on that hard-scrabble farm in Missouri. Matthew will make it, and I'd not be a bit leery of him standing alongside me in any gunfight."

"I wanted you to know," the rancher closed the subject.

Smoke nodded his head. "Stash fully loaded rifles and pistols in the buggy, Walt. Cover them with a blanket. We're not going to have time for reloading once the fight gets to the creek."

"We have enough weapons, for sure," Walt said with a grin, his eyes twinkling. Then he sobered. "I'm going to lay the rules down to the boys. They are to remain on this ranch come the night of the party. Anyone who disobeys that order loses his job."

"Good. I think they'll stay put." Smoke met the eyes of the men. "We're only going to have one chance at pulling this off, people. So let's do it right the first time. That's it."

21

"My, my, what a grand place," Rusty remarked, as the huge mansion of Jud Vale came into view. "Looks like a palace for sure."

Smoke's Colts were hanging from his saddle horn, as were Rusty's guns. Both men felt naked without the weight of the pistols. The buggy was loaded with rifles and pistols, the arms covered with a blanket.

"Well, we're certainly not the first to arrive," Alice pointed out. "Even though it is early."

Susie had stayed at the Box T to look after Mickey and the boys.

Smoke looked at Walt and saw that the old rancher's eyes were sad.

"My brother had it all," Walt said. "But he couldn't stay away from crime. And now he's as crazy as a loon, surrounded by men on his own payroll who plot to kill him. It's tragic."

Smoke disagreed with that summation, but then, it wasn't his brother in question. He kneed Dagger forward, moving toward the mansion.

They were conscious of many eyes on them as they entered the ranch grounds. Hostile, murderous eyes—everyone thinking about that ten thousand dollars on the head of Smoke, and wishing that Jud hadn't lifted it for this event.

Smoke swung down from the saddle and looped the reins around a hitch rail, with Rusty doing the same, and looked up at the sky. He read the sun at about half-past five. The invitation had read from six to ten. Smoke figured to start his own party at seven.

"Mr. Vale said that all hosses was to be put in the corral," a surly puncher told Smoke.

Smoke turned and grinned at the man. "His name is Dagger. He killed the last man who tried to do anything with him. But you're welcome to try."

The Bar V hand eyeballed the walleyed stallion. Dagger showed the man his big teeth and the puncher made up his mind.

"Hell with that hoss." He looked at Rusty. "What about yourn?"

"They're brothers," Rusty told him.

"Hell with him, too!" The puncher walked off.

Walt and Alice were already climbing up the steps to the porch. Shorty DePaul was there, standing by the door, collecting invitations, looking very uncomfortable in his stiff new black suit.

Smoke grinned at him. "You do look awfully cute, Shorty."

Shorty told Smoke where to go, how to get there, and what to do with his comment along the way.

"Feller's plumb testy, ain't he?" Rusty said.

Shorty had a few words for Rusty, too.

Smoke and Rusty followed Walt and Alice inside the mansion.

It was a grand place, Smoke noted, no doubt at all about that. Imported chandeliers and French furniture and all sorts of knickknacks and assorted gewgaws scattered all over the place.

"What's all this stuff good for anyways?" Rusty questioned.

"For people to look at and admire," Smoke told him.

"Looks junky and sissy to me."

Smoke grinned at him. "Your mind will change after you're married." Rusty blushed at the thought.

The punk gunfighter who called himself the Pecos Kid walked up, carrying a tray of little crackers and a bowl of dark-looking stuff. "Gentlemen," he said, speaking the word as if it hurt his mouth. "Some whore-derves?"

"What the hell is a whore-derve!" Rusty said, leaning over to take a sniff.

"That is Russian caviar," Smoke told him. "Louis Longmont used to keep some on hand at all times. Try it, it's good."

"How do you eat it?"

"Take a cracker and use that little spoon to dab some caviar on the cracker."

Rusty spooned a glob on a cracker. "Well, ain't I the fancy one, though? My, my." Rusty took a nibble and grimaced. "You got any ket-chup, Pecos?"

Smoke thought Rusty and Pecos were going to tie up right then and there, and if they had, Rusty would have shoved that whole bowl of caviar up the nose of the Pecos Kid. He pulled Rusty away and told him to behave himself; they had a more important mission that came first.

One of the ranchers who had been in the trading post when Matthew shot it out with Smith walked up to him. His face was ashen.

"What's the matter with you?" Smoke asked.

"Have you seen Jud?"

"No."

"He's walking around with a crown on his head and all dressed in a fur robe. He's carryin' a stick that looks like a good-sized saplin'. The man is insane!"

"That's what some folks have been trying to tell you people for months. Don't you people even care that he took Doreen by force and is holding her here against

199

her will?''

"I heard that but I didn't believe it." He sighed. "All right, gunfighter. I believed it. But what could I have done?''

"Join in the fight against Jud?"

But the man shook his head. "No. He has too many hired guns on the payroll. He'd roll over us like stepping on a bug."

There was contempt in his eyes and scorn in his voice when Smoke replied. "Do you look under the bed at night for ghosts and goblins before you blow out the lamp?"

The rancher flushed but wisely contained his sudden anger and kept his mouth closed.

Smoke turned his back to the man and then stopped short when he spotted Jud. Rusty was standing with his mouth open, staring at the man as if he was sure his eyes were deceiving him.

Jud was quite a sight. He looked to Smoke like he'd just stepped out of a Russian opera. Jud cut his eyes to Smoke and hate filled them. He snarled at Smoke and walked away.

"You seen Doreen, Smoke?" Rusty said.

"No. I expect she'll be making her entrance just a tad after six. That's the way the fashionable ladies do it, so I been told."

"Why? Hell, she can tell time, cain't she? She ain't stupid."

"No. I mean, yes, she can tell time. No, she isn't stupid. Ladies do that so all the people will be present to look at them when they make their entrance."

"I shore don't know much about wimmen."

"Rusty, after you've been married for five or six years, you'll discover something."

"What?"

"That you don't know any more about women after all those years than you did when you got married."

"Well, ain't that just something to look forward to?"

Smoke laughed at him and moved on, walking through the lower part of the mansion. He spoke to several of the farmers that he knew. Ralph's father took his arm.

"I don't know what you got planned in the way of gettin' Miss Doreen out of this place, Smoke. But I'm with you all the way. Me, and about a half dozen other men."

Smoke started to tell him to stay out of it, then changed his mind. Somebody had to be the first ones to stand up to Jud and his army of hired guns. If the cattlemen in the area wouldn't, then maybe the farmers would shame them into joining them.

"All right, Chester. Here's what you do: when you see Walt and Alice leave, you and the others follow them. I'll tell Walt that you boys are with us."

Chester smiled. "I put rifles in the wagon. The wife can shoot nearabouts as good as I can."

"Good man!" Smoke gripped his arm and walked on. They stood a chance if he could just get Doreen out.

Smoke declined a glass of champagne being offered by the German gunfighter, Jaeger, who was minus the top part of an ear, thanks to Smoke. The German glared pure hate at Smoke.

"I ought to take off the other ear, Jaeger," Smoke told him. "So you'd have a matched set. But then you'd have a hell of a time wearing a hat, wouldn't you?"

Jaeger growled something at Smoke in German and moved on, toting his tray of drinks.

Smoke moved over to stand by Sheriff Brady's side. The sheriff gave him a curious look.

"Have you decided whether this is in your county, or not, Sheriff?"

"I don't know. I didn't come here to arrest anyone. I didn't bring any men with me. Why? Are you planning on starting something?"

"Me?" Smoke managed a shocked look. "Heavens no, Sheriff. I'm just here to have a good time."

"Right," the lawman's reply was drily given. "Sure,

you are."

"Have you seen Jud, Sheriff?"

A pained look passed over the sheriff's face. "Yes, unfortunately. But there is no law against a man wearing a fur robe and a jeweled crown."

"Oh, I never said there was, Sheriff. But it might make a person question Jud's sanity—right?"

"Like I said, Jensen: I'm not here in any official capacity."

"Enjoy yourself, Sheriff." Smoke moved on, snaking his way through the growing crowd. Somewhere in the house, a clock chimed six o'clock.

He caught the eyes of several farmers; they gave him a slight nod and a wink. Chester had done his part; the men were with him. Smoke returned the nods and found a place next to a wall. Rusty soon joined him and with their backs to the wall, they waited.

At ten after the hour, the bugler started tooting, the guitar player started strumming, and the fiddler started sawing.

"Sounds like a cat fight to me," Rusty said.

Then Doreen made her entrance, and the crowd oohhed and aahhed. She was dressed to the nines, all done up in silks and satins. She was playing her part to the hilt, acting like a queen as she moved through the crowd, smiling and offering her hand to the folks.

Jud stood to one side, a big grin on his big face. He looked like a damned idiot.

Walt and Alice offered their congratulations to Doreen and then Walt glanced at Smoke. Smoke nodded his head. The old rancher and his wife slipped unnoticed out the front door and climbed into their buggy, heading back toward Box T range.

In pairs, the farmers and their wives began slipping out of the mansion. At a quarter to the hour, all those who were on Smoke's side had left. Smoke found Rusty.

"Start staying close to the Pecos Kid, Rusty. When I

202

make my move, you grab his guns and watch my back."

The cowboy nodded and moved off into the milling crowds.

The band was doing their best to play a tune that Smoke could but vaguely recognize. Sounded to him like they were all in different keys.

Smoke moved over to a table near the hallway where the grandfather clock was located and took a glass of champagne just as the chimes donged out seven o'clock. He finished the glass then walked up to Jud and Doreen, jerked both Jud's guns out of leather and placed the muzzle of one in the man's ear. Jud's bodyguards froze, not knowing what to do.

The band stopped playing; the milling crowds were still as the word spread throughout the ground floor of the mansion.

Rusty had clobbered the Pecos Kid with a silver platter of fried chicken and grabbed his guns. The Kid lay on the floor, his head on a pile of chicken.

Smoke said, "Tell your men to start tossing their guns out the windows, Jud. If just one of them tries anything, I'll kill you where you stand."

"See that they do it, Jason," Jud managed the words out of his fricasseed brain and past his anger.

Six guns began sailing out the open windows.

"Get horses out front for Doreen and King Vale," Smoke ordered.

Jason nodded at one of the bodyguards.

"Make your speech, Doreen," Smoke told her.

Doreen spun around to face the crowd. "Jud Vale kidnapped me and brought me here against my will. I've been a prisoner in this house." She looked straight at Sheriff Brady. "Do you hear me, Sheriff?"

"I hear you, girl."

"I hate this man," Doreen said, pointing to Jud. "I would sooner marry a grizzly bear. I planned this whole party so's Smoke and the man I really love, Rusty, would come and rescue me."

Rusty was grinning and blushing. He looked like a lit railroad lantern.

"I'm ashamed of you people!" Doreen yelled at the crowd of men and women. "Not a one of you would help Walt and Alice or Smoke and Rusty stand up to this nitwit!" She glared at Jud, standing with his crown tilted to one side of his big head. "To hell with you all!" Doreen shouted.

"Let's go!" Smoke said, shoving Jud toward the door.

Outside, Doreen hiked up her expensive gown and showed Rusty bare legs as she stepped into the stirrup and mounted up. The cowboy did his best to look away, but the sight was just too tempting. One eye was going one way and the other was on a shapely leg.

"Settle down, Rusty," Doreen whispered. "Your time is coming. I promise."

"Have mercy!" Rusty said.

Smoke prodded Jud into the saddle. Jud hiked up his robe and showed some leg, too; but it was definitely not a scintillating experience for anyone. Especially the horse, who swung his head and tried to figure out what it was on his back.

Smoke stepped into the saddle. "Jud dies if anyone follows," he warned the crowd. "Tell them, King Vale," Smoke said sarcastically.

Some lucidity had returned to Jud. Having the muzzle of a .44 laid against one's ear can do that. He twisted in the saddle. "Stay back. Our time will come. Just stay back."

"Let's go, King," Smoke said. "Your royal procession is about to parade."

The Pecos Kid woke up with a chicken leg stuck in one ear, wondering why the band had stopped playing.

204

22

"You'll die hard for this," Jud warned them all, as they clip-clopped along, Jud's crown bouncing from one side of his head to the other. "Especially you, Doreen. I'll turn you over to my men and let them have their way with you. And that's a promise."

Doreen turned in the saddle, balled her right hand into a fist, and busted Jud square on the nose. His crown flew off his head as the blood began to trickle, leaking down into his beard.

"You can pick your crown up on the way back," Smoke told him.

Jud cursed them all.

Smoke turned at the sounds of a single horse coming up fast behind them. It was the young reporter from the paper at Montpelier.

"I'm on my way to get this story written," he shouted at them. "I'll see that this is printed all over the state."

He galloped on past and then cut north, toward the town.

"He's dead, too," Jud growled.

"Give it up, Jud," Smoke advised the man. "Send your gun hands packing, break up your outlaw gangs, and settle down."

Jud mouthed a few choice words at Smoke, none of them the least bit complimentary.

Smoke rode on for another mile and then twisted in the saddle and knocked Jud sprawling, on his butt, in the road. Smoke grabbed the reins of the riderless horse and shouted, "Let's go, people!"

Jud sat in the dirt and squalled at them, shaking his fists and cussing.

"They'll be coming after us now!" Doreen yelled over the pounding of hooves.

"We'll make the crick," Rusty told her.

Jud jumped to his feet and began loping up the road, back to his ranch. He reached the spot where his crown lay in the dust, the jewels twinkling under the starry light. Jud plopped his crown back on his head and stomped on, his anger and hate growing with each dusty step. A mile farther on, he met a large force of his men, hanging back a couple of miles.

"They're heading for the creek!" Jud shouted, pointing. "Get them. Kill them! Kill them all."

Jason rode up, leading a horse. "I figured they'd set you afoot, Boss." He handed Jud a brace of six guns.

Jud swung into the saddle. "Somebody give me a piece of rawhide," he ordered.

A piece of thin rawhide was found and handed him.

Jud made a chinstrap for his crown, tying it tightly under his square jaw. He rode to the head of the group and paused, looking back. At least sixty riders. He lifted his hand into the air. "Forward!" he shouted. "Slay the infidels!"

"What the hell's an in-fidel?" Gimpy asked.

"Beats me," Jake Hube told him. "Must be something like a Injun, maybe."

The riders surged forward, with King Vale in the lead waving a six gun and shouting curses.

But many of the smarter gunfighters had either stayed

back at the ranch or were bringing up the rear of the force. They were too wise in the ways of Smoke Jensen to think Smoke would not have a backup plan in Doreen's escape. Probably he had set up an ambush.

John Wills, who had been wrapped up in poison ivy by Smoke, and his buddies, Dave and Shorty and Lefty, trailed a good mile behind the main force. Jaeger and Chato Di Peso and Hammer, along with Blackjack and Highpockets and DePaul and about a dozen others had not even left the ranch area. They sat on the long front porch of the mansion, eating fried chicken dunked in caviar and drinking champagne. All of them had a very strong hunch that many of those chasing after Smoke this starry night would not come back at all. The rest would come straggling back in, all shot to hell and gone.

But that would be all right with them. They were professionals in this business, and hardened to the ways of their chosen profession. This night would probably see the end of many of the punks and two-bit gunslingers who had hired on, looking for a cheap and fast buck and a few quick thrills to take back home and boast about. What they would get is a shallow grave. If they were lucky.

The crowds had quickly departed after Smoke had made his move. All but the bugler; he was now drunk as a cooter and blowing cavalry calls into the night. Some of the gunslingers had dumped him, bugle and all, into a horse trough. But that had only slowed him down for a few moments. He had shaken the water out of his bugle and kept right on tooting.

Jaeger spread some caviar on a cracker and nibbled. "Only ting de damn Russians ever did dat vas any gut was make caviar," he growled.

"What's this stuff made of anyways?" Pike asked.

"Vish eggs."

"What the hell's a vish?" Highpockets paused in the lifting of a caviar-spread cracker to his mouth.

"A vish is a vish. Swim in wassar."

About half of the men threw the caviar to the porch floor and stayed with the fried chicken.

"Here they come," Jackson announced.

Smoke, Rusty, and Doreen had just made the creek in time to dismount and take positions. Alice and Doreen had told Walt and the others they were staying and to shut up about it. They had taken rifles and squatted down behind logs with the other farmer women.

Matthew stood by a cottonwood, Cheyenne's long-barreled Colt in his right hand. The boy was calm as death, and his hand was steady.

Smoke earred back the hammer on his Winchester; he heard the sounds of others doing the same. As the charging riders came into range, Smoke lifted his rifle and took aim at Jud's crown. He squeezed off a round and drilled the arch of the crown, blowing off the arms and the dangling pearls.

"Huugghh!" Jud croaked, as the chin strap momentarily tighted, cutting off air due to the force of the impacting slug.

Those on the Box T side of the creek began filling the night air with hot lead. The first volley cleared half a dozen saddles and wounded that many more.

Spooked horses began bucking and jumping, sending another half-dozen riders to the hard ground. One gunslinger, afoot, his hands filled with Colts, tried to ford the creek. Young Matt took careful aim and squeezed the trigger, dead-centering the man, putting the slug right between his eyes. The gunny pitched face-forward into the creek.

Rusty shot the punk Glen Regan just as the kid was turning. The rifle slug went right through both cheeks of Glen's buttocks. Glen dropped squalling and crying to the creek bank, losing his guns, both hands holding onto his injured backside.

"Fall back, men!" Jud yelled. "Regroup but don't lose courage. They are but riffraff and swine who face us. You have the power of royalty on your side."

Jackson put another dent in Jud's crown, knocking it down to one side of the man's head, giving the man a thunderous headache. Jud's horse spooked and tossed him into a thorn bush and royalty's bare legs and backside took the full brunt of long thorns.

"Yowee!" Jud hollered, jumping to his feet. Holding his ermine robe waist high, he beat a hasty retreat up the bank and jumped over the crest.

"Let's get gone from here!" Cisco Webster shouted, just as Walt put a slug into the man's saddlehorn, tearing the horn from the saddle and knocking it spinning. Cisco's horse panicked and went snorting and racing into the night. Unfortunately for Cisco, the horse stampeded the wrong way, taking him right across the creek. "Whoa, goddammit!" Cisco yelled.

Rusty reversed his Winchester and knocked Cisco slap out of the saddle, the butt of the rifle catching the man on the jaw. Cisco was unconscious before he hit the ground, landing amid what was left of his broken teeth.

The fight was gone from Jud and his men. Jud screamed in pain as he was lifted into a saddle. He was still yelling and cussing and waving his arms as what was left of his army rode back toward the mansion.

The night fell quiet, broken only by the moaning of the wounded.

"What do we do with them?" Alice asked, listening to the pleadings for help.

"Leave them!" Chester's wife said, bitterness making her voice hard. "Would they help us if the situation was the other way around?"

Smoke booted his Winchester and swung into the

saddle. He turned his horse's head toward the Box T ranch house and his back to the wounded bounty hunters.

That ended any further discussion as to the fate of those who chose to take fighting wages from Jud Vale.

Smoke stepped out of his room the next morning and stood in the pre-dawn quiet, drinking his first cup of coffee. He had an odd feeling, a premonition, that matters would be coming to a head very soon. Why that jumped into his mind, he didn't know—only that he felt it to be true.

Jackson walked out of the bunkhouse, a mug of coffee in his hand. He joined Smoke on the bench by the side of the barn and built him a cigarette, passing the makings to Smoke.

"I got a funny feelin'," Jackson said. "Come on me sudden-like; woke me up."

"That Jud Vale is going to bring this war to a head real soon?"

"Huh? You been readin' my mind. Yeah. Reckon why we both come up with that?"

"We've made a fool out of him too many times, Jackson. Last night was probably that much-talked about straw that broke the camel's back. Now he knows that peole are laughing at him. With his ego, he won't be able to tolerate that. He'll have to do something to reinstill the fear that people once had for him."

"By killing us." Jackson's words were offered in a flat tone.

"That's it. Or part of it, at least."

"He ain't gonna get it done."

"I believe that. I just don't want to see the women or the kids get hurt."

They drank coffee and smoked their cigarettes in silence for a time. "What are you gonna do when this mess is over?" Jackson asked.

"Head south. My wife and kids are down in Arizona. The youngest took a lung infection. Had to go there for health reasons. You?"

Jackson took a moment before replying. "Walt's asked me to stay on. Says he'll give me a working interest in the ranch if I do. And . . . well, me and Susie been eyeballin' each other. I might do it. I backed into gunfightin' like a lot of other men. Never set out to hunt me no reputation. It just come on me. One day I looked up—I'd been punchin' cows for a man over in Nevada Territory—and these two men 'bout my age come into the saloon where I was havin' a beer and braced me. Said they was gonna kill me. I asked them why? They said 'cause of who I was. Surprised the hell out of me that I was anyone special. They grabbed for iron and I was faster. The boss said he didn't want no gun slicks on his payroll and paid me off the next day. I drifted. Hooked up with some men headin' for Utah to draw fightin' wages. I reckon the rest is history."

Rusty had walked up to stand quietly and listen. When Jackson fell silent, Rusty said, "You ought to stay, Jackson. Me and Doreen is gonna get hitched up soon as the trouble is over. The ranch is damn sure big enough for the both of us."

"I been thinkin' on it for sure."

"Light's on in the kitchen," Smoke said. "Breakfast pretty soon."

"Dolittle's up. He'll wake the boys," Rusty told him. "What's up for today?"

"Going over every inch of this ranch compound and making sure we can stand off a heavy attack. It's got to come. Jackson, I want you to take some of the boys and start clearing off all the brush from the hills and ridges around this place. Make damn sure we can't be burnt out. That'll also cut down on the risk of any riflemen slipping in on us."

211

"Good move," Jackson agreed.

"I'm hungry," Rusty said, one eye on the light coming from the kitchen window.

"I've never seen you when you weren't," Smoke said with a smile. "When you and Doreen get married, you best plant a big garden."

"You do know how to use a hoe, don't you?" Jackson kidded him.

"I 'spect, the way you and Susie is calf-eyin' each other, you'll be hoein' right along 'side me," Rusty fired back.

Jackson laughed. "Yeah, if it all works out. Be a welcome relief from gunfightin'."

"Don't ever pack those guns too far out of sight, Jackson," Smoke warned him. "It doesn't work. I know. I changed my name and tried it for a time. You'll always have to keep a sharp eye on your backtrail."

"I know," Jackson's words came after a sigh. "But I do wish that some of us could get that message through to young Matt."

"Could anybody tell you anything when you were his age?"

Jackson smiled ruefully. "Nope. I heard all the words, but they never sunk in."

"Matt will have to find his own way," Smoke said, standing up from the bench. "Just like we did. But I think Old Cheyenne—in the time he had to spend with him— taught Matt a thing or two."

"Walt is talkin' about hirin' the boy on as a full-time puncher," Rusty said. "Matt says he's through with schoolin'."

"That's a good idea. I imagine Matt will stay for a year or two. Then he'll get ants in his pants and drift. All we can do is wish him well."

Rusty looked toward the ranch house and the lighted kitchen window. "Damn, I'm hungry!"

23

Jud Vale lay on his belly in bed, while a doctor from Montpelier probed and dug and pulled out thorns, some of them more than three inches long. Jud hollered and squalled and carried on all through the procedure.

But the pain seemed to have done one thing: it had cleared Jud's mind, at least for the moment. His ermine robe and crown had been tossed to the floor. He was still as nutty as a pecan pie but some lucidity had crept through the madness.

Through the open window of his bedroom, Jud could see men digging graves to bury the recent dead. He cursed Smoke Jensen, his brother, his bastard son, and everyone else he could think of.

Especially Doreen. He cussed Doreen for playing him for a fool until he was breathless. Long after the doctor had left, doing his best to hide a grin, Jud was still cussing.

Jason came to his room and waited until his boss and long-time partner in murder, rape, and robbery had calmed down some. "What do you want me to do with them royal duds and that bent crown?"

"Put them in the closet. I might decide to wear them again."

"Jesus, I hope not!"

"I lost it for a while, didn't I, Jas?"

"You were off your trolley for a fact. I thought I was going to have to shoot you there for a time. You was becomin' unbearable."

"Was I that bad?"

"You turned into a plumb idiot."

"It's so hazy. I don't remember much of it."

"Be thankful for that." Jason pulled out a chair and sat down. "You think you're all right now?"

"Yes. For a time. But I don't know when I might go off again. Or for how long. It's frightening, Jas. It really scares me."

"You want me to bring one of them newfangled head doctors in to take a look at you? I could have it done on the sly."

Jud thought about that. It was tempting. Finally he shook his head. "No. Let's see if I can't lick this thing on my own. Did Luddy and his boys come in?"

"Early this mornin'. Phil and Perry and Rim is on the way. Be about thirty more men."

"How many did we lose last night?"

"Six dead. A dozen wounded. A couple of them ain't gonna make it." Jason was beginning to feel better; Jud was starting to talk like he had good sense.

"How many quit us?"

"That's surprisin'. Nobody. Yet."

"I figure it's gonna be a week before I can sit a saddle. Then we're going to wipe out the Box T. We're going to kill everyone there, bury the bodies deep, and burn all the buildings. Scatter the ashes with rakes; carry off the stones. Level the well and fill it up with rocks, cover that with dirt. Plant some trees and bushes. Not a sign is to remain that anyone ever lived there. I am Walt's only living relative. And I can prove that in a court of law. Everything will go to me. The land, cattle, money, and all that gold that's over there."

214

"Sounds good to me." He grinned at Jud. "Good to have you back, Boss."

"It's good to be back, Jas." He moved and grimaced, his southern exposure throbbing with pain. "Pass me that bottle of laudanum."

The hills and ridges around the ranch complex of the Box T were cleared of brush for a half mile in any direction. In heavily timbered areas, the timber was thinned and cut up for firewood. Wagons were put into use to haul dirt from far out in Box T range, the dirt used to fill up any depressions in the earth for five hundred yards from the complex. It kept the boys busy and Smoke and the others close to the ranch.

But when the week was drawing to near a close, Smoke was told by Walt they had to make another supply run to the post for food.

"Let's do it," Smoke told him. "We have time to do it now and get back before dark. I'll tell Jackson to stay here at the ranch. We'll take Rusty. If we run into any of Jud's men, they might try to prod Jackson into a fight for changing sides."

"And you don't think they'll prod you, Smoke?"

"They'll die if they do," he replied simply.

"Any trouble?" Smoke asked Bendel.

The owner of the trading post shook his head. "I ain't seen hide nor hair of any Bar V hand all week and I have been expectin' them. I got the word that they was gonna come in and bust up my place." He smiled. "But I understand King Jud Vale is havin' to sleep on his stomach of late."

"Oh?"

"Yeah. Seems like his horse throwed him and he landed

in a thorn bush. He was wearin' that silly-lookin' robe. Doc Evans from over Montpelier way spread the tale, to use his words."

Smoke and Rusty and Walt—the rancher was having a rare drink of whiskey while the shopkeeper filled the order—all had a good laugh, at Jud's expense.

Walt wiped his eyes with a bandana and smiled. "I guess any feeling I might have been carrying around for Jud has finally left me. God might punish me for the way I feel, but I can't feel anything except contempt for the man now."

"He doesn't deserve anything else, Mr. Burden," Bendel told him. "He's made life miserable for everyone around here for years."

Rusty had taken his beer to the batwings. "Riders pullin' up outside," he announced. "'Bout a half dozen of them. I don't know none of these old boys. Don't look like I'd really care to get to know them all that good, neither. Damn, but they is *ugly!*"

Smoke walked to the batwings. "The Almond Brothers. Killers. Call themselves bounty hunters. Barry, that's the oldest, he's got a few brains. The rest of them are close to being morons." Smoke finished his beer and set the mug on the plank. "I'm going outside. No point in having your place shot up."

Rusty stepped back into the store, exited that way, and pulled a rifle from his saddle boot, jacking in a round. At the sound of the cartridge being shucked into the chamber, Barry Almond looked over the saddle at him.

"You huntin' trouble, cowboy?" the bounty hunter asked.

"Naw," Rusty told him. "I just seen me five big rats. I like to shoot rats."

"Rats? Where'd you see five rats?"

"I'm lookin' at one of them," Rusty told him, just as Smoke pushed open the batwings and stepped out on the porch. Walt was right behind him, holding Bendel's double-barreled express gun.

Barry smiled, a slight cruel movement of his lips. His eyes did not leave Smoke. "I seen you work once, Jensen. You're fast, all right. I'll give you that much. So I reckon some of us, including me, will probably take some lead. But they's five of us ag'in you, that ugly redhead, and one stove-up old man."

"Ugly!" Rusty blurted. "Me! Why, you so ugly you ought to wear a sack over your head! And I ain't real sure them brothers of yours is even human. I've seen bears that was better lookin' than them."

"I'm a-gonna kill that freckle-faced puncher, Barry," an Almond brother said.

"You can sure have him, Race," Barry said. "But Jensen is all mine."

Smoke had stepped off the porch to stand in the street. He didn't want Dagger to catch a bullet. And there was something else: the stallion was alert to trouble, and he had sensed the situation building. If Cal Almond, who was standing next to the big horse, put a hand on him, Dagger was going to kick him into the next county.

Cal shoved roughly at Dagger. "Git the hale outta the way, horse!" he said, stepping around to Dagger's rear.

Dagger let him have it. Both rear hooves lashed out, one steel-shod hoof catching the killer in the groin, the other in the belly. Cal went sailing out into the middle of the street, screaming in agony.

"One down," Walt said.

Leo drew on the old man. But Leo never really knew the mettle of the men who came to the West when it was really raw. And he had failed to notice that Walt had earred back both hammers of the 12 gauge.

Walt shot the bounty hunter in the belly. Really, he shot him all over the place as rusty nails and ballbearings and other assorted bits of hand-loaded metal tore his body apart.

Rusty stepped out and leveled the Winchester just as Max turned, drawing. Max caught a slug in the belly that bent him double and spun him around. Max pulled the trigger and shot himself in the knee. He tumbled to the street, screaming rage and hate and pain.

Smoke palmed both Colts and began putting lead into Barry and Race. The .44 slugs dotted the trail-dusty dusters, pocking them with blood as the slugs tore into flesh.

Race went down first, sinking to his knees in the dirt, dropping his guns as life left him.

Smoke felt a bullet tear his cheek and another slug rip a narrow gouge on the outside of his left thigh. Smoke and Barry Almond faced each other, guns belching fire and death. Smoke had known that Barry was going to be hard to put down, and the bounty hunter was livng up to his reputation.

As the fourth slug from Smoke's .44's hit Barry, the man went down to one knee, cursing as he slumped to the dusty and rutted road. Using all his strength, he lifted his left hand .44.

Smoke shot him between the eyes just as Cal managed to work his way past his terrible pain to lift his guns. Smoke turned and fired twice just as Rusty's Winchester barked and Walt's express gun roared. The last of the Almond Brothers died on his belly in the dirt, torn to bloody bits by the three guns.

The silence was shatteringly loud for a moment. Then Smoke broke the stillness as he ejected empty brass and began reloading. The spent brass tinkled as it struck small rocks in the road. Loaded up, Smoke holstered his Colts and turned to face Walt, still standing on the porch of the trading post.

"Thanks, Walt."

"Felt good," the old rancher said. "In more ways than one. I knew that night back at the crick I'd misplaced my backbone for too long."

Max groaned and cursed as he lay in the dirt, his blood staining the earth under him.

Rusty walked over to the killer and kicked his guns out of the dying man's reach. "He ain't got long," the puncher said, glancing at Smoke.

Max looked up at him and cussed the redhead.

"If I was a-goin' where you're goin', partner," Rusty told him, "I believe I'd try to clean up my mouth some."

The last words to pass the bounty hunter's lips were curses.

"You boys put them down," Bendel said, coming out of his saloon with several shovels. "You can damn well help me plant them."

They looked up at the sounds of hooves clip-clopping up the road. Several gun hands from the Bar V were riding out, bedrolls tied behind the saddle and their saddlebags bulging full.

"We ain't huntin' no trouble," one told Smoke, eyeballing the carnage sprawled in the dirt. "We're pullin' out."

Smoke knew the man and knew he was no coward. Something had happened at the Bar V. "What's the problem, Jake?"

"The mainest thing is you, Smoke. This here poker game has done got too rich for my blood. I'll hire my guns out to whoever pays the price, and you know that. But I ain't no thief. I ain't never stole nothin' in my life." That curious moral streak that so many men who lived by the gun surfaced in Jake. "That damn Luddy Morgan and his bunch of no-goods come in. Rim Reynolds and Perry Simmons and that crazy Phil What's-His-Name is due in anytime. I ain't havin' no truck with that trash."

"If we're lucky, Jake, we'll never see each other again," Smoke told him.

"You're gonna have to ride clear over to Oregon if you want to see me, Smoke. And since I ain't on Vale's payroll no more, I can tell you this much without be-trayin' no confidence: Jud's gonna attack the Box T—I don't know when or I'd tell you. He's gonna burn the place to the ground, kill ever'body there, and then bury the bodies deep . . ."

Walt's lips tightened at that.

"He's gonna remove all sign that there was ever a building on the place," Jake continued, "and he ain't prancin' around wearin' that stupid robe and crown no more, neither. He's come to his senses . . . for a while, at least. But the fool is liable to go off agin any time. He's worser than any cow who ever et loco weed when he drops off the deep end."

A hired gun pulling out with Jake spat a stream of tobacco juice into the dirt and said, "Them ol' boys that's comin' in is all bad, Smoke. And the ones that's stayin' is just as bad. Jud's gonna take this here fight right down to the killin' end." He noted the thin trickle of blood oozing down Smoke's cheek. "You lucked out agin, Smoke. An inch over and somebody would be plantin' petunias on your grave."

Smoke nodded in agreement. His leg hurt but he knew it was not a serious wound. He'd had enough lead dug out of him to fill a good-sized gunnysack. "How many men does Jud have?"

"I'd say nearabouts a hundred," Jake told him. "Maybe more. He's promisin' them the moon and the stars and wimmin and apple pie and ever'thang else 'ceptin' his drawers iffen they'll stay with him and see this thing through. I reckon most of them will do that. Me and the boys here just couldn't see to do that. I never did like the idea of fightin' wimmin and kids." He looked at Rusty. "You got yourself a good woman with that Do-reen. She'll stand by a man when the goin' gets rough. Wish I could find one like that. See you boys." He lifted the reins and Jake and his buddies rode on.

"Well," Rusty said. "Let's plant these ol' boys and get back to the ranch. Looks like we're in for some excitement. Lord knows," he added drily, "we been so bored of late."

24

Walt had doubled the supplies and borrowed pack horses to bring the additional staples to the ranch. There, Smoke made a slow walking inspection of the area surrounding the complex. There could be nothing else done to make the place any more secure.

After supper, he called a meeting in the lantern-lit barn.

"Here's the way it's going to be, people. No one leaves this area. No one. Not for any reason. Jud is going to hit us, and he's going to hit us hard. When? Very soon, I'm thinking. He should be able to sit a saddle most anytime." He noticed the smiles at that and had to join them in the rough humor. But his smile faded quickly. "I thought that after the so-called party at the Bar V the other night, and what happened afterward, that Sheriff Brady would do something—anything! But that doesn't appear to be the case. I don't know whether Jud has bought him off, or what. Maybe the sheriff just doesn't want to get involved. Whatever the reason, it looks like we're in this thing all by ourselves. We can handle it. But it's going to get rough and dirty. Any of Jud's hired guns with an ounce of mercy in them have pulled out. What's left is the crud. That's what's going to be hitting us. Be ready for it. That's it."

Smoke looked at the young kids, kids that were growing

up fast. Too fast, probably, for he saw no fear in their eyes. Did they really know the danger that faced them, or was this just kid excitement? Probably a combination of both, he thought.

"I'll stand the first watch," Walt said. "Then Smoke and Rusty and Jackson can divide up the rest. We're going to have to do this every night. Three-hour pulls for each of us until it's over."

"Anybody seen or heard anything from Clint?" Alice asked.

No one had.

"The last time I spoke with him," Smoke said, "he said he was having one of his spells—one of his moods is what he called it. He wouldn't come close to me."

"That's probably good for you," Doreen said. "He gets murderous when those things take hold of him. He thinks everybody is his enemy."

There was nothing else to say, so Walt broke up the meeting by telling everyone to go to bed. He got his rifle and took up a position by the corral, taking the first watch.

Smoke slept a few hours and then went out to relieve the rancher. It was one of those Idaho nights that inspire poets to write the loftiest and most eloquent of verses. The heavens were filled with stars that clung so close to earth one could almost feel they were touchable.

"Quiet," Walt said, standing up and stretching. "Everything is at peace with the other, I reckon. Well, almost. Even the birds stopped calling a few minutes ago."

Smoke tensed. "No birds are calling?"

Walt was silent for only a few seconds, then he cursed himself for being an old fool! "Dammit! What's the matter with me? I'll alert the others." The old rancher took off in a bowlegged lope.

Smoke ran toward the bunkhouse, catching up with Walt and telling him to get to the house and get Little Micky into the root cellar; he'd alert the others.

Smoke knew better than to bust into the bunkhouse with everyone on the alert. That would be a good way to catch a bullet. He paused at a window.

"They're here, boys!" he called softly. "Get to your positions and keep the lights out doing it."

He rousted Jackson and Rusty and they ran to preset positions around the compound. None of them saw the youngest of the kids leave the bunkhouse and race across the area, stopping by the side of the barn for a moment, and then slip into the darkness of the huge barn.

Chuckie and Clark and Jimmy and Buster grinned at each other. They'd had the very devil of a time getting just the rocks for their slingshots; but they'd finally found some with just the right texture and their weapons were strongly made, their pockets bulging with smooth little stones.

They knelt down in the darkness and waited. They could hear Smoke up in the loft on one end of the barn, talking to Jackson who was up in the loft on the other end.

The boys waited in silence, slingshots in their hands.

Smoke searched the darkness of his perimeter but could see nothing out of the ordinary. If Jud and his men were out there—and that was still iffy—they were on foot and staying very quiet.

Chuckie thought he heard something behind him, at the far end of the barn. He looked at the others. Their eyes were wide; they had heard it, too. Then the very faint sound came again, but this time it was closer.

Someone was in the barn with them, and it wasn't anyone from the Box T. The boys knew all the positions of those friendly.

Chuckie slipped a rock into the pocket of his slingshot and ever so slightly shifted positions. Then he saw the clearly outlined figure of a man. And the shape of the hat told him it was no one from the Box T. Chuckie lifted his slingshot, pulled the rubber taut, and took aim. He let the rock fly and his aim was true. The rock struck the man in the center of his forehead and knocked him off his boots. The man made one grunt of pain as the rock hit him and then lay still on the barn floor.

Smoke was down the loft ladder in seconds. He looked at the slingshot-armed boys and sighed. It was too late to send them back to the house. But he couldn't help but feel proud of them. They were a gutsy bunch.

Smoke moved to the fallen man. He didn't know him.

"What's goin' on down there?" Jackson whispered from the hayloft.

"One of Jud's men," Smoke returned the whisper. "The boys dropped him with a slingshot."

Jackson chuckled softly.

"That means they've infiltrated us. Look sharp, Jackson."

Smoke cut several lengths of binder twine and securely tied the hired gun. He stuck the man's guns behind his belt and took his rifle. He looked at the boys looking at him. "I ought to spank you," he whispered. "But I feel too proud of you to do that. Now, dammit, boys, stay down and out of sight! This is not a game."

"Yes, sir," Buster said, as Smoke headed for the ladder.

Smoke had just cleared the landing when Rusty's rifle barked from his position in the bunkhouse. A man cried out in pain as the bullet struck true. Smoke ran to the hay door as gunfire began pouring in from all sides of the ranch complex.

Below him, the boys readied their slingshots as they crouched down behind bales of hay.

Jackson sighted a running figure, fired, missed, and fired again. The second slug dusted the man and sent him sprawling to the ground, side-shot and out of it.

Then the compound was filled with running men as they left their positions on the near-barren hills and ridges around the ranch and charged. Smoke could hear, over the gunfire, the sounds of horses coming hard.

The first wave of running men were cut down by the savage fire from the house, the barn, and the bunkhouse. Their bodies lay sprawled under the starry sky. One man, only slightly wounded, tried to make the barn. He was knocked to his knees by slingshot-propelled rocks and then knocked unconscious as a rock fired by Buster hit him on the side of the head and dropped him to the ground.

The boys grinned at each other.

Doreen sighted in a man and pulled the trigger, the Winchester slamming her shoulder. The slug caught the hired gun in the chest and ended his career.

Susie turned one around with a rifle shot and Alice finished him with a pistol. The rancher's wife was calm and steady, this being nothing new to her. She'd fought Indians for years before this.

One of Jud's men reached the outside bunkhouse wall. Jamie shot him between the eyes as he carelessly poked his head up just a tad too far.

Then the hard-running horses came into view, the riders carrying burning torches. The first half-dozen to reach the compound were blown out of their saddles by rifle fire. The boys in the lower level of the barn then went to work, sending rocks which impacted with horses' butts.

One man was knocked out of the saddle as a rock struck him on the jaw. He fell on his torch and quickly became a living firebrand. He rose screaming to his feet, his clothing ignited, and tried to run. Walt ended his agony with a bullet to the head.

The horses went into a panic as the rocks pelted them, stinging and confusing and angering them. The horses began bucking and jumping, trying to escape the hurting stones. Riders were tossed to the ground and shot down by rifle and pistol fire.

One managed to reach the house and jumped in through a window. Doreen picked up a pot of coffee from the stove and tossed the contents on the man, the scalding coffee catching him flush in the face. He dropped his guns and began screaming in agony, running around the room, crashing into furniture in his frantic rush to get away from the awful pain.

Alice shot him in the head and permanently ended the wailing.

A bounty hunter ran into the barn as rocks from slingshots pelted him, stinging but not stopping his charge for cover.

Little Chuckie grabbed up a pitchfork, tines out, and braced himself against the impact. The gun hand ran right into the pitchfork, knocking Chuckie down as the tines tore into his belly. Screaming in pain, the gunny ran toward the other end of the barn. The handle of the pitchfork, sticking several feet out of his belly, hit a wall and stuck there. The gunny screamed his life away, unable to pull the handle from the crack in the stable wall or free himself of the tines.

Chuckie got sick.

A torch hit the roof of the bunkhouse and lodged there, soon catching the roof on fire.

Smoke lit the fuse on a stick of dynamite and tossed the bomb into the milling and panicked scene below him. The explosion knocked several horses to the ground, busting a couple of riders' legs and creating even more confusion in the fire-lanced night.

Smoke began tossing stick after stick of dynamite from loft to the ground, as his eyes spotted Rusty and the boys running from the bunkhouse to a storage shed. A Bar V rider turned his horse as he spotted the boys, lifting his pistol. Smoke shot him out of the saddle. His boot hung in the stirrup and the frightened horse took off at a gallop, dragging the screaming, flopping, and helpless man.

All the steam seemed to leave the Bar V men at once. Those still mounted wheeled and raced from the fire-lit ranch. Those on foot ran away into the darkness.

"Cease firing!" Smoke yelled. "Hold your positions!"

The crackling flames from the bunkhouse became the only sounds in the bloody night.

"I'm gonna let it burn itself out!" Walt yelled from the house.

"You all right, Jackson?" Smoke called.

"I'm okay. How about the boys down below?"

"We're all right," one called. "Chuckie got sick, is all."

Smoke climbed down the ladder. He stopped as his eyes saw the pitchfork-impaled gun hand, the man's hands still gripping the handle in death.

"I had to do it, Mr. Smoke," Chuckie said. "I didn't have no choice."

"You did fine, Chuckie," Smoke assured him. "You boys stay down behind those bales of hay."

Smoke found a sack and then eased his way out of the barn. Staying close to whatever cover he could find, he began working his way to the storage shed. On the way, he passed men who were moaning and twisting in pain. He took their guns from them and dropped them into the sack. Rusty saw what he was doing and stepped out to begin calming and corralling the milling Bar V horses. Jackson stayed where he was, keeping a sharp eye out for any return raiders.

But Jud's hired guns had apparently had enough for one night. No more hostile fire came.

Susie and Doreen rolled the dead man out of the living room and off the porch. A couple of the boys dragged the man out of the front yard.

"Rusty, at first light, I want you to ride for Montpelier and get that reporter and then find Sheriff Brady. Bring them both here. If Sheriff Brady won't come, send a wire to the governor's office and one to the Army up at Fort Hall. But I think Brady will come."

"Right. What do we do with the bodies?"

227

"Lay them over by the side of the barn and cover them with whatever you can find. Use their own bedrolls and ground sheets if they were carrying any. We'll put the wounded in the barn."

Walt walked up. "I count twenty dead and twelve wounded. Some of them ain't gonna make it."

"I guess you better bring Doctor . . . what's his name, Walt?"

"Evans. He's a good man. He'll come." Walt looked up at the sky. "I hope they come quick. It's gonna be a warm day and these bodies'll start to bloat in a hurry. Flies will be awful."

25

Sheriff Brady took one look at the lined-up bodies and paled under his tan. Doctor Evans and his assistant began working on the wounded.

"I'm filing charges against all these men," Walt told the sheriff. "And I'm filing charges against Jud Vale. They worked for him, they acted under his orders."

"Can you prove that in a court of law?" Brady challenged. "And I ain't tryin' to be a horse's butt about it, Walt. Just askin' what the judge will ask."

"I understand. We can prove it if some of these men will talk."

"Fat chance of that," Brady said. "But we'll give it a try. Walt, I'm going to call in the U.S. Marshals. It'll take them about two days to get in here by train. I just don't have the men to handle this by myself."

"Then why not deputize all the farmers and such around here?" the rancher suggested. "Form a posse. We'll go in and arrest Jud and his men."

"First I got to find a judge to sign them papers authorizing such a move. I think it's best if we let the marshals handle it. And I ain't tryin' to back out of my duty, neither."

"I understand. All right, Sheriff. We'll play it your way."

Brady looked around him at the carnage, the burned-out bunkhouse. "This has got to end. I just ain't gonna tolerate it no more. I'll be back with the marshals, Walt. And that's a promise." He looked at the doctor. "You need some help with these wounded, Doc?"

"A few of them can sit a saddle. Walt's lending us a wagon to transport the rest. Help me load them up and we'll be on our way."

The wounded bounty hunters and hired guns were loaded into a wagon, and not too gently either. With Sheriff Brady leading the way, the wagon rolled out, those sitting saddles doing so with their hands tied to the saddle horn. Smoke didn't hold out much hope of any of the hired guns talking.

And as for the U.S. Marshals coming in . . . Smoke didn't think they'd be coming in anytime soon, although he believed that Sheriff Brady would certainly try to get them in. The U.S. Marshals' force was a small one, with a lot to do. They would probably look at the sheriff's request as just another flare-up between ranchers over water or graze, and promptly forget it.

The reporter had indeed written his story about the kidnapping of Doreen and her rescue, but nothing had come of that report. This was still the raw West, with lawmen few and far between. Communities were still expected to handle their own problems without crying for outside help.

Smoke said as much to Walt and the others.

Jackson was the first to agree. "I've seen this happen time and again. In the end, it's all gonna boil down to men facin' men with guns. That's the way it's always been, and that's the way it's gonna be . . . for a while yet."

"I'll cling to a small hope that the marshals will come in," Walt said.

"Cling to a gun with your other hand," Smoke told him.

Chuckie and other smaller boys went down to the creek, looking for more small stones for their slingshots. None of them had ever seen a U.S. Marshal and didn't expect to see one anytime soon.

Jud Vale took his afternoon coffee on the front porch of his mansion. He was feeling much better—physically and mentally. But he had enough sense to know that his mind could flip him back into madness at any moment, without warning.

He sucked at his coffee cup, with some of the hot brew trickling out of his mouth and dribbling onto his shirt front. Jud didn't pay it any attention. He hadn't gone on the past night's raid against his brother; Blackjack and Molino had assured him they could handle it. They handled it, all right. Came straggling back in with half their men either dead or wounded and captured, talking about kids with slingshots—*slingshots*, for Christ sake—and dynamite and all kinds of other excuses for having failed.

Jud shook his big head. Slingshots!

He mentally laid aside his burning hate for his brother and forced himself to think rationally.

A frontal attack, a mass attack of the Box T had failed for the second time, so Jud had to discard any further thoughts along that line. He knew that at one time, and not that long ago, a couple of weeks back, maybe a month, he'd had several plans in mind. Now he couldn't think of a single one, and that scared him. Was he losing his marbles again?

He thought hard; sweat broke out on his forehead. Then it came to him. Burn the damn nesters out. Yeah, that had been one of them. There had been other plans, but the burning out of the nesters was the only one he could think of at the moment. Pretty good plan. Instead of striking at

231

the head of the beast, the head being his brother and Smoke Jensen, start chopping away at the arms and legs.

He called for Jason and told him of the plan. Jason thought that it might work.

"No one will be expecting any trouble this soon after the raid on the ranch. Send some boys out this afternoon. Start with that damn interferin' Chester and his old woman. He was one of them at the creek, wasn't he?"

"Sure was."

"Kill them and burn them out."

"We won't even have to send any of the top guns to do this," Jason pointed out. "I'll send them three punks that come in on the train with some of Perry's bunch."

"Sounds good. Do it."

The six hired guns were in good spirits as they rode out of the Bar V range, heading for Chester's farm. This was going to be good fun. And maybe the nester had a good-lookin' daughter . . . that would be even more fun. They'd hogtie the farmer and his old woman and make them watch while they had their way with the girl.

The punk kid who called himself Tucson Bob vocalized his plan.

The outlaw known as Cline grinned, exposing a mouthful of rotted teeth. "I like that idea, Tucson. You all right." Then he sobered. "But what if they ain't no young girl?"

"Then we'll hang the nester slow; make it last and watch him kick and choke."

"I'd druther have me a young girl who don't want to give it up, but the second idea is a right good one. How far did Jud say this pig farm was?"

"It's just up ahead. Do we ride through the garden first and tear it up?"

"Might as well. They'll get 'em so scared they won't know what to do."

The six hired guns hit the small farm at a gallop, whooping and hollering and firing into the house, riding right through the neat garden.

Chester's wife stuck a shotgun out of a window and blew the would-be gunfighter called Randy out of the saddle just as Chester came out of the barn with a Winchester and emptied another saddle, ending the life and career of the outlaw called Fox. The farmer's wife let loose with the other side of the double-barrel and the punk who should have stayed home and learned his father's dairy business back in Wisconsin hit the ground, landing hard amid the green beans and cabbage, half of his left arm torn off from the buckshot.

Cline leveled his pistol at Chester just as the farmer pulled the trigger. Cline felt a hard blow to his chest and slipped from the saddle, his world dimming just as neighbors galloped up, all armed.

"Don't shoot!" Tucson Bob yelled, his eyes wild with fear.

A neighbor knocked him out of the saddle with the butt of his shotgun just as a gun hand tried to jump the fence and get away.

A half-dozen guns barked and the outlaw hit the ground, right into the pigpen. The hogs moved toward him.

Chester walked up, his eyes hard and his face grim. He stood over the scared punk. "Somebody shoo them hogs away from the body 'fore they eat him. And then get a rope," Chester added.

Tucson Bob started screaming.

"Where'd you hang him?" Walt asked.

Chester and a few of his neighbors had ridden over to the Box T with the news of the attack, after they had returned from the creek.

"Down at the line separating your range from Jud's.

Right at the crick so's he can be found. We dumped all the bodies there, too."

"Kinda bothered me hangin' that kid," a farmer said. "He sure blubbered and hollered and begged, callin' for his ma. But then I had to think about what he told us they was gonna do if Chester's girl had been found. Then it didn't bother me so bad."

"How about the kid with his arm shot off?" Jackson asked.

"He didn't make it to the crick 'fore he died."

"After he died," Chester said, "the other kid started talkin' his head off, tellin' us 'bout what they had in mind to do with any girl they found at farmers' homes they was plannin' to raid. He said that's what Jud's men was goin' to do from now on out. I guess he thought by tellin' us ever'thing he knew we would spare him from the rope. He thought wrong."

Walt told the men about Sheriff Brady's try to get U.S. Marshals in.

Chester shook his head negatively. "You been out of touch too long, Walt. And I ain't sayin' that it's all your fault. Brady is a good man, and he'll make his request for help. But it ain't gonna come in. Somebody higher up will block it. We done tried to do what you're tryin' early last year. We sent Jim Martin to see the governor. He didn't get in to see him and was ambushed on his way back home."

"I remember," Walt said, shaking his head. "Another good idea shot all to hell."

Smoke cut his eyes to Jackson, remembering the gunfighter's words: "In the end, it's all gonna boil down to men facin' men with guns. That's the way it's always been, and that's the way it's gonna be . . . for a while yet."

Smoke couldn't agree more.

Several days drifted by, and it was as Chester had predicted: nothing was heard from Sheriff Brady. One week after the night raid by the gunmen, Brady rode slowly up to the Box T. He looked like a man with the weight of the world on his shoulders.

Walt waved him onto the porch, where the rancher was sitting with Smoke, Jackson, and Rusty. Brady took a chair and the cup of coffee that Susie brought out to him.

"You look like a man whose best horse just died," the rancher remarked. "What's the matter, Sheriff?"

"It's worse than that, I'm here to tell you. There ain't gonna be any help comin' in from the government, Walt. And that's just the beginning of it." He sighed and took a sip of coffee. "I been ridin' all over this county. I can't find a judge who'll sign papers against Jud. One of them outright laughed at me. And I had to turn all them gun hands loose. Judge's orders. He says that since you didn't personal come in and swear to the truth of the raid, I can't hold them."

"Judge Monroe?" Walt asked.

"You got it."

"I always knew he was takin' money from my brother."

"I don't think it would have made a whit of difference if you had come in and signed them papers," the sheriff said. "I've had to open my eyes these past few days and look at things I guess I been avoiding over the years." He sighed. "The mainest thing being that Jud Vale's got a lot of people with their hands in his pockets . . . and some of them hands has been there for a long time. I'm finding out, really finding out, what it means to butt your head up against a stone wall."

"I hate to be the one to ask you this, Sheriff," Walt said, "but how about your deputies?"

"Can they be trusted? Yes. They been with me for a long time and they'll stand. I've bet my life on that too many times not to be totally sure of them." He looked at Smoke and Rusty and Jackson. "You boys want a badge?"

Smoke shook his head. "Not me. Too many restrictions go with a badge."

Rusty and Jackson also declined the offer of being deputized.

Brady said, "I'm about to do something that I ain't never done in all my years of totin' a star around." He was thoughtful for a moment, then drained his coffee and stood up, hitching at his gun belt. "You boys handle this anyway you see fit. I won't interfere in no way. If Jud starts squallin' for the law to come in, I'll tell him I'll get to it as soon as possible. Then I'll toss his complaint into the trash can. If the judges get on me about my foot-draggin', I'll tell them the people elected me, not them, and if the people don't like the way I'm doin' things, then come election time, they can vote me out of office as easy as they voted me in."

Brady stepped off the porch and walked to his horse. After swinging into the saddle, he looked at the men on the porch. "Good luck, boys. If you need help, holler, and I'll come a-foggin'."

Brady turned his horse and rode out of the ranch without looking back.

Smoke took out the Colts, one at a time, and filled up the empty chamber under the hammer. Rusty and Jackson did the same. Walt rose from his chair and walked into the house. When he returned, he had his gun belt in one hand and a box of .44's in the other. He sat down and began filling up the loops in the belt.

"I fought for this land," the old rancher spoke. "Fought hard for it. But until you boys come along, I reckon I'd misplaced my backbone. I'd turned into a scared old man. That scared old man ain't no more. Maybe it takes me a little longer to get goin' in the mornings, but there ain't nothin' wrong with my eyes nor my trigger finger. And I made up my mind about something else: my brother can go right straight to Hell! And if it has to be me who sends him there, so be it."

26

Days after the disastrous attack against the nesters, Jud was still having trouble accepting the fact that most people, from the territorial line west to the Little Malad River were no longer going to bow and scrape to him. Jud had not only lost his power base, but now he felt his mind going again. He struggled to maintain control. He managed to hold on, but it was becoming increasingly difficult to make rational thoughts work their way through the fog that clouded his brain.

Jason was talking to him, but Jud was having a hard time understanding the words.

"Jud!" Jason shouted at him.

Jud turned his head. Blinked his eyes. "Yes, Jas. I hear you."

"Can you understand me, Jud?"

"Yes. Now, I can. What were you saying?"

"It's time to pull in our horns. We got enough money to last us ten lifetimes. It's time to quit. Break up the gangs and send them packing. Stick with ranchin'. The people has turned ag'in us. It can't do nothin' 'cept get worser."

Jud didn't believe the words he was hearing. This wasn't like Jas. Jas had been his strong friend and supporter for years—long, bloody, murderous, and savage years. Together they had raped and murdered and stolen and savaged from Illinois to Idaho. Now the man was telling him it all had to come to an end. Jud shook his head. "No way, Jas. It's too late for that." Lucidity was returning to Jud's darkened brain. "Far too late. We are what we are. We can't change. The people won't let us. We've got to stay strong, and we've got to show the people that we're still the kingpins of this area."

"For God's sake, Jud—how? You haven't ridden around the area like I have. Every move I make, they's anywhere from five to fifteen guns on me. The people have had it, Jud. We've come to the end of our string."

Jud looked at the man. "You want to ride, Jas?"

"You mean leave?"

Jud nodded.

"No. You know me better than that. We been together since we was young bucks, full of piss and vinegar. If you say we're gonna stand and fight this out, then I'll be right beside you."

"How many men are still on the payroll, drawing fighting wages?"

"Seventy."

Jud's eyes were hard and savage. "Then tell them to start earning it."

The riders struck at night, wearing masks and dusters. They struck a small farmhouse near the Wyoming line and burned it to the ground, killing the farmer and abusing his wife and oldest daughter before tying them naked to a tree and leaving them. Then they vanished into the night, scattering, leaving no trail that Sheriff Brady and his men could follow. The raiders did the same thing the next night, miles away from the first scene of horror and degradation.

The third night the raiders struck, Sheriff Brady and his

men were at the extreme south end of the county while the raiders were working the northern tip of the county. It was the same operation: a farm was burned, the man was killed, the women abused.

But what Jud didn't know was that after the first raid, Smoke had been absent from the Box T, roaming mostly at night, looking for tracks, and holed up during the day. Just before dawn on the morning of the fourth day, he watched the raiders return to the Bar V, still wearing their dusters. He waited until he was certain that all who were coming in were in, then began slowly and carefully backtracking the trail.

By eight o'clock, he had found where all the raiders came together after scattering. It was on the Bear River Range, but he wasn't certain it was on Bar V holdings. He felt this might be public range.

He began following the main body of the raiders, finally discovering where they had built a hidden corral to keep their spare horses. Smoke backed off a good half-mile, rubbed down Dagger, and cooked himself a meal. He stretched out on the ground to sleep for a few hours. This night, the raiders would be in for a surprise when they came for their horses. A very deadly surprise.

When he opened his eyes, he guessed the time to be about four o'clock. Smoke built a small fire and made coffee, frying some bacon to go with the last of his bread. After eating, he leaned back against his saddle and rolled a cigarette, enjoying his coffee and the peace and quiet. Come the night, it would not be a bit peaceful, and it sure as hell wouldn't be quiet.

Before dusk settled over the land, Smoke put out his small fire and saddled up, moving closer to the hidden corral. He dismounted and carefully picketed Dagger, hopefully out of the line of fire. Taking his rifle, he moved to well within throwing distance of the corral and found himself a good position. He chambered a round and eased

239

the hammer down, then Smoke settled in to wait for the first of the raiders to arrive.

He didn't think they would come all in a bunch, but instead come drifting in by two's and three's. The first bunch of outlaws would wait until the last had arrived, then take off to do their dirty work.

But Smoke had some dirty work of his own in mind, and he was confident that the number of raiders who rode out would be considerably less than the number who rode in this night.

The first bunch rode in almost carelessly, certain that no unfriendly eyes were upon them.

Smoke waited and watched through the gathering gloom as the assorted scum on Jud's payroll checked the corral to see if their spare mounts were still there. One man busied himself building a fire and making coffee.

Then the damning evidence showed itself as the men began unrolling white dusters from behind their saddles and shaking out the black bandanas they would use to cover the lower half of their faces.

More men began drifting in until the number had reached twenty. They drank coffee and began slipping into their dusters. The talk was rough as the conversation drifted to where Smoke lay hidden. The Bar V hired guns laughed as they casually talked of murder, rape, and torture. Another man tossed more wood on the fire.

Smoke had carefully gauged the distance between his location and the main body of men. With a grim smile on his lips, he lit the fuses and tossed two sticks of giant powder into the group.

It took a couple of seconds for the men to react, and a couple of seconds was all it needed for the short fuses to burn down. When the dynamite blew, the din was enormous in the night.

Outlaws were hurled off their boots, some landing hard and breaking bones, others with the wind knocked from

240

them. Horses reared up, screaming their panic, breaking loose and galloping off into the darkness. Those hired guns who were still on their feet were stumbling around, cursing and disoriented and momentarily deafened from the huge explosion.

Smoke knocked half a dozen men sprawling with fast but well-placed rifle shots, then shifted locations, reloading as he made his way toward the corral. The outlaws began pouring lead into the area Smoke had just vacated.

Smoke jerked the rawhide string holding the gate to the post and fired into the air, stampeding the remuda. The frightened horses ran right into and through the milling gun hands, knocking a few screaming to the earth before the steel-shod hooves mangled flesh and broke bones.

Smoke took that time of painful confusion to run back to where he had picketed Dagger and swing into the saddle. Smoke got himself gone from that area, feeling very confident that the raiders would not strike against women and children this night.

He did not head for the Box T, instead pointing Dagger's nose toward the Bar V. He had not gone a mile before a horseman rode onto the trail and waved at him.

Clint Perkins. Smoke reined up and looked at the man.

"Heading for the Bar V to do some mischief, Smoke?"

"That was my plan."

"I'll ride along with you."

"Your funeral."

Clint laughed in the night. "Oh, not just yet, Smoke. Oh, my, no! I have that auspicious but final event all worked out in my mind. And the time is close, but not this night."

"Whatever you say."

"Your plan for the Bar V?"

"Lay up on the ridges and put about a hundred rounds into the house and bunkhouse. Just let Jud know that I haven't forgotten him."

241

Clint laughed. "Let's ride!"

They rode hard for a couple of miles, then slowed to a walk, sparing their horses but still covering the distance swiftly. They did not talk until they were about two miles from the mansion.

"I'll take this side, Clint," Smoke told him. "The other side is all yours."

"That's fair. How long do we keep it up?"

"Oh, ten or fifteen minutes. We'll wait about half an hour before we start. That'll give our horses time to catch their breath and for some of those behind us to make the ranch and spread the news. There'll be lots of lanterns and lamps lit when they return. That'll give us better targets."

Clint smiled. "See you around, Smoke Jensen." Then he was gone into the night.

Smoke angled off into the timber and carefully made his way to a ridge overlooking the great mansion. He picketed Dagger and settled in behind a tree, just at the crest of the hill.

The minutes ticked by, turning into half an hour. What was left of Jud's raiders began trickling back to the ranch complex, about half of them belly-down over a saddle, tied in place. Smoke brought his Winchester to his shoulder, compensated for the downhill shooting, and sighted in a man, squeezing the trigger.

The slug went high and knocked the man's hat from his head, sending the hired gun to the ground. Smoke's second shot was true. The gun hand tried to rise up on one elbow, then fell face-forward, neck-shot.

From across the way, Clint opened up, the outlaws clearly visible under the light of the moon and the starry night. Smoke joined in, concentrating his fire into the mansion.

Jud, Jason, and the bodyguards hit the floor as .44 slugs began tearing through the walls and windows of the mansion.

A slug shattered the knee of a bodyguard, bringing a howl of pain. Clint was pouring rifle fire into the running men in the yard. He quickly punched more cartridges into his rifle and began peppering the bunkhouse. Smoke shifted the muzzle of his rifle and put two fast rounds into one of the newly built outhouses. A man came rushing out, trying to run while holding his britches up with one hand. One knee caught in his dangling suspenders and sent him sprawling to the ground.

Smoke tried for a lamp in the mansion, his third shot finally striking true, sending coal oil and flames worming across the floor like a flaming snake. Jud and Jason and the bodyguards began stomping at the flames before they caught and burned the place down.

There was little the men around the mansion could do except curse the birth of Smoke Jensen; they knew it was Smoke on one of the ridges. And probably Clint on the other ridge.

Smoke decided he'd pressed his luck to the maximum for this night, and began working his way back to Dagger. It would take Clint only a couple of minutes to understand that Smoke was gone.

Inside the mansion, hopping mad, jumping around like a huge frog, his eyes bugged out, cursing at the top of his lungs, and just barely hanging onto what little sanity was left him, Jud began screaming orders to get Smoke Jensen, declare war on everybody, burn down Montpelier, assassinate President Arthur; do whatever needs to be done . . . just kill that damned Smoke Jensen!

Clint fired one more round before he pulled out, putting his shot into the living room and plugging a suit of armor Jud had imported from England.

"Another day, Father," Clint muttered, slipping back to where he'd tied his horse. "Soon."

*   *   *

Smoke slept soundly the remainder of that night, in his room in the barn at the Box T. He had stopped at several small farms, telling the people what had gone down and also that he doubted Jud's raideres would be out doing their dirty work that night. But keep a guard posted just in case.

He slept late; it was nearly six o'clock when he awakened and put on his hat, then his pants and boots and shirt, slinging his gun belt around his waist, and stepping outside.

"What went down last night?" Jackson asked, handing him a cup of coffee.

Smoke took a sip of coffee before replying. Jackson was smiling when Smoke finished.

"Wish you had invited me along," he said wistfully.

"I didn't know what I was going to do until the last minute. But it will be interesting to see what Jud does next."

"Interesting is one way of puttin' it, for sure."

27

"Jud's sellin' his herds," the farmer said, dismounting in front of the ranch house. Walt led him to the porch and offered the man coffee, as Smoke and Jackson and Rusty joined them.

It was just past dawn and three days after Smoke and Clint had assaulted the mansion.

"He's pulling out?" Walt asked, a hopeful note to the question.

"No," Smoke said. "I'd say he's gearing up for a long and expensive war. Putting his hands on as much hard cash as possible." He glanced at the farmer. "When did you find out about this?"

"Late yesterday evenin'. My neighbor, Jim Morris, had been up to Montpelier. Stopped in for a drink and heard cattle buyers talkin' about it. Them buyers done sent men in to move the cattle."

"Knowing we wouldn't harm any innocent party," Smoke mused aloud. "Good move on Jud's part. Then they've begun moving the cattle out?"

"Oh, yeah. Job's might near half done, I reckon." He cut his eyes to Smoke. "Them bounty hunters—Wills is one of them?"

Smoke nodded. "I know them."

245

"I heard some talk, Mr. Jensen; heard it this mornin'. Word is they're pullin' out on Jud's orders. Goin' down to Arizony, lookin' for your wife and family."

"It would be something Jud would do," Walt said. "That would be one way to get you away from here."

Smoke stepped from the porch, his face tight and his eyes hard. He walked to the barn and saddled Dagger. The road by the trading post would be the one they would be most likely to take. Smoke would be waiting for them. It was time to bring this boil to a head. Crazy or not, when Jud Vale started threatening Smoke's wife and family, Jud Vale was a dead man.

Doreen had a poke of food waiting for him when he rode up to the ranch house. Smoke stowed it in his saddlebags. There was a gunnysack filled with dynamite tied onto the saddle horn. One side of his saddlebags was stuffed with ammunition and spare pistols. Smoke looked at Rusty and Jackson.

"Jud may be doing this trying to pull us all away from the Box T. Well, it isn't going to work that way. You boys stay here. This is my show. I'll be back."

The farmer grabbed hold of the reins. "No, sir," he said firmly. "That ain't the way it is and it ain't the way it's gonna be. This is *our* show. They's men comin' here right now. Farmers and hired hands and shopkeepers and such from all over; as far away as Montpelier. Sheriff Brady and his men is comin' in, too."

"Riders comin' for a fact," Rusty said. "Horses and wagons. Looks like a regular parade."

Smoke cut his eyes. It did look like a parade. He picked out Chester and his wife, and a dozen other farmers and family. He smiled as he saw Doc Evans's buggy. Right behind it was the editor of the Montpelier paper, Mr. Argood. Coming up to intersect the line of horses and wagons and buggies, was Sheriff Brady and his men. Chester whoaed his team and stepped down, helping his

246

wife to the ground.

The farmer had a gun belt around his waist and his wife carried a rifle. He walked to Smoke and looked up at him. "We ain't no good as gunfighters, Mr. Smoke. But we can damn sure defend this ranch while you boys is gone."

"I can't interfere or condone this, Smoke," Sheriff Brady said. "But I can stay right here and then sort out the pieces when it's over."

"And I'll be here to patch up the wounded," Doc Evans told him.

"I'll get my guns." Walt turned toward the house.

"Walt!" Alice said.

"Hush, woman," the old rancher told her. "A man's got to do what he's got to do. You just keep the coffee hot. I'll be back."

Rusty and Jackson were walking toward the barn to saddle up.

Matt walked his horse toward Smoke. There was a grim look on Smoke's face as he noticed the way the boy was wearing his guns. He carried his Peacemaker on his right side, and Cheyenne's old Colt on his left side, butt-forward for a cross draw.

It was like looking into a mirror that reflected years back. Like looking at himself as a boy.

"I'll be comin' with you," Matt told him.

"I can't stop you."

"That is correct, sir," Matt said politely.

They waited and watched for a few moments, as the farmers took up positions around the ranch and the women gathered on the porch. Rusty and Jackson rode up, leading Walt's horse. The rancher stepped out of his house, kissed Alice on the cheek, and swung into the saddle, booting his Winchester. The four men and the boy headed out, Smoke in the lead.

It was to be the start of the bloodiest day in that part of Idaho Territory.

247

They reached the trading post, coming in from the back of the long building, dismounting and tying their horses in the rear of the store. Jackson had pointed out the bounty hunters' horses in front of the saloon.

"Jackson and me will handle this," Smoke said. "The rest of you stay here."

The shopkeeper's wife rushed out the back door. "They got my husband and Bendel all trussed up like hogs," she whispered hoarsely. "They're waitin' on you, Mr. Jensen. And there's eight or ten more gun hands just over that ridge," she said, pointing.

"Thank you. Hunt some cover, ma'am." He looked at Jackson. "First things first," he said, then pushed open the back door and stepped into the gloom of the storage room.

Smoke had made up his mind that this battle and as many others as he could arrange would not be stand up, face, and draw. The odds were just too high.

He had both hands full of Colts, hammers back, when he kicked in the door to the saloon and went in shooting, Jackson right behind him, doing the same.

Lefty went down with the front of his shirt stained with blood and smoking holes. Smoke dropped to one knee, partly to give Jackson better shooting room and partly to show a smaller target, and put two slugs into the head of Shorty Watson. Jackson had knocked John Wills and Dave Bennett spinning. Bennett went down to the floor, blood leaking from his mouth, dying and cursing as Wills staggered out the batwings and fell off the porch, landing on his back.

Smoke stepped outside just as Wills was lifting his guns. Smoke shot him between the eyes just as the sounds of galloping horses reached him.

Walt, Rusty, and Matt stepped around the corner of the building, rifles in their hands, and emptied some saddles. The charging gun hands did not slack up.

Smoke lifted his Colts and let the hammers down just as

a hired gun galloped past the trading post. The .44's knocked the man from the saddle. Jackson was beside him on the porch, guns blazing. The badman turned good man emptied two more saddles.

The early morning became eerily quiet as Smoke and Jackson began punching out empties and reloading. The shopkeeper's wife untied her husband and Bendel. The saloonkeeper was furious as he joined Smoke on the porch.

"By God, I've had it!" he yelled. "I'll not tolerate anymore of Jud Vale's highhandedness."

"Nor will I," the shopkeeper said, taking the shotgun his wife offered him. "From now on, I see a Bar V brand, I blow the rider out of the saddle."

"That goes double for me," Bendel said, stripping the guns from Wills and loading them full.

Matt led the horses around front.

"Let's ride!" Walt said.

Three miles from the trading post, Smoke and his little force rode right into a group of Bar V riders. There was nothing gentlemanly or honorable about the fight. Smoke just dragged iron and started shooting, Walt and the others doing the same.

They looked up from the body-littered road as Clint Perkins rode up, a wild glint in his eyes. "It is time, is it?" he called. "Very well. I recall an Indian saying: It is a good day to die." He turned his horse's head and rode off toward the Bar V.

"I didn't know we was just gonna ride up to Jud's front door and start shootin'," Rusty said.

"I didn't either," Smoke said. "But maybe that's the way it's got to be." He put Dagger into a gallop and the others followed, leaving the bodies in the road without a second glance.

One hired gun groaned and rolled over in the road. Finally he sat up, his head bloody and throbbing. He gingerly touched the wound and winced. It was painful, but not serious. He got to his boots, found his horse, and crawled into the saddle.

"Hell with this!" he said. "It's gone sour." He reined up when the trading post came into view, and watched Bendel and the shopkeeper and wife digging holes in the back. The gun hand wisely changed his mind about having a drink and carefully skirted the trading post. He thought California ought to be a real good spot to head for.

He knew there had been four or five men at the trading post, about ten more lying in ambush out from the post, and five with him. That was twenty men dead or dying at the hands of Smoke and them others, all in one morning—and the morning wasn't even half over! Yeah, California sounded real good.

"Move, horse. Jud Vale's number is comin' up this day, I'm thinkin'."

Cisco Webster, the Texas gun hand whose teeth had been knocked out by Rusty back at the crick, looked up at the road, just at the point where it crested the hill. He felt a touch of fear clutch at his belly.

Six men sat their saddles, looking down at the mansion, and Cisco didn't need a crystal ball to know who they were.

Highpockets noticed the direction the man's eyes were taking and looked up. Like Cisco, the gunfighter felt a slight lash of dread touch him at the sight.

The yard crowded with bounty hunters and gunslingers, all looking at the crest of the hill.

Smoke urged Dagger forward, riding with the reins in his teeth and his hands filled with Colts.

"What the hell are they goin' to do?" Hammer asked.

"It's over," Buck Wall told him. "I woke up with a bad feelin' about this day."

"You quittin'?" Chato Di Peso asked.

"I shore am." Buck walked toward the bunkhouse just as Jud appeared on the front porch.

"Where the hell do you think you're going?" Jud yelled at him.

"I'm quittin'," Buck called over his shoulder. "Like right now."

Jason had appeared on the porch beside his boss. "The hell you are!" he said, and shot Buck in the back.

The gunfighter pitched forward, dead before he hit the ground.

Smoke picked that time to charge. They split up, with Smoke and Clint riding right into the front yard, the reins in their teeth and hands full of Colts.

Matt and Walt went to the right, Jackson and Rusty to the left.

Hammer grabbed for his guns. Smoke shot him down, the slug taking him in the chest. Hammer died sitting on his butt in the road, his hands by his sides. After a few seconds, he slowly toppled over.

Shorty DePaul came out of the bunkhouse just as Walt and Matt were galloping past. Shorty sighted in Walt. Matt's gun crashed and Shorty felt the sledgehammer blow take him in the belly, about an inch above his belt. Matt fired again, his second slug striking the gunfighter in the chest and knocking him down.

"Kilt by a punk kid," were Shorty's last words.

Rusty and Jackson rode right into a knot of startled gun slicks. Pike and Becket went down under bullets fired at almost pointblank range. Molino stepped out of the barn and put a slug into Rusty's shoulder. Rusty border-rolled his Colt and shot the man in the throat. Molino hit the ground, coughing and gurgling.

Jaeger and Chato Di Peso saw very quickly the outcome of the fight and slipped through the dust and confusion to the bunkhouse, quickly gathering up their possessions. They grabbed horses—neither one of them giving a damn whose horse it was—and pulled out.

Cisco Webster watched as Smoke jumped from the

saddle, and ran behind a building, reloading as he ran. Dagger trotted to the corrral and began harassing the mares.

Cisco ran to the storage shed, flattening out against a wall. He stuck his head around the corner just in time to catch a bullet right between the eyes. He sank to the ground, a very curious expression on his dead face.

Clint, out of the saddle and down on one knee, doubled over the Colorado gun hand, Barstow, with two .44 rounds to the belly, then shifted his Colt and ended the career of Highpockets.

Jackson had helped Rusty out of the saddle and left him behind good cover with a half-dozen Colts taken from the dead and dying. Jackson went headhunting. He walked right up to Rim Reynolds and several of his men and began shooting as fast as he could cock and fire. Rim went down screaming in pain with two slugs in his belly. Jackson was burned on one arm and took the loss of part of one ear but he was still standing when the others were down. He calmly and swiftly reloaded, shook the blood from his face and stepped back out in the fracas.

Walt and Matt were standing side by side, the old and the young, their guns taking a terrible toll. Crazy Phil was down on his knees, with four of his men on the ground with him. Old Walt winked at young Matt as they reloaded.

Clint was working his way closer to the house. He had but one thought in his demented mind.

The Pecos Kid and Glen Regan—Glen was walking slow due to the gunshot wounds in his butt from back at the creek—tried to make the corral and get away. Rusty dropped them both midway.

Blackjack Morgan stood with legs spread wide, his hands over the butts of his guns, facing Smoke, who still held his Colts in his hands. "I'm faster, Jensen!" he called over the din of battle.

"No. You're just dead," Smoke told him. He lifted his right hand and shot the gunfighter. There was a time for discretion and a time for valor, but at no time was there a moment to be wasted on fools.

Smoke stepped over the dying man and walked on.

A searing pain in Smoke's left leg turned him around and slammed him up against a wall. Gimpy Bonner and Scott Johnson faced him. Smoke lifted his Colts and let them bang. When the dust and gunsmoke cleared, Smoke was bloody but still standing.

Smoke reloaded, checked his wounds, and bound a bandana around the leg wound. He walked on as the sounds of galloping horses came to him over the shooting. About a dozen men were hauling their ashes away from the ranch. Smoke lifted his right-hand Colt and ended life for Ben Lewis who had lined up Jackson with a rifle. Ben danced for a moment, his spurs jingling his death chant, then slumped to the ground.

"Jensen!" the voice turned Smoke around to face Luddy.

Smoke didn't hesitate. Just lifted both guns and began firing and walking toward the man. He stood over the bloody outlaw, their eyes meeting.

"I thought you'd give me fair chance, Jensen!" Luddy gasped.

"Did you ever give anyone a fair chance, Luddy?"

Luddy laughed humorlessly. "Can't say that I ever did, come to think of it." He shivered once. "Cold. Mighty cold all of a sudden." He closed his eyes and died.

Smoke turned away.

The gunfire had all but faded away. The grounds around the great mansion were littered with bodies. Jason was sitting on the steps, his shirt front bloody, but he was holding on to life long enough to see the outcome of what was about to take place in front of him.

Clint and Jud faced each other, both of them with the

same wild light in their eyes.

"Hello, Daddy!" Clint said sarcastically.

"You son of a bitch!" Jud snarled at him.

"You sure got that right," the son told the father, then grabbed iron.

Father and son stood ten feet apart and put lead in each other. Both went to the ground on their knees at the same time. Both continued firing. Jud toppled over and Clint was only about one second behind him.

Walt walked up, one arm dangling useless from a .45 slug. He looked at the scene in front of him then lifted his eyes to Jason.

"I reckon it's over and done, ain't it, Walt?" the man gasped.

"I reckon it is, Jason."

"I reckon Jud just tried to toss too big a loop. Is that the way you see it?"

"Why did you and Jud kill my son?"

Jason laughed, a nasty bark of dark humor. "'Cause we wanted to, you old bastard!" Jason closed his eyes as the pale rider came closer.

Walt lifted his Colt and earred the hammer back. Then he slowly lowered the weapon as Jason tumbled down the steps to lie on the ground.

"Ride for Doc Evans and the sheriff, Matt," Smoke told the boy.

"They're comin' up the road now, Smoke," Matt told him, pointing. "And it looks like the Army is with them."

28

Smoke had to hang around for the hearings—both state and federal government, since the Army had finally gotten involved—but that was all right, his wounds needed the time to heal. He watched as Rusty and Doreen, then Jackson and Susie got married. Since Walt was Jud's sole living survivor, Walt took possession of the Bar V. He signed over the Box T to Rusty and Doreen and gave the Bar V to Jackson and Susie. Matt stayed on as a hand for Rusty. Walt and Alice were going to build a little place on Bear Lake and retire.

Jackson was having the great mansion torn down on the day Smoke rode out. The couple planned to build a smaller, much more practical ranch house.

Smoke stopped by the trading post for a beer and to say good-bye to Bendel.

He was halfway through his beer when Jaeger and Di Peso pushed open the batwings. Smoke sighed and set the mug down.

"Your time to die, Jensen," Di Peso told him.

"I don't think so," Smoke replied, turning and drawing both guns.

Smoke stepped over the bodies and walked to Dagger, swinging into the saddle and pointing Dagger's head south, toward Arizona and Sally and the kids. Bendel's voice stopped him.

"Smoke!"

He twisted in the saddle.

"If you ever plan a return visit, do me a favor, will you?" Bendel yelled.

"What's that?"

"Please bring a damn shovel!"